Reincarnations of Rose

MARY SAURER-SMITH

ISBN: 979-8-88640-364-0 (sc)
ISBN: 979-8-88640-365-7 (hc)
ISBN: 979-8-88640-367-1 (e)

One Galleria Blvd., Suite 1900, Metairie, LA 70001
1-888-421-2397

Contents

Introduction v

Chapter 1 Flashbacks and a New Life 1

Chapter 2 Atlantis 5300 B.C. Rose 18

Chapter 3 Mwa 46

Chapter 4 Aaron 1671 B.C. 62

Chapter 5 Thusydyas 73

Chapter 6 Miriam 82

Chapter 7 Milah 111

Chapter 8 Lee-Si-Yan 134

Chapter 9 Shi-Ge Shu 148

Chapter 10 Nisha 158

Chapter 11 Maria 177

Chapter 12 Tessie 197

Chapter 13 Melissa 208

Chapter 14 Rose 212

Chapter 15 Rose 221

Introduction

Reincarnation is a subject that fascinates many, and one that more and more people in the United States are willing to discuss. A belief in reincarnation is part of the spiritual heritage of many religions, and for a growing number of people it is a personal experience of knowing. For some, the remembrances might come as those delightful de-ja-vu sensations, but for others they are vivid memories coupled with other bits of knowledge, as real as a memory of their childhood.

This book presents 12 fascinating and progressive short stories of Rose's life as reviewed from her current incarnation as Rose. In watching her flow from one incarnation into the next with the same concerns and questions about life we witness the subtle and sometimes dramatic changes that take place within her consciousness.

A spellbinding process takes place internally as Rose meets the challenges and difficulties of human existence, life after life. Her story leaves every reader with a feeling of joy, hope and something to think about.

Chapter 1

FLASHBACKS AND A NEW LIFE

Throughout her cross-country drive, Rose replayed the sound of her husband's sorrow in her mind, "I can't let you go. I don't know how to live without you."

She had kissed him gently on the forehead, knowing that her forgiveness for his years of infidelity was as sure as was the end of her attachment to him. "Then you'll have to learn how to live without me. How long do you think that will take?"

"At least a year," he had replied, clinging to her.

Rose had known that a postponement could cause her to lose a window of opportunity that could mean divine timing for her future, yet she felt an urgency to leave the marriage gracefully.

"Then I will wait a year," she had promised.

She and Eddie had continued to live together as housemates with separate bedrooms. Eddie had often gone out at night, and sometimes she had not seen him for days. Six months later, on one of the after-dinner walks that she and Eddie had begun sharing in lieu of sex, Eddie took her hand. She could feel him trembling, and her heart wrapped love around him to give him courage. She wanted so much to have him feel strong and confident, but it must come from within him. it was not a gift that she could give.

"It scares me to death to say this," he began, his voice shaking to reflect the trembling of his body, "but, every day that we're together is a bigger torment for me. I wake up each morning to realize what

I have lost, and am losing forever. I know now that as long as you're here I won't be able to believe I can live without you. Your presence works just the opposite, and every day I feel more desperate to hold you here. I guess what I'm trying to say is that I'll never be ready to let you go, so now is as good a time as any."

He shook with great gut-wrenching tears, and she stopped to hold him in her arms. If he had asked her then to stay, she might have. The core of her original love for him had been stirred in that moment of his anguish. but he had not asked. The window had closed, and with it went all potential for a reversal of her decision. they had continued their walk in silence, and when his trembling stopped she felt a peace come between them that had not been there for a very long time.

When they arrived home, she made a pitcher of lemonade. It was a warm evening in late September, and they sat on the patio by their swimming pool, talking about the beauty of the landscaping they had done and the home they had made.

"Will you be asking me to sell the house?" he asked. "how will we divide the property?"

With a sense of freedom from time consuming and problematic legalities and negotiations she had said, "This place is your greatest love, and the institute of mind science will be my new partner in life. Once i get a job at the school it will provide for me just as you've done so freely for twenty-three years, but probably not so generously.

"I would never expect you to continue contributing to my livelihood." she continued. "You have a life to live, and you've worked hard for what you have. I'll take my clothes and jewelry and close the door softly behind me."

Jim had put his arm across her shoulders to draw her close, and this time he did ask her to stay, "I wish we could start all over again. I'm sure I could do it right next time."

The comfort of his shoulder was solid and warm and they had cuddled for a while before she felt the strength to gently release herself from his embrace. "Let's not cloud this time of peaceful parting, Eddie. There's no bad guy here, just the end of our journey together. I'll remember the good times and the lessons we both learned. Please have faith in your future, and try to be true to what those years taught you. I know I will."

Turning to look into his eyes she had pleaded, "Promise me you won't carry guilt into your future. I'll always be your friend, and you'll find someone else to love. Life always brings us new opportunities to use what we think we've learned."

They had tasted the final embers of their relationship when she stood to kiss him on the cheek and say goodnight. Touching her hair in the old familiar way he had gazed at her with eyes of anguish and whispered, "Stay with me all night. This is the last day I'll ever know you as mine."

She nodded consent and they had sat for hours in the glider, reviewing the good times, remembering the beauty, the passion and the laughter they had shared. They had ended the night with a moonlight swim, sleeping in the comfort of each other's arms until morning.

The sound of a horn blowing impatiently startled Rose, just as a dog ran across the road. She shook her head and turned on the car radio in an attempt to rise above the memories. To bridge the gap between past and future, she turned her attention to where she was going.

Rose's first goal for her new life was to apply for employment in the prayer ministry at the institute and to develop and practice her teaching skills through the school and other opportunities that might arise. She had no plans beyond that. She had written to the manager of the prayer ministry, and he had promised to let her know when there was a job opening. "But," he had assured her, "Don't let that delay you. Come when you are ready. See the associate minister of our chapel as soon as you arrive. She has a knack for helping new arrivals find employment."

Rose smiled as she recalled the hope that had filled her. Having no one with whom to celebrate that encouraging response, she had turned to the wall of full length mirrors in her bedroom. In a symbolic gesture of rebirth she had undressed slowly and deliberately, looking at her body as if she had never seen it before. "I'm brand new!" she had sung to herself, dancing around the room.

Taking the next exit to go a few miles out of her way, Rose turned her car onto the grounds of the university where her son, Keith, had attended college. She drove slowly to the bank of the river. This was a planned detour, and she hurriedly took a blanket and her picnic basket out of the back seat for a picnic brunch. It was autumn, quiet and cool under the shade of a huge Magnolia tree that stood nearby. Settling into this hour of rest and reminiscence that she had afforded herself, Rose sipped hot coffee from her thermos cup and filled her paper plate with cut fruit, a boiled egg and cottage cheese.

She had said her final goodbyes to family members the day before, and this morning when Eddie had hugged her possessively on his way out the door to work, he had given her an envelope. She assumed it was a letter of farewell and waited until now to open it. It was not a letter. It was a note of thanks for the good years, and a cashier's check for $10,000.

Rose was in shock, then she felt delight. With a rush of gratitude she thought, "If I don't find a job right away, this will see me through a few months of classes. It feels like my timing is perfect."

She poured herself another cup of steaming coffee and smiled with nostalgia as she remembered the day she had driven here with Keith to register for classes. She and her son had always had a sense of gentle comfort with each other, as if they had been friends forever. They had enjoyed a picnic in this very spot that day.

Keith was married now and living in Alaska. Though he had never had a good relationship with his Dad, still he had counted the permanence of his parent's marriage as a constant in his world of change. He had been heartbroken when Rose called to break the news in July and had asked her to stay until his time in Alaska was over. Her answer had been firm.

"Honey, I can't promise that. Divine timing is about making choices and changes at the appropriate time so the invisible energies are all working in synchronicity. By making this choice, I've already made the change in spirit, and my life is now moving in that direction. When the time comes to walk through that door of my future, I'll know it, and I can't let anything or anyone delay the flow of my life changes. Wherever I am, you will always be loved and wanted there."

His voice broke as he whispered, "Okay," and he put his wife on the phone. She had said with mock sternness, "You can't go anywhere that I won't find you, Mom. When Keith gets out of the Air Force we're comin' to live close to you, so don't get yourself too busy for family."

Rose packed up her breakfast things, shook out the blanket and stashed them in the car. Then she strolled along the river bank with thoughts of her daughter, Marie.

Marie had been the hardest thing to leave behind. She was just nineteen, six months out of high school, working at what she loved and out on her own for the first time. She had said no to Rose's invitation to come with her, promising to keep in touch. Rose had told her the door was always open if she decided to come to Missouri and was proud of Marie's confidence in making her own life-changing decisions.

Rose blinked the tears away, walked briskly to her car, took the driver's seat, started the engine and turned up the radio volume. The next few hours of her trip were filled with cheerful music, curiosity and the questions that only her future could answer. She had taken her time and the sun was setting when she saw the welcome to Missouri sign. This time, the tears that filled her eyes did not stem from pain but from a feeling of pure ecstasy.

She drove straight to the office of the apartment complex in which she had rented a small apartment by phone. The manager looked up from his book when she walked in, greeted her warmly and gave her a key with a little map to her apartment.

It was a second floor apartment with a nice sized private veranda that overlooked a beautiful wooded area. The apartment was small but adequate, and it took her no time to unload her car and settle in for the night.

The next day she reported to the academic offices of the school to sign up for classes and then went to see the associate minister of the chapel.

"Who should I tell her is here?" the secretary inquired.

No sooner had she given her name than the minister, herself, came out.

"I've been waiting for you," she said enthusiastically. "John told me about you. Come in and I'll give you the name and location of a friend of mine who's hiring people for a small business he just started."

Rose knew without a doubt that she had made the right decision and that she was fully immersed in the stream of Divine Order for her new life.

After only a year, as new friends were found and her new way of life became more and more familiar, Rose felt that she was indeed someone new and the old had passed away. She had worked joyfully at her first job in Missouri during that year, while completing her studies and practice teaching. Many opportunities for both service and socialization had opened to her. She had recently married an accountant who was also a student at the Institute, and she had been hired to work as a prayer counselor in the prayer ministry. Except for the fact that her children had moved to Missouri to be near her, she would have been sure the former Rose was a figment of her imagination.

One morning Rose woke with a feeling of impending danger and reached for the phone. "Please, God, let her be there," she prayed as she counted the rings.

Her aunt picked up on the fourth ring. "This is Virginia," said the cheerful, girlish voice.

"Aunt Virgie," Rose blurted out as if grasping for a lifeline with her last breath, "I've been having those memory flashes again, this time in my dreams! They come more and more often. I can't sleep o meditate or concentrate on my studies. If I pay for your airfare will you come out to see me for a few days?

Virgie, I've been having those memory flashes again, this time in my dreams! They're coming more and more often. I can't sleep or meditate or concentrate on my studies because of them. If I pay your airfare will you come out to see me for a few days?"

"Interesting," said the voice on the other end, "you haven't had one of those flashbacks since you were 15 years old. When did they start up again?"

"Only since I've been here in Missouri," said Rose. "I know you told me to ignore them, but I can't anymore. I need to either bring them into focus or find a way to put them behind me. They are annoying me and distracting me from my new life. Do you have any suggestions?"

Virginia was of American Indian descent, and both she and Rose's mother had been well known psychics in their hometown of Lafayette, Louisiana. Virginia's skills as a hypnotist and interpreter of dreams had benefited many seekers of inner peace and had made an ample contribution to the family income. Throughout her childhood, Rose's aunt had unmasked many frightening dream characters for her by revealing them as harmless messengers. She could use a big helping of that assurance now.

"Why are they so disturbing to you, Dearie?" asked Virginia in her gentle Southern drawl. "After all they're only memories."

"They just seem so real," groaned Rose, "and I feel like something unpleasant is about to happen, something related to one of the memories. If I could shake off these vague half-glimpses into the past maybe I could avoid whatever is coming."

"I could hypnotize you and have you forget them temporarily if you insist," said Virginia with her usual calmness, "but I think this a good time for them to surface." You went out there to that New Thought School to become a full-blown spiritual teacher. Doesn't that school teach that the more self-awareness you have, the easier it is to be true to yourself? Any spiritual leader worth his salt has to live the truth he's teaching. If the memories are coming, it is their time to come. Be brave now, and face your past lives. They've helped to shape you into who you are today. I'd be curious as all get-out if I were you."

Rose stifled an impulse to laugh at her aunt's country clichés.

"It would be a mistake to turn your back on these past-life memories," Virginia advised. "If you let the memories come now, then later you might be able to help other people who are going through the same thing. There's a reason for everything under the sun, my Pretty Girl."

Rose was encouraged, "You're right. I guess if I'm going to try to help others understand how the mind works, it would be good to understand it more fully myself. I can see myself counseling with someone in a future time about their de-ja-vu experiences."

"Now you're thinkin'," chuckled Virginia. "The reason we forget from life to life is because of the confusion old memories might cause, but when the time comes for those deeply buried memories to take their place in your personal history, they come back begging to be reviewed."

"All at once, or just the one that is most relevant to my current life?"

Her aunt sighed impatiently, "Oh, honey. That depends on whether you have completed your cycles of spiritual development. If this is your final incarnation on earth, you will have all your past life memories in this lifetime. Remember your NDE's? Each of those two near death experiences came with a review of your life. Well, the final incarnation is like a time of transition from the physical body to the spiritual body. There's a kind of knowing that you will not walk this earth again. That final life review is not just of this incarnation like the NDE reviews. And it's not just about one or two incarnations but of the whole string of connected stories that brought you to this moment.

Since this total life review is not accompanied by physical death, it seems reasonable to me that it would use the path of dreams or meditation."

"Are you saying you think I'm in my final incarnation?" asked Rose.

"Only time and the memories will tell, My Beauty. If it turns out that you just have one or two incarnations to recall, I would say no. But if you have them all, you can bet your bottom dollar that you won't be coming this way again, unless it would be to teach others how to get off the merry-go-round."

Rose had to laugh. And what about you, my all-knowing Auntie. Have you received the full range of your memories yet?"

There was silence.

"Aunt Virgie, are you there?"

"No. I have seen only three former stories of my life, but if I can use those memories to make better choices in the future, my next life may be the last."

"And how can we use the memories in a positive way?"

"Forgiveness is the only way," said Virginia, her voice sounding far away and strangely depressed. That's what has been hard for me to do in some cases. "We have to face the unfinished business and handle it different this go-round. Until you can handle it different, it just keeps on coming' again and again like the same game with a new name. You forgive those who are messin' with you along the way, and you forgive yourself. Then you move on into your future with no blaming or regret that hooks your mind into the past."

"Well, I've had lots of practice in letting go," mused Rose.

"Are you spiritually mature enough to handle unfinished business that might be coming?" asked her aunt.

"What else could life throw at me that I haven't already learned to forgive?"

"More of the same, my Dear, more of the same."

"I doubt that," thought Rose, knowing she was no longer vulnerable to the same naïve illusions that had led to her painful but necessary divorce. She knew now that loving someone is not enough to instill in them a consciousness that they have not yet achieved.

Pouring love into them can influence, but they still will live their lives according to their own values and beliefs.

"More of the same," reiterated Virginia with a solemn certainty that sent chills along her niece's spine.

"Are you coming out here to help me, or not?" demanded Rose, feeling irritated at her aunt's unshakable confidence.

"Baby Girl, there's nothing I would like better, but you're trying to make your own way now, and it's probably best if you work through this with someone who doesn't know you. I would be much too prone to analyze and interpret everything for you. You know how opinionated I am. Pray about it and keep your eyes open. Now that you are ready, you will meet just the right person to guide you in remembering."

Rose was reluctant to hang up the phone. "Okay," she whispered, holding back a temptation to beg. "I'll be on the lookout for my guide. Send some prayers my way.

"Bye, Darling, I love you," said Virginia. "Keep me posted on your progress." The line went dead.

Rose felt like a child on her first day at kindergarten; abandoned, unsure, close to tears, but brave. She had seldom needed Aunt Virginia's counsel after she grew up but had always counted on it being there when she wanted it. "This must be how my adult children felt when I told them their Dad and I were divorcing," she thought.

It was not yet noon and she had errands to run. Rose slipped into jeans, a woolly red sweater and soft brown moccasins, grabbed her shoulder bag and stepped out into the morning. She felt happy and receptive to whatever the day might bring. A bird was chasing a cat. Rose laughed. It seemed symbolic of what was happening to her. The "bird" was her past life memories and she was the "cat". "Or is it the other way around?" she mused. "Could it be that the memories are the cat and I am the bird, chasing those memories?"

"Either way, it's time to stop running and face it head on," she said firmly to herself. In that decisive moment a wisp of hope moved softly within her, like a tree bending in a tropical breeze. A rush of appreciation for The Institute warmed her blood. She recalled the surge of joy that she had felt upon discovering an organization whose philosophy was compatible with her own and the joy she had felt in being accepted into their teachers program. Soon afterwards her dream job had come, bringing a happiness to the impersonal life of spiritual service that even her greatest happiness in personal living had never produced. She still loved Eddie but not at all in a romantic way, and she knew her forgiveness of him was real.

Her current husband was a wonderfully romantic man who said his dream was to share a ministry with her. They were immersed in the activities of the school, enjoying classes together, singing with two choirs, and she was working as a professional story- teller and teaching classes in three local churches.

"If not for these nagging half-memories that get all mixed up together, I would be perfectly happy," she thought. Then, as if to will herself out of the somber mood, Rose said loudly to herself, "Forget that for now! This is registration day for next semester. I wonder what's on the menu for elective courses."

The walk to the education building from where she worked was only a few steps. Hungrily she scanned the list of available classes. A thrill spread through her mind, raced up her spine and tickled the pit of her stomach as she read the description of the fourth class on the list:

Parapsychology and the Spiritual Life

A Twelve Week Course facilitated by Reverend Cherry Fleming, Ph.D.

Reverend Fleming came to our Ministry from a fifteen-year career of teaching Parapsychology at the University level. After receiving her ordination last year, she immediately applied for an instructor position at the Seminary. While her request is being processed, we have accepted her offer to present this fascinating subject. Agenda for the course will be:

- *Instruction and practice in the Art of Regression*
- *Sharing of past life memories*
- *Facilitated discussion and examination of the impact of your past lives on your current Spiritual Consciousness.*

Acceptance in this course is based on personal interview with Reverend Fleming. Call today for an appointment.

Rose rebelled at the idea of waiting for a formal appointment and was determined to test her theory that Reverend Cherry Fleming, Ph.D. was destined to be her guide to the past. The next morning at seven she rapped lightly on the new instructor's office door.

A tall, gorgeous, red-haired woman in her mid-forties opened the door. A single maroon rose, matching her silvery V-necked silk shirt, adorned the lapel of her gray flannel business suit. Her eyes were a brilliant green and she radiated an aura that was magnetic yet warm and comfortable. If the Reverend had not been in her stocking feet, Rose might have felt intimidated by the contrast in their appearance.

Rose's small, shapely figure, exquisitely sculptured features, high cheek-bones and mounds of curly, long pale-blonde hair had brought her a lifetime of admiration from suitors and green-eyed jealousy from other women. "Elegant" and "beautiful" were the adjectives most often used to describe her. Her best feature was her sky-blue eyes, which were rimmed with a darker blue. They radiated light and an inner glow of delight that acted as a charismatic attraction to men, women, children and animals alike. Rose's unruly hair was caught at the neck with a rubber band, and her nails were crying out for attention. She felt anything but elegant at the moment.

"Good morning," said Cherry Fleming in a warm but assertive voice that supported her mesmerizing charm. "Did we have an appointment?"

"Yes, a Divine Appointment," said Rose with faked confidence. "You are the one I am to see for help with my situation."

The Reverend Fleming raised her eyebrows in amusement and opened the door wider. Walking toward the coffee-maker near her desk, she said, "Then, by all means, come in and have a cup of coffee with me. We can't keep God waiting if this is a Divine Appointment. What's the situation I'm to help you with?"

Cherry listened intently to Rose's story of the recurring dreams, then beamed a friendly smile in her direction. "I sense that you're ready to remember far more than bits and pieces of your former incarnations. I can help you review them in depth, if you will work with me every Monday evening from six to eight. I would also expect you to attend my Tuesday evening classes for a deeper understanding of the regression process and the evolution process of the Soul."

When Rose tried to speak, Cherry raised her hand in a gesture that commanded silence.

"That's not all," she continued. "You would be required to journal after every session and to put your memories into writing as if they are stories about someone else. This will assure objectivity so you won't get caught up in old emotions."

Rose hugged Cherry enthusiastically. "I knew it was a God-thing!" she gushed. "Monday and Tuesday evenings are free time for me. I am so excited! Will this review include all the lifetimes I have ever lived, Reverend Fleming?"

The charming red-head laughed with a musical sound that was as lovely as everything else about her. "No, my dear," she said. "That would be far too many. The lifetimes prior to your first Enlightenment experience were only stepping stones to the point of your earliest encounter with the Divine Light. The lifetimes we will review are those that began with your first enlightenment stage--when you first awakened to yourself as a spiritual being living in a physical body. I would expect you to begin by telling me about this current lifetime. It is only after a certain pinnacle of spiritual maturity has been reached that all the details of the segments of your life are available for review. You obviously have reached that pinnacle, and it is time to look back on where you have been so you can celebrate how far you have come. Now, just one more thing; I intend to call you Rose, so please call me Cherry."

Rose blushed with pleasure at the invitation. "Thank you; I'll do that, Cherry.

But, why aren't the earlier incarnations remembered?"

"Because you were living in the darkness of unawareness," explained Cherry. "Spiritual unawareness is ignorance of the true nature of God and of the Holy Spirit within yourself. Those earliest lives have no bearing on the path one takes toward progressive stages of enlightenment after consciously realizing that punishment, jealousy, vengeance and preferential treatment are not a part of God's nature. When all fear of God is put aside, and faith in God's love and goodness illumines the mind, we are ready to see life through the subjective experiences of Divine sight."

Rose gave Cherry an overview of her life story up to that point while Cherry listened without comment except an occasional chuckle or grimace to show she was listening.

When she had finished, Rose said, "I can't tell you how grateful I am, but we haven't talked about payment yet. What is your fee?"

"For Divine Appointments there is no fee," laughed Cherry, opening the door to end their visit. "See you on Monday."

On the evening of their first session, Rose arrived promptly at six. The room was cozy and inviting, with soft lighting and the gentle scent of Adara. Cherry led her guest to a comfortable chaise lounge and presented her with a steaming hot cup of Jasmine green tea laced with honey.

As if by agreement, the two women sipped their tea in silence. Placing her empty cup on a table, Rose noticed the pens and notebooks neatly stacked there. She looked expectantly at Cherry.

"Cherry sensed the question in Rose's mind and said, "Our weekly ritual will be like this: After you have had your tea, you will close your eyes and silently count backwards from fifty to zero. Then you will open your eyes and follow my guidance. Today, I will guide you to the memory of an incarnation in which you had your first experience of a direct vision of Divine Light. You will merely write the story as an objective observer and put it aside.

Each week we will proceed in this way until we arrive again at the current incarnation. At that point you will begin sharing all the stories with me for the insights they might produce."

"But I thought you would be guiding me through the memories, telling me what they mean," protested Rose.

Cherry smiled indulgently, "If I guide you too strongly, my Dear, I am likely to influence your memory pattern. These incarnations are pieces of your spiritual journey, and you are the only one who can know what they mean to you. I'll critique them with you after they've been recovered. Until then, just enjoy reminiscing about the places you have been in past times, and hold the knowledge as sacred. I want to caution you not to tell your stories to anyone before we've reviewed all of them together."

"Can't I tell my Aunt? She's my primary confidante other than my husband." Rose asked timidly.

"No one!" repeated Cherry sternly. "Only your journal, until it is time to tell me." Placing her cup on the table, Cherry caught Rose's eyes with hers and said, "Let's begin."

Rose closed her eyes and settled deeply into the soft chair. She counted backwards from fifty to zero, then opened her eyes, feeling very relaxed. Serenity had taken the place of her resistance.

"Now, close your eyes and imagine that you are going down twelve steps into a large, clean, well-lit, circular basement. It is completely empty and safe. Image the twelve steps and count them as you descend."

Cherry's voice became slower and seemed far away. "You are standing on the basement floor. Your steps echo as you walk. Suddenly you notice there are doors about six feet apart, on the walls of the basement. You are curious about what is behind them. Every door has a series of numbers on it. You look closely and realize that these series of numbers are dates. There is no month, just the year of a time in the past on every door. No two have the same date. You pause to think about the significance of this. Then you realize that behind each door is a lifetime that you have experienced during that time period. You want very much to open one of the doors. But wait. Look around until you find the oldest date. It could be hundreds of years ago or even thousands. Take time to find it. When you have found the oldest date, stand in front of that door and open it slowly. Step across the threshold.

See yourself as a young child in that life. Are you male or female? What kind of clothes are you wearing? Look around at the environment. You have nothing to fear. Start from the point of your childhood now, and walk slowly through that lifetime. Notice the people, the places and the significant situations along the way."

Rose was no longer aware of Cherry's presence or voice. She saw herself in another body, another time, another place, another life. And she relived it as both a witness and as herself. She felt as if it had happened only yesterday. When Cherry touched her gently on the shoulder, Rose was so startled she nearly jumped out of her chair. It took a few seconds to get her bearings and remember who she was and where.

"The memories were so real," she blurted out.

Cherry's finger to her lips reminded Rose to make some notes before speaking.

As she was walking out the door, Rose turned to look at Cherry. "I thought it would be a subjective experience of being transported to that time and place, but it was just like a vivid memory that I might have of this lifetime, only I was observing at the same time I was remembering."

"Thank you for sharing that," said Cherry with amusement. "Regression into a past life is not an out of body experience, and it's not time travel. And contrary to popular thought, it is not merely remembering what is stored deeply in your subconscious mind. It is a combination of subjective and objective realization. The subjective realization is your subconscious memory, but that only tells your part of in the story. The objective realization comes from the Akashic records, which are stored universal holograms. You perceived both simultaneously and were able to witness situational events along with your personal memory. What you said convinces me that your memories are authentic. Now, go and tell your journal the time and story of that life; then come back next Monday for another."

Beaming with gratitude, Rose hugged her guide so tightly that Cherry squealed!

Then she went directly home to make the first entry in her journal.

Chapter 2

ATLANTIS 5300 B.C. ROSE

This vision is of my life more than seven thousand years ago. What a delightful place to be born. It is the Northern Mainland in Atlantis, banked on one side by a river that is used as an entry into the open sea for purposes of travel and trade between coastal land areas. For over a thousand years the vast continent of Atlantis has been subjected to earthquakes, floods and storms that have steadily increased in frequency and duration.

The Southern half of the continent has been fragmented into large islands, but this northern half remains intact. Every Atlantean Island as well as the Northern Mainland of Atlantis has a separate government, each with a Senate in charge.

Throughout Atlantis, land travel is accomplished by the use of solar power; and all utilities are powered by the sun. Outdoor escalators are abundant, as well as small vehicles which can hover above the ground for land travel or be set for air travel at higher altitudes and speeds. Another form of travel is by the use of solar-powered vests that have a small engine with controls worn at the waist. These vests are very popular and are used for recreation as well as individual air transportation. They permit a person to "fly" with out-stretched arms just above tree-top level. Use of the flight vests requires some skill, but it is by far the preferred method of travel when weather conditions are favorable. Many use these for short trips to villages on a nearby continent.

Due to a variance of energy, the larger air travel vehicles cannot operate properly over the open Sea. Consequently, submarines are the usual vehicle of lengthy sea travel for Atlanteans while barges or boats powered by steam are popular for recreational and trade excursions.

The culturally advanced Atlanteans often appear in less developed land areas, seemingly from "out of nowhere", and refuse to speak of their homeland. Because of these mysterious appearances, they are believed by inhabitants of the villages and cities they visited to have magical powers. Their enormous physiques and golden skin-color have brought upon them the name of "giants", "gods", or "demons", depending on the name-caller's experience and perception of the mysterious travelers. Speculations about their opulent life-styles and stories of their amazing strength have become legend in other cultures.

Atlanteans go to great lengths to assure the purity of their race. On the islands and on the mainland, guards are posted at every accessible entry point, and visitation or immigration from other land areas is not permitted. Atlanteans believe that they are a superior race, placed in a region of the world that was designed just for them by the Great Creator. Keeping the blood-lines pure and free of contamination from non-Atlanteans is their way of showing respect and appreciation for the gift of life, land, and the superior qualities and intellect that have been bestowed upon them. They believe that to have children with non-Atlanteans will risk the loss of their physical strength and mental superiority as a race; and the laws of every Atlantean area strictly enforce adherence to this ideal. Breaking this law is punishable by permanent exclusion from the mainstream societies of Atlantis. An offender is immediately tattooed with the image of a closed eye, and then is blind-folded and taken to a specific Atlantean Island that is reserved for criminals. On the criminal island, a governing party of six guards and six resident criminals maintain an orderly and peaceful social structure. Prisoners provide for their own survival needs, living a simple life of farming, shore-line fishing, and hunting.

If citizens of another land should sneak into Atlantis, they are not permitted to leave, but are given full citizenship and immediately sent to a clinic for rendering them incapable of producing offspring. With permission they may even intermarry with Atlanteans if certain requirements are met.

Rose's mother has now come into view.

She was an immigrant from the Valley of the Nile who stowed away on a ship with her husband to come to the land of the Golden people. Her husband died of a fever on the trip. A lovely, small, frightened dark-skinned woman, she was taken to the Council immediately upon leaving the ship. She was granted full citizenship, but did not receive the sterilization procedure because she was already pregnant with me.

I, Rose, and a male infant named Jahu were born on the same day at the same hour in the same birthing clinic.

During the hours of their labor, while waiting for their time to give birth, the mothers became acquainted. The woman from the Valley of the Nile shared with Jahu's mother that she and her husband had hidden beneath the cargo on a trader's barge that had the insignia of the Children of the Law. For the past few months, she had earned her living in Atlantis by mixing and selling exotic oils and herbs, using formulas and ingredients that she had brought with her.

Jahu's mother, Adara, felt very warm toward this lonely woman who had no kin with whom she could communicate. She was the wife of a wealthy merchant who traveled from island to island six months out of every year collecting artifacts to sell in their elaborately beautiful shop.

When Adara learned from the clinical attendants that the woman of the Valley had died giving birth, she appealed to her husband to adopt the tiny, dark-skinned girl.

"It's doubtful that anyone else will want her, and I feel somehow responsible since it was my own husband's barge that brought this woman to the mainland of Atlantis."

Her pleadings continued for a full day until her husband agreed. The formalities were completed within a week, and Jahu's parents claimed the woman's few belongings as a legacy for her daughter. They gave the child her Mother's name, Rose.

Adara was accustomed to traveling with her husband as a buyer on his six-month excursion to the coastal lands, and after adopting Rose, she was especially interested in their annual trip to the Valley of the Nile. Instead of focusing on the cosmetics and jewelry that she was accustomed to selecting from there, she now sought to purchase the exotic oils and herbs that were described in the formulas. During these six months of travel, it became the custom of Adara and her husband, Aaron, to leave the children and the shop to trusted employees who were members of their religious group, which was called Children of the Law.

When they were not on buying trips, they enjoyed managing the operation of the household and the shop but still left the actual work to their employees, who were overjoyed with the opportunity to be employed by one of the adept leaders of the Children of the Law. Their religion, their friends, their work, and their elaborate home defined the lifestyle for Rose's family.

All members of the Children of the Law celebrated when they heard the story of Rose and her stowaway mother on the barge of the very ones who were to become her parents. It was agreed that the Law had sent Rose to all of them for a very special purpose. It was obvious to all, and a source of great pride for his adept parents, that Jahu had been born an adept, having developed his psychic skills through many incarnations. Adara held a secret belief that the birth of Rose and Jahu at the same moment was a sign from the Law, and she felt sure that she knew what it meant. As the children grew older, she encouraged Jahu to treat Rose not only as a sister but as a twin, sharing all his secrets and thoughts with her.

Meetings of the Children of the Law were frequent but not routine, almost like a party. Invitations were sent by telepathic invitation, and all the local members delighted in anticipating how many or how few might gather. At times the invitations were by name only so that selected small groups could study the Universal Law and practice their Psychic Skills for the delight and amusement of one another. Their object of worship was the Universal Law, which they perceived as the formative energy that created and moved everything in the Universe. While "Great Creator" was the name used throughout Atlantis for the Deity or that which we call God, there were many religions and each had its own concept of that Great Creator. To the Children of the Law, Universal Law was the identity of that Deity. The Law was not perceived to be conscious, but a formidable force that operated automatically and that was available for conscious creatures to use.

Cooperating with the Law would produce betterment of one's life, while ignoring or discounting it would be devastating to one's life. The goal of life was to increase in understanding of the Law, cooperation with the Law, and respect for the Law so that one could fulfill the purpose, which was to have a good life while helping other Children of the Law to do the same.

Parents belonging to the Children of the Law were required to have their children trained in methods of basic Psychic Skills such as astral projection, telepathy (both transmission and reception), reading the Akashic Records and finally White Magic (using Creative Visualization for producing a desired effect). Through home-schooling, Jahu and Rose were provided an excellent education relating to a variety of subjects, including the basics of Universal Law and psychic experimentation.

Jahu was adept in White Magic even before he had his first lesson, therefore, quite skilled in all the other practices. No Atlantean ever questioned Rose's small stature, which was quite strange in comparison to the tall, blonde willowy frames of Atlantean women and the massive physiques of Atlantean men. Even though she was not of their superior race, the girl was a good student with a preference for Jahu as her mentor rather than her teachers or her parents.

Children of the Law was not the most common religious practice among Atlanteans by any means. With complete religious freedom, there were dozens of religions to choose from. Only the belief in reincarnation and the belief that they were a special race of people were universally accepted among Atlanteans, regardless of their Religion.

The most predominant religion of all was worship of the God of Light. In all of Atlantis there were no more than twelve hundred members of the Children of the Law, but there were thousands worshipping the God of Light.

The Children of the Law prided themselves in their exclusiveness. They did not accept all who applied, and their knowledge of the Law was given only to members.

Membership was attained only by birthright or recommendation by one of the Adept members.

By contrast, followers of the God of Light hungrily welcomed all sincere seekers of the Light into their membership and even sought converts. They were quite judgmental concerning the teachings and practices of the Children, saying that was a good name for them since they were so childish in their beliefs. In turn, the Children of the Law playfully ridiculed the worshippers of the God of Light as delusional and deliberately avoided all personal interaction with them.

As Rose grew older, she became intrigued with the study of various cultures and Religions. From her parents she learned that her ancestors in the Valley of the Nile worshipped the sun. In her classes on different beliefs, she learned that the worshippers of the God of Light believed that the whole purpose of life is to enjoy the sensation of "witnessing the Light" while sitting in silent meditation. Their claim was, "When this is accomplished then one is happy, no matter what happens."

The prospect fascinated her. A further thought of this philosophy of happiness was that when a meditator becomes of age to be free from the requirement of earning a living or caring for a household, the ideal is to give as many hours as one can tolerate to witnessing the Light in rapt meditation upon it. This will gradually produce a disinterest in all things and people of the world.

Rose felt a harmony with this philosophy, and she brought it into conversation when she and Jahu were alone.

"They teach that eventually the ultimate joy will come to one who sits in witness of the Light and not even the world can distract the meditator from the ecstatic rapture of constant absorption of his mind in the Light. The Enlightened One would then be liberated from all mundane responsibilities and exempt from pain and suffering. They also account for reincarnation by teaching that an Enlightened One would be repeatedly reincarnated as an Enlightened One, with no responsibility except to entice others by his or her example of one who depends on nothing but the Light. Such a fully Enlightened One would need no food, no liquid and no human affection. They say that teaching the first step toward developing this experience of Total Enlightenment is to sacrifice everything that one takes pleasure from except the Light because the Light is jealous of your other pleasures. The more enjoyable a human pleasure, the more important it would be to sacrifice that pleasure.

The second step is to sacrifice work. To sacrifice all work except for basic survival needs is said to be evidence that the Enlightenment is expanding. The refusal to partake of any pleasures, other than the pleasure of Meditation upon the God of Light, is accepted as a testimony of the seeker's commitment to gaining Enlightenment."

"Humph!" was Jahu's comment, and he wrinkled his nose to make a funny face. "The first pleasure I would have to give up would be you. And, I have to say that I don't ever want to be in a state of consciousness in which I have no work to do and no need for a mate."

Rose snuggled close to him. She was both amused and fascinated by the contrast between this belief and the beliefs of the Children of the Law, which taught that human beings were a product of the Law of Mental Action, brought about by an intense energy that became a mass of concentrated energy in the Universe. Desire was the name of that mass. Desire then continued to expand until it produced a human form with a mind. This allowed the Desire energy to be connected to Mind (they had no explanation of the source of Mind or Consciousness). As she understood it, the Children of the Law taught that the whole purpose for human life was two-fold: Primarily, it was to experience personal pleasure through the harmless satisfaction of personal desires, without interfering with the rights of others to satisfy their own personal desires in the manner of their choice. And, secondly, it was to practice a work that was pleasurable to oneself and beneficial to both the worker and other members of the society.

Rose laughed and thought to herself, "Indeed if one gives up personal desire and work one must also give up this religion."

Another major belief of the Children was that the Psychic Ability, and the degree to which it was possessed, was a gift from the Law and a testimony to one's relationship with the Deity. Once a promise was made under the Law, it must never be withdrawn in the current incarnation. A lawful promise was for life. To withdraw or be disloyal to a lawful promise was to sever one's personal awareness of the Law and lose the Psychic Ability. It was not known whether this loss of Ability was for just that incarnation or for all time, but few dared to take the chance. Loss of Psychic Ability would create enormous Karma for that soul in many lifetimes to come.

A Lawful Promise was made by toasting to an agreement and to the Law in the presence of one or more Children of the Law. Once made, no matter what occurred, the promise could not be undone. Because of the serious consequences of it, no one was permitted to toast to the Law until their 18th birthday. Until then promiscuity and every other form of human pleasure, except those that are dangerous and harmful to the body or the mind, was not only acceptable but encouraged. The idea was that this early freedom provided the young ones sufficient experience for making adult choices about lawful promises when they came into the age of responsibility for keeping their word.

"It is strange," thought 11-year-old Rose, as she reviewed the two concepts. "To one group, desire and pleasure are that which keeps us from the Deity, and to the other they are to be honored as the Deity's gift to us. I wonder which is really true."

Jahu and Rose were inseparable, and when they were 12 years old two important changes occurred in their lives.

Jahu became an apprentice in his father's business to learn first about the artifacts, geography and artisans of various regions. And he announced to their parents that he and Rose had become lovers.

They were overjoyed.

"Did we not envision it, my husband?" said Adara, embracing her husband. "The hope for this was my winning argument for getting you to adopt the girl. We had hoped for a strong alliance between them and that Jahu would find Atlantean women unattractive by comparison. Our vision has been realized. Praise to the Great Law."

Aaron glowed with pride, "This means that Jahu will not be distracted by other girls and the social nonsense of mate selection. He will be more inclined to focus on the retention and further development of his Psychic skills. With freedom to concentrate, he will be assured of happiness and success in life."

They drank a toast to the future marriage of their children.

And another change took place when at age 13 Jahu began the second stage of his apprenticeship. He was to be included in the buying trips each year until he was 18. This would assure his practical development in learning to apply his Psychic Skills to manipulating business affairs and trade.

Rose had also been offered the opportunity for apprenticeship, but she politely refused. "I will surely miss Jahu when he is away, but I must be true to myself and to you, my beloved parents. My interests lie in the use of my psychic skills for helping enhance the life experience of others. And I must confess that I thoroughly enjoy working with exotic oils and my Mother's formulas."

Adara was disturbed by Rose's decision. She worried, "What if he is tempted toward another woman in his time away?"

The thought crept frequently into her mind, and she voiced it to her husband who shared her concerns. But no amount of pleading on their part could distract Rose from her interest in oils and herbs and dabbling in psychic activity.

Jahu had been traveling six months of every year for five years, and now they were on another return trip to Atlantis. It was a clear, sunny day, and as Jahu stood at the railing of the cargo barge, observing the depths of the water below, he realized that soon he and Rose would be 18 and he felt his life was empty except for her.

He remembered some of their deep conversations, and nostalgic feelings of loneliness and love consumed him. He thought, "The Sea is beautiful and eternal. If I did not know the Law, I might worship the sea that stretches as far as the eye can see and has no beginning or end. But it stirs up a loneliness in me for the warmth of my Rose. The sea is cold, but she is warm and feeds my desire for love."

Looking at the Sun, which was believed by some to be the God of Light, he continued to muse, "The magnificent Sun! How beautiful is he and how wise. He knows when to move and when to shine, when to wake and when to sleep. He brings sweetness to the unripe fruits and color that pleases the eye. But the sweetness of Rose and the ripeness of her tantalizing fruits put all the berries to shame. Her colors outshine the most brilliant hues of nature."

With an aching heart he cried inside himself, "Rose, Rose, I am coming, sweet love. Together we will play in the sun and bathe in the sea. But I am done with traveling! My work will be on shore. For I love the softness of my billowy bed, and the opulence of a table spread with fine foods, and the familiar scents of my own garden and my wife to be."

At the same time, Rose was sitting by the shore, gazing into the sky and projecting a message to Jahu: "My heart is as if shattered until you return to me, my beautiful Jahu. I see the ocean through your eyes as I gaze into the sky. Do you see my heart? It is divided between sea and sun, earth and sky, for I know not where to find you in this moment."

She stayed there for hours until the darkness came; then whispered to him again, "Now the sky is dark. One star peeks through. Will you meet me on that star as we dream and share our sleep together?"

When the barge docked a few days later, Jahu leapt from the deck and ran to sweep Rose into his arms. Nuzzling her long dark hair he groaned, "I could find you nowhere, except in my heart and in the first star of each night. The star drew me up from my pallet on the deck and wrapped me warmly in love. Were you there?"

Rose whispered through tears of gladness, "I was there."

That night they lay on the grass under the stars, planning their life together. It was a dream of sharing work that they would accomplish as partners for life. They would begin as soon as they were permitted to marry.

To celebrate the eighteenth birthday of Jahu and Rose, a telepathic invitation was sent by his parents to all Children of the Law. It was not their actual birthday but the night of the nearest full-moon. They had been born under the sign of the Bear. A great feast was prepared, and over one thousand people were there in a great circular auditorium with candles around the entire outer wall. The two lovers were amazed at the number of people attending. A birthday celebration traditionally involved only family and close friends, but these "Children" seemed to have come from all parts of the Continent. Jahu and Rose were dressed in white. toga style, indicating that they were virgins to their new life of emancipation from parental control. They were seated in the auditorium on white velvet chairs upon a raised platform in the center of the room.

Everyone else was standing.

Their father raised his silver goblet for a toast, "Praises to the Great Law for sending Jahu, the adept, into my family and into our circle of friends. May he prosper profusely and see nothing but happiness and pleasure all the days of this life and in his lives to come."

Everyone raised their silver goblets toward Jahu, saying in unison: "Praise be to the Law for placing an adept among us to reinforce our Faith in the Power and our Love for the Law."

After they drank, Aaron raised his hand to quiet the crowd, saying, "A second toast to another gift from the Great Law to my household. She was a gift at her birth, directly from the Great Law to Adara. Adara, in turn, gave her to Jahu with hope that they would find pleasure in one another. Rose was mentored by Jahu in all the ways of the Children of the Law. Through her studious efforts she proves herself to be worthy of membership in our company. In return, she gave him a love that saved my son from distraction and aided in his remembrance of the Practice."

Everyone raised their goblets toward Rose, "Praise be to the Law for giving us the joy of raising Rose among the Children of the Law.

Wild music burst forth with dancing in the great hall. When the dance was over, Aaron raised his cup again: "And a third toast to complete the power of the first two. Let us celebrate the emancipation of both Jahu and Rose from these former years of parental control. And knowing their first wish of the state of emancipation is to know each other as mate, I hereby pronounce that they are free to be wed! It is the wish of the Law and the fulfillment of their desire."

Everyone raised their glasses toward the astounded couple and in unison they recited the wedding ceremony and blessing, "Will you promise under the Law to be faithfully wed to one another for all of this life?"

Jahu and Rose lifted their cups, "We promise."

Cups clinked as the crowd shouted, "Praise be to the Law for mating of Soul to Soul. It is done."

Rose and Jahu were overjoyed. They had not expected approval for marriage at the time of emancipation. The general waiting period was one year from emancipation to the requesting of permission to marry.

In keeping with the marriage ritual of the Children of the Law, Jahu and Rose turned to one another and chanted in unison: "My public life is devoted to doing a work with you. My religious life is devoted to keeping my word to the Law and using the gifts the Law has given me. My personal life is devoted to giving you pleasure and adding to the joy of your life, and I promise to accept the pleasure you give to me as you add to the joy of my life."

The music resumed while the traditional "Wedding Vat" was brought out on a round wooden platform with wheels. It was a huge, gleaming, flat-bottomed vat, actually made of gold to represent the wealth of their family. In less wealthy families the Wedding Vat was made of brass, or even wood. As the Vat was sent spinning around the room from one person to another, it was filled to overflowing with great sums of money. Finally, it rested in front of the newlyweds. A fortune had been collected for beginning their married life, in keeping with the tradition of the Children of the Law.

Aaron lifted his cup toward Jahu for another toast: "One more toast. Now that Jahu is no longer my apprentice, I declare him a full partner in my business, free to buy, travel and trade at will."

Startled, Jahu leapt to his feet and raised his hand in a gesture of protest, "Wait! Do not drink to seal my fate. I am grateful to you, my father, but Rose and I have a dream."

Placing his hand on Jahu's shoulder, Aaron said, "Speak, my son. "You are free, and your dream for yourself is my dream for you."

Jahu announced with confidence, "Rose and I will be partners in a business to sell not wares but services of our Psychic Skills. Even those who are not Children of the Law are interested in success and pleasure and health. We can earn a handsome living by helping to improve their quality of life while finding a meaningful outlet for our skills.

Rose has become adept in many areas of the Practice. She will work in one element and I in another. Each of us will want six adept helpers to start our service, and with this fine fortune collected on our wedding day, we will purchase the stone house at the bend of the River. If your sons or daughters between 18 and 25 qualify as adepts, send them there to inquire before the next full moon."

More than 50 adepts inquired of the positions, and 24 were selected to take a test.

The test was the same for everyone. It was a simple test of telepathic skills (both projection and reception) because communication of thoughts was acknowledged by the Children of the Law to be the basis of all Psychic Practices.

Of the 24 who tested, six women were selected by Rose and six men by Jahu.

Jahu's service was to be in two categories. In one area he would offer business advice and political predictions. In another he would offer healing touch and health readings, balancing of energies and recommendations for dietary change, with a focus on mental and physical strength; all skills in which he was greatly adept.

Within two years, he was recognized as the greatest Practitioner of Psychic Ability in the territory and was invited to contract as a direct advisor to the Senate. Soon he was spending most of his personal "work" time with the advisory activity, while leaving the business advice and predictions and the healing work to his employees.

Rose viewed her work as much more exciting and glamorous. She and her workmates provided a "Lover's Service" and a Healing Service for both men and women. Jahu's workmates referred healing customers to Rose's service for emotional healing, after the healing touch and energy balancing was done. She and her workmates would then provide anointment with exotic oils from the Valley of the Nile, and herbal teas to drink. Rose used the formulas that had been given to her from her mother's belongings. The Lover's Service was available to any person age 18 or over who had a lover or mate, or who desired one. For a fee they offered a month of Psychic chanting for the purpose of increasing the customer's animal magnetism and seductive powers. They also offered readings of every kind for helping customers with their personal issues of life, including astrology charting. They gave advice on improving personal magnetism and taught mannerisms for attracting the opposite sex. They taught a meditation form designed to seduce when performed with the partner of choice. As a result, dull marriages were revived, self-confidence blossomed, the quality of pleasure in their customer's love affairs was enhanced, and Rose's work group made a great deal of money.

The relationship of Jahu and Rose was both erotic and sacred to them because of their serious commitment to their word and the promise to the Law. Their great love for one another was pointed out as an example of what the Law could do for those who became adepts and married adepts. Their religion stated that the Law requires of its married "Children" that they be bound to fidelity of thought, word and deed in order to avoid any interest in another. Because of this they were forbidden to take another mate in this life even if the other were to leave or die or become disinterested in them. If the Law brought about circumstances of separation or estrangement, it was to be accepted as the path for one's life. To choose another mate or to enjoy sexual pleasure with another would be to break one's conscious connection to the Great Law. This would result in immediate loss of psychic ability. And, as was said before, it was not known whether that severing of the psychic ability would be just for the current incarnation or permanent, but few were willing to test it.

One evening, seven years after her marriage, while focusing upon her third eye, a necessary skill for controlled psychic practices, Rose saw in her mind's eye a white cloud of Light swirling toward her face. As she observed, spellbound, it drew near, "melting" into her eyes and causing a momentary sensation of euphoric buoyancy to swell inside her mind. A sensation of being immersed in harmony permeated her being, as if she had just listened to a grand orchestra presenting a piece that touched her to the core, only more than that. Then it was gone. But the memory of the experience lingered, leaving a gentle sense of deep peace and joy.

She felt different, as if she knew something that she had not known before, but could not put her finger on what it was. She concluded that this cloud of Light she had seen must be none other than the God of Light that she had heard and read about. How could she deny it now? It seemed that the God of Light, for some reason, had selected her and invited her to learn about him.

Rose knew that many believers in the God of Light taught that the Sun is the true Deity. They pointed out that the Power of the Sun is used to activate everything from the cell regenerators to the air vehicles. They acknowledged the Law as a reality but reasoned that the Sun generated the activity of the Law, and that without the Sun the Law would have no Power, therefore; the Law was a secondary Deity to the Sun. This seemed logical to Rose as she pondered the meaning of her experience.

The worshippers of the Light taught that the Law had rebelled against the Sun, seeking to press desire upon the human mind, while the Sun had created the humans simply for his own companionship and to give them the sole enjoyment of witnessing the Light. She remembered that the requirement for claiming the God of Light was to sacrifice every pleasure except that of experiencing the Light beginning with the greatest pleasure that one enjoyed.

For weeks Rose struggled with this shift in her concept of the Deity. She felt a growing revulsion toward her former understanding of the "Great Law", along with a fear of what it would mean to her and Jahu if she should decide to accept the God of Light.

But to think that she had once considered the Law to be God was now ludicrous to her since she had witnessed the pleasure of knowing the Light for herself. She did not know that it was the Divine, Harmonic Vibration of her own Spiritual Energies that she had seen; and she did not think to look for other interpretations of her experience. All she could perceive was to accept the interpretation given by the worshippers of Light.

Rose struggled with the idea letting go of sexual enjoyment and the joy of mental, emotional, and telepathic joy that she shared with Jahu. It was as Jahu had said when they were but 13. Her intimate association with him was her greatest pleasure in life, and she decided that she must begin by giving up her sexual pleasures. But desire was still there; and guilt for it now consumed her with a burning shame, taking the place of joyful expectation.

She began giving Jahu excuses day after day when saying no to his advances because she was afraid to tell him the real reason. She knew how to shield her thoughts from his psychic probing, and she wrestled with the question without consulting him.

"How can I tell Jahu of my need to give up all human pleasures? Perhaps I can convert him to the Light, and then I will not be required to give up my association with him. I could still enjoy our mental and emotional intimacy."

Yet, even these thoughts produced a burning guilt in her. The guilt was compounded for having betrayed Jahu's trust and her promise to the Law, that she would live for his pleasure and bring joy to his life. She was not afraid to lose her Psychic Skills through breaking her promise to the Law, but she was afraid of losing an even greater source of pleasure for her: Jahu's approval and respect.

After weeks of attempting to recapture the sensation of Light in her third eye, Rose realized that she was neglecting her part of the business. Rose began to cry with the pain of confusion, guilt and loneliness, emotions that she had never felt before. When she was exhausted, and her crying was done, she turned her attention once more to her mind's eye. Then she saw a glow of pale light developing, just a bit above her third eye, and the sight of it sent waves of harmony and peace throughout her entire being, bringing forgetfulness of her former misery. Now she was convinced that the worshippers of the God of Light were right, for if she had not been willing to accept the agony of her sacrifice, she might not have seen the Light again. She celebrated its return quietly within herself, thinking, "It is true. The pleasures of body and mind surely must be the antipathy of pleasure in the Light. Sacrifice of one type of pleasure in order to have the other is required by the Deity. One must choose between human pleasure and Spiritual pleasure and cannot have the pleasure of both."

Rose arranged for Jahu to meet her at their favorite picnic spot near the sea. With an unapproachable dignity she told Jahu about her experiences with the Light, apologizing for her neglect of him, while appealing for his forgiveness. "I no longer can believe that the Law is God, for I have seen the God of Light for myself."

Her husband was stunned. At first he laughed at her, thinking it was a joke. But when he saw that she was sincere, he felt agony for the first time in his life.

Jahu begged, "Surely, you will change your mind. To see the Light is one thing. But to believe all that is said of it is another. Find another way to explain it to yourself. I beg you. With the help of the Law, you can do it. Ask and the Law will reveal to you a way to reconcile this to your own way of life!"

"There is nothing to ask. I have decided the meaning, and I cannot change my mind," said Rose. "My mind now belongs to the God of Light and is no longer my own to use."

Jahu wept. Rose did not hold him and stroke his hair as she was tempted to do because it would have given her pleasure, and because she would have been guilty of producing pleasure for another. If he were ever to come to her again, it would be through his sorrow not through his pleasure. She waited until his tears were spent.

Jahu tried again to reason with her. "You are my wife, given to me by the Law, and no mysterious Light can undo our promise to each other and the Law. You are not free to change your Deity. You made a promise to the Law that you would work with me and live with me in pleasure as long as we live."

"Yes, I made the promise," said Rose, "and I am sorry for the pain this will bring to your life. You must understand that to ignore my desire for you and follow my desire for the Light is the first work that I must do for my new way of life. I have no more love for the Law or desire to live as a Child of the Law, but I do still love you and I do still desire pleasures with you."

Jahu pleaded, "Your love for me and your love of the Law must be one and the same. I have no use for one without the other. I am an adept loving my affiliation with the Law, loving my gift of Psychic Powers, loving you and loving our belief in the Law. How can you separate this into parts? It is all about our life."

"You must think about only your life, now," said Rose in a monotone voice. "My life is as if the old Rose never existed. I ask the Light to give me the strength to ignore your pain and to go into my new way of life with peace."

Recovering his own dignity in the face of her coldness, Jahu spoke at length, "Then you have left me and betrayed our agreement and our parents. You are free. I release you to be a new person in your love with the Light. But I am not free because I honor the Law.

Children of the Law do not intermarry with worshippers of the God of Light. I will be married to my Rose until the day I die and let no other entertain my mind. But you say she is no more. I wish that you would change your name to make it more complete. We are but 25 years old and I am true to the Law, with only my memories of pleasure in the one who was my Rose. My happiness is at risk, but my power will never be at risk."

He looked deeply into Rose's eyes as if probing to find a spark of the woman who had shared his life. "By the Law, I am forbidden to take pleasure in my own wife if she abandons the Law!"

Rose showed no signs of reversal.

Jahu looked beyond her, toward the sea, "Go in peace to our house at the River's Bend, and let the household servants care for you. Your workers and the proceeds of their labor will provide the necessities you require. I will establish my residence in our place of business. Unless you come to me with a renewal of our wedding vows which accepts the Law, I will view you no longer as my wife."

In the weeks and months that followed, Rose alternated between euphoria when in deep meditation upon the third eye and an unshakable sadness and sense of deprivation and guilt when not in meditation. Her desire for Jahu was a smoldering fire within her, and she prayed fervently that it would be dissolved.

One day while in meditation, she questioned the Light using a process that she formerly had used when questioning the Law. She had become concerned about the increasing frequency, severity, and volume of floods and earthquakes being experienced on the mainland. Even though she felt guilty for desiring to know, still she wanted to know. To her surprise the place where she went to join the Light seemed to become illumined, and she sensed that the Light had responded. She had a psychic impression that a great flood would come soon to totally engulf the mainland of Atlantis. With hope for reforming his beliefs, she visited Jahu to plead her case.

"The Law has not abandoned me or taken my psychic skills away even though I am a worshipper of the Light. It has shown me what is happening to our world. There is nothing to fear. You would not lose your psychic abilities. You, too, can break your vow and join the worshippers of the God of Light."

Jahu simply stared at her with disbelief as she continued her plea.

"I saw the breakup of the mainland into smaller islands and valleys under the sea.

It is going to happen sometime soon with a great earthquake and engulfing flood. Please leave with me. It is not safe for anyone to stay here."

"Are you asking that I leave with you as your husband in the Law?" Jahu asked.

"No. I cannot accept the Law as God. The Light has sent me to rescue you from the perils that will come upon Atlantis,"

Jahu was decisive but gentle in his response, as if speaking to a child, "I am surprised and pleased that your betrayal of the Law has not cost you your psychic powers, but to share time with you that requires avoidance of pleasures would provide nothing of value to me. In fact, it would cause me more anguish than to be without you. I wish you well, my beloved one, but you can tell your Light that I still enjoy my love of the Law, and I trust the Law to bring my knowledge to me at the appropriate time. I need no messengers to interfere with my fate. Go to safety as you see fit, and I wish you good health. I will be needed here by those who employ me for advice, and here I will stay until the Law reveals to me that I must go."

Rose cried, pleading with him, "But you might die, then how can you be of help to anyone?"

Jahu said, "Show no fear, my wife. I have work to do here. If I die, then perhaps in my next life we will share our dreams again. If you must leave Atlantis, take what you need and go."

Rose whispered through her tears, "Will you kiss me good-bye?

He held her tenderly. "It is Rose who has asked me. I will gladly kiss my wife at any time."

Jahu kissed her deeply, then turned away in sorrow. He could tell that she felt guilty for the pleasure she felt in that exquisite kiss.

Rose went to the meeting place of the worshippers of the God of Light. She announced what she had seen and selected 15 female worshippers to accompany her in her escape to the Valley of the Nile. She had booked passage for them on a trading barge that was owned by her adopted Father. She had heard that on the other side there was a river flowing from sea to shore and back again, but it did not flow daily as did the river here. That river rushed closer to the Valley week by week and at one point of its surge, depending on the size of the moon and the seasons of the stars, it would dump its water into a shallow Valley below. People had settled along the shores of the Valley and it was divided by landmarks into Kingdoms, with each Kingdom having a ruler of its own.

Rose had been told that the Kingdom nearest the shores of Atlantis was ruled by an altruistic King who paid no attention to who entered or left by boat. Everyone was welcome to come or go as they pleased. It was rumored that people from many different lands lived there in harmony.

"We will let the river take us from the sea, then walk the remaining distance to this open Kingdom," she said to her friends. "The barge captain has secured a piece of land for us to occupy and set three tents upon it."

Their journey was long and hard. By the time they arrived at the Fertile Valley of the Nile, the thought of living in a tent on dry land seemed a great pleasure compared to life on a barge. She could see that it was worth the suffering they had endured.

Upon entering the land of their new home, Rose and her friends followed the boat captain to the place that he had arranged for them.

Wishing to reassure Rose of their freedom and safety, he said, "Belief in the God of Light is a well-known religion, just one of many religions in this kingdom. There is no need to hide your beliefs or practices from the inhabitants. No one is offended by what anyone else believes. The governor here believes that there is a power behind the sun that generates both the light of the sun and the Law, and that this power is the Deity. That means that neither the light nor the law is God. What do you think of that?!"

Rose was startled by such an extravagant belief. "How absurd!" she laughed.

Her pleasure in the laughter was followed by guilt, and she congratulated herself for the progress she had gained in recognizing quickly when she had sinned.

"I will be back in a year," said the boat captain. "May the Law provide for your every need."

On their first trip to market, the small band of women discovered that the boat captain had failed to tell them their money had no value here among the common people. Being ignorant of the availability of conversion from one form of money to another, they took this as a sign that the God of Light was requiring another sacrifice of them. To demonstrate their willingness to accept poverty, they went in unison to the riverbank and tossed all their coins into the river. It was a considerable sum, but worthless to them here, so they believed. Proud of their new ability to survive poverty, they took to sitting in the marketplace to beg. All of them except Rose were very large compared to the locals and were obviously from Atlantis, "the land of the golden giants." The locals would give her associates a few coins to tell about life in Atlantis, and there was enough food to eat as long as two of them were willing to go to the marketplace to sit each day. Rose was exempt from the begging, and she spent her active time in preparing the food and training converts in meditation upon the Light.

By the end of their third year, all of Rose's original friends had experienced the beauty of the Light in their meditations. Because this was the only pleasure they permitted themselves, they decided to call themselves, "Brides of the God of Light."

In the next seven years they attracted more than 50 new members. Newcomers were required to bring their own tent or share the tent of a willing Bride. There were now 30 tents on the site. Solitude and silence were encouraged and, except for taking turns at begging, shopping and food preparation, no one worked at all except to keep themselves, their clothes and their tent clean. Needless to say, all of the members were women because of the name they had taken.

During those first 10 years the boat captain who had helped Rose escape made one trip each year to the fertile Valley of the Nile and back again to Atlantis. He got a good laugh out of her story about the useless coins, the begging and the converts. And he brought news to Rose of Jahu, their parents and the ravages of nature upon not only her former home but the entire mainland. Her greatest concern was for Jahu's safety and well-being. She did not wish him happiness because she knew that only sorrow and loneliness would urge him to join her.

The same boat captain took news of Rose to Jahu. Jahu's only concern was that she be safe and well. He did not wish her happiness because he knew that if he were to have her back it would be because of disillusionment in her change of beliefs.

Atlantis was now almost completely under the Sea. Sensing it was time to go, Jahu left on a barge with a bag of clothing and as much gold as he could carry. Not one other person could have fit on the barge. He praised the Great Law for providing him with the opportunity to hop aboard and the friend who had told him of this barge one of the last few vessels escaping the storms. He brushed away tears as he thought of Adara and Aaron. They had been lost in a great storm at sea three years before on one of their buying trips to the Western Islands.

Jahu's reputation as the most adept psychic practitioner in all of Atlantis went before him as well as the news that he was coming. Dozens of citizens waited for his arrival to get a glimpse of this golden giant. One of the government officials took his bags and offered him a bed for the night. In conversation at dinner, he was told that there was an opening in the Senate and was encouraged to apply. His request to meet with the governor was fulfilled that same day, and after hours of conversation he was appointed to the first seat of the senate as the governor's confidante and psychic advisor. A part of his generous salary was a grand house with beautiful landscaped gardens and servants to care for his daily needs.

"Praise the goodness of the Great Law for this wonderful new start," he said. His heart was overflowing with gratitude. "I am but 35 years old, strong and healthy, with my wits about me still. What more does a man need, but a good wife to share in his bounty?"

Tears stung his eyes with a mixture of gratitude and loneliness. "At least I am in the same city with Rose again. Perhaps she has missed me too," he thought. Hope fluttered through his soul, and he felt charged with enthusiasm to begin his new way of life.

While he was becoming oriented to this new land with its backward ways, Jahu often walked through the marketplace. In the years since Rose had left, many Atlanteans had fled to this Valley of the Nile, and his size was not such an odd sight in the city.

The old boat captain, who had brought Rose here before he was swept away in the floods, had told Jahu about the daily begging as a way of life for Rose's people.

Strolling through the marketplace one day, Jahu saw several Atlantean women begging in the square, and he inquired of each, "Do you know a woman named Rose who is a Bride of the God of Light?"

They shook their heads and continued their begging chants.

Then a day came when he noticed that one of them was not chanting but sitting silently with her bowl. When he inquired, she nodded in response. A flush of joyful expectation spread across Jahu's face. "Where can I find her?" he asked.

As if afraid to speak, or perhaps her years of silence had caused her voice to be weak, the woman pointed toward a brass ornament in her hair. It was designed after the sun. Then she whispered, "See someone who is wearing this and follow her home, but do not follow me, lest you wish to be cursed."

Jahu put a large sum of money in her dish, and she left immediately to shop for food. Every day for a week Jahu went to the marketplace, found a beggar with the sun in her hair and filled her dish with coins to take to her camp. One day he found he could hold himself back no longer. He must see Rose or die. He followed 10 paces behind a woman with the sun in her hair, and when they were near the tented area he shouted, "Madam, tell Rose that Jahu has come to see her."

Rose heard his voice, and overcome with joy she ran from her tent and leapt into his arms, showering his face with kisses. He dared to hope that this meant a renewal of her wedding vows to him.

But when he had set her feet on the ground and their eyes met, she adjusted her shawl, pulling it tightly around her head and looked at her feet.

Jahu asked tenderly, "Are you well, my wife? Do you and your friends have everything you need?"

She answered in a whisper, as if not trusting her voice, "I am well, my friend and brother. I give praises to all powers that be for your safe escape from Atlantis."

Still with a remnant of hope he asked boldly, "Are you ready to renew our wedding vows?"

"I cannot," she murmured almost too softly to hear. Then she looked at him and said, "Will you come into my tent for tea?"

"Is that what you desire?" challenged Jahu.

"It is the only desire that I will permit myself. Perhaps it is an innocent desire, if there be such a thing."

Jahu declined. His heart was filled with a suffering that he did not want to reveal. "If you ever change your mind, go to the office of the senate. You can find me there."

Every day after that he would go, or send someone, to the marketplace to find a woman with the sun in her hair and fill her dish with coins. He never attempted to see Rose again.

That same year, the governor became quite ill. Jahu was able to sustain him with healing touch and energy balancing, but he could tell psychically that the man would be dead within 10 years unless something more effective were done. In Atlantis, pyramids had been commonly in use as conductors of energy rays from the planets and stars. They were positioned differently in order to conduct the vibrations in different combinations.

Jahu had spent considerable time in pyramids to receive the energies for cellular reconstruction and to transmit them psychically for various purposes. He proposed to the governor that a healing pyramid be built for the personal use of the governor, his family and the senate. The governor readily agreed, and the first pyramid in the Valley of the Nile was completed within eight years of that date. It was a small pyramid, open at the top with steps from bottom to top on all four sides.

Once these outer steps were climbed, one could descend into the various chambers of the pyramid by way of a wooden cage that served as an elevator, capable of being lowered by a solar- powered pulley. At different seasons of the year, the vibrations inside the pyramid would change, causing a need to descend to a lower level or ascend to a higher chamber within the structure. On his first visit inside, the governor was barely able to crawl up the steps with Jahu by his side. He was invited to sit on the floor of the first chamber while Jahu intoned specific sounds that were meant to aid the activity of the healing rays. Upon being deposited at the top again by the ascending elevator, the governor literally ran down the steps. Through these efforts Jahu became known as a miracle worker, and the governor lived an active life for five additional years after the pyramid was built.

Jahu had become very friendly with the governor's son, and upon the governor's death, the son took his place as Monarch of the province, proclaiming himself, not as a governor, but as King of the Province. He announced that Jahu would continue to hold the number one position in the Senate as advisor and confidante of the King.

Almost two years later, just before their 50th birthday Jahu received the news that Rose, of the Brides of the God of Light, had died of malnutrition.

For days he was overcome with grief. "How dare she starve herself to death when I was providing for her and her friends every day!" How could she be so stupid as to forget about health and nutrition or to ignore all the things she knew?" he raged.

But he did not know that after he had been there, Rose had longed for him with burning desire every day and confessed it to her friends. Because she had not been able to stop her desire for him, she decided to let it live while she chose a different desire to sacrifice, one that would be easier to accomplish. She gave up her desire for food. Very soon she was able to sense no physical hunger whatsoever, so she ate only a crumb or two every day and sacrificed the delicious teas for water. Some days she forgot to eat at all. One day she went to sleep with the desire for Jahu on her mind, and the next day she did not wake up.

Jahu was angry about the pain and agony he was feeling. "I have been loyal to the Law. The promise of the Law is that those who live in harmony with the Law will never experience extreme displeasure, so how can this be?"

Now he knew it was not true. Had he been wrong about the Law? He wrestled with this question as well as with the knowledge that Rose had never lost her psychic skills. Disillusionment threatened his peace of mind and he felt a need to sort things out.

In an effort to do just that, Jahu stayed in seclusion, in his home and gardens, for the rest of his life. He continued to support his commitment to the king, but with the provision that the king would come to him for service. He was not happy, but he was resigned to his way of life and therefore content. He adapted to his situation and found it very pleasant, but he always felt expectant, as if he were waiting for something. He could not have told anyone, especially not himself, what he was waiting for.

Fifteen years later Jahu died in his sleep on the full moon following his 65th birthday. There was no evidence as to the cause of his death. It was as if he had merely grown tired of waiting and willed it to be.

Chapter 3

MWA

Egypt 2500 B.C.

> **Journal Entry #2**
>
> *The place of this incarnation is exactly the place in which Rose of Atlantis died. As I witness my birth in this incarnation, I am saddened to see that again I am not to know my birth mother. Compassion for my former ignorance fills me, as I look in on the beginning of this lifetime to see that the result of my former withdrawal from the act of reasoning, intimate relationships, and the normal comforts of life is a poverty-ridden beginning. It is accompanied by the painful experience of being shunned. This land on the banks of the Nile River is now a beautiful, wealthy and powerful kingdom under the rule of one monarch, a Pharaoh. The Pharaoh amuses himself with frequent travel across the land in a large, ornate carriage that is manned on four corners by his servants.*

Mwa was born in Egypt in 2500 B.C. of an unwed peasant woman. Her father was an Aryan traveler whom the woman had met walking on the shore in dim moonlight. After their brief encounter, he had gone back to his boat and sailed away. One look at the strange appearance of her child with white hair and pink translucent skin convinced the dark-haired, olive skinned, superstitious Egyptian woman that she had been cursed by the gods because of her promiscuity. Her family worshipped the Sun-God above all the gods of their culture, and she feared the girl was a demon sent to torment her as vengeance for her sexual pleasures. The fact that this child did not cry or make a sound added to the mother's fears. This white girl seemed to have no voice, just eyes like blue stones that watched as if in a trance and yet did not see. She gave the child no name; and when the infant was six weeks old, her mother ran away in terror and was never heard from again.

The woman's relatives lived in fear of the planetary gods with a strong sense of duty toward the burdens that the Sun-God had placed in their lives. This demon child, abandoned by her mother, was thought to be one of those inescapable burdens. Because none of them wanted to take on the responsibility of raising her in their own home, they quarreled among themselves until they devised a solution.

"After all," they murmured among themselves, "we must pay penance to the gods so that they will know we are not cruel enough to let a living thing starve. We will feed her on the milk of a goat and pass the goat with her from house to house each month." They called her "White Girl", and still she was given no name.

As she grew older, White Girl observed everything with watchful eyes but did not speak. For fear of being shunned, her relatives had never let anyone outside the family see her with them or near their shanties. They believed she was incapable of learning and they wanted nothing more than their freedom from this curse. The truth is that the power of reasoning had become dormant in the soul's consciousness by its lack of use for so many years in her incarnation as Rose of Atlantis. She was not stupid at all but found it difficult to connect her thoughts to words or to relate her ideas to what she witnessed.

On the rare occasion that someone did see White Girl near them; her relatives treated her with kindness, pretending she was a beggar. The family assigned her no chores, and they encouraged her to roam about the streets. She was warned to avoid letting anyone see her leave the house or return. Secretly they hoped that someday she would not return. White Girl pretended that they really did care for her and that their gift of freedom was a sign of trust, yet she knew they had no interest in what she did as long as she kept away from them. The child spent her time day-dreaming, sitting and staring, observing people and playing in the busy marketplace among the crowds, then sneaking home just after sunset so that no one could find out where she lived. Each night she would climb the outer stairs to the roof of whichever house was her home for the month, and nibble at the fruit and bread that had been left for her, before curling up on her straw mat to sleep.

When she began to be conscious of her own emotions, the girl with no name was plagued with a sense of guilt, deep sadness and loneliness that seemed to have no origin. These feelings just seemed to be a part of her existence or her "self". She hungered for approval, acceptance and acknowledgment, and found self-approval by disciplining herself to the practice of strict obedience to her relatives.

The beggars in the street seemed to have a familiarity among themselves that she envied, and she longed to be part of their group. She was fascinated with one beggar who played the flute in order to attract attention from passersby. One day, while watching him play his lovely melody, she began to dance as if she were a butterfly being carried on the wings of his music. A small crowd gathered, and when her dance was over the flutist's bowl was full of coins. He smiled at her and beckoned her to sit beside him with a beggar's bowl.

Tears stung her eyes, and she felt acknowledged as a person for the first time in her life. Somebody wanted her.

Every day she sat with him and danced for the crowds, and at the end of the day she felt pleased when he would empty her bowl of coins into his and pat her on the head. He had no idea where she came from or where she went, and he had no interest in her outside the bowls of coins to which she seemed to have no attachment. Still, he gave thanks to the many gods for sending this stupid girl to hear his flute and attract the crowds. This "partnership" started when White Girl was only eight years old and continued undisturbed for six years. She was happy being a dancing beggar, pleasing the crowds by day, and a silent stranger to her family by night.

When she was 14 her relatives built her a hut in the row of huts occupied by outcasts. They placed in it her sleeping mat and a basket, then ended all direct contact with her. Each day while she was gone, one of them would come, posing as a benevolent god-fearing citizen interested in helping the wretched outcasts. He would fill her basket with food and be on his way.

Even at this young age White Girl was a well-developed, curvaceous young woman, with soft, shining white hair that hung to her waist, and eyes that seemed to hypnotize. She had perfected her beautiful dance that imitated a butterfly or an eagle, a horse or a hummingbird. On other occasions she might mimic a bee or a stinging wasp, a grasshopper or frog. Her antics produced everything from rollicking laughter to an exalted sense of beauty in the minds of her audience. Many people came to the marketplace just to watch her and toss a few coins into her bowl. The flutist now gave her a portion of the coins daily to buy clothing and costumes for her dances. Still, no one knew where she lived or how she came to be there; and no one inquired.

One warm day the Pharaoh was traveling in his carriage chair near the outcast region of Thebes. When he approached the busy center of the town, he had his carriers take him into the marketplace for amusement. Soon he heard a flute, laughter and applause.

Curious, he commanded to his carriers, "Tell the crowd to step aside. I want to see what is so amusing."

White Girl was performing her butterfly dance. Never had he seen anything so lovely. The great Pharaoh stepped out of his carriage to watch the dancer, mesmerized by her waist-length white hair that swirled and bounced as she moved. He had never seen anything like it.

She stopped her dance in front of the fine gentleman, bowed low, and then raised her eyes to meet his. He gasped at the blue color, the bottomless depth and the attraction he felt at her gaze, and thought her the most desirable and beautiful woman he had ever seen.

"Who is this girl?" he demanded of the crowd. "Where does she live?"

"She's not my kin," the flutist announced loudly, hoping to receive a reward for his quick response. "She's a homeless peasant girl who has no kin, no voice and no name. An idiot who knows nothing but to dance."

Upon hearing this, the Pharaoh picked her up bodily, threw her over his shoulder, placed her in his carriage, climbed in beside her, and gave the order to return to his Palace immediately. White Girl was in shock. Her mind began racing with fear and with questions about what his intent might be.

Touching her hair tenderly, as if it might break, he said to her, "Now you have a home, and I give you the name of Mwashw because you dance as if moved by the wind. It means lover of the God of Air. I will call you Mwa. Henceforth, you will dance only for the Pharaoh and never have to beg again."

Mwa felt overwhelmed but also excited and grateful as she was bathed and dressed in colorful clothing with jewels in her hair. Again, someone had acknowledged and wanted her. "I like the name he has given me," she thought with gratitude. "And if there is a God of Air, I do love the God of Air."

At first, she was kept in the quarters of the concubines and called for each night to perform a private dance for the Pharaoh in his bedchamber. Each night he watched with rapt attention from a great couch while sipping an intoxicating beverage. After the dance, he would have her sit at his feet while he stroked her hair until he fell asleep on the couch. This was his bedtime ritual. To his surprise, she did have a voice, and as her trust in him grew she would sing and talk quietly to him in the evenings. As a reward for her talking to him, she received tutoring in language, conversation, reading, art, singing and the ways of a lady of the court. Mwa was becoming very happy.

Pharaoh's physical desire for her was extreme, and his original intent had been to make her one of his many concubines, but she had such an air of innocence and trust that he could not bring himself to touch her in a sexual way. He decided that the Great God had brought her to him in order to test his strength of will and his ability to be a faithful husband if ever he were to take a wife. His intent, now, was to claim her secretly as a virgin bride for one full year. This meant that he would spend no time with concubines for that year and have no sexual activity. Such a sacrifice would purify his body to make it worthy of such a bride. His proof that the Great God had ordained this would be that she would eagerly agree to become his wife at the end of that year. If she refused him, it would be a sign that he had been mistaken about her worthiness; then he would take her as a concubine.

Mwa knew nothing of his plan, and as the months passed her pleasure in his company and passionate desire for his tender words and touch grew to such heights that she could barely endure just sitting at his feet or dancing for him. But no matter how she tried to entice him by looks, gestures, songs or flirtatious conversation, he never made a move toward the slightest embrace.

The old guilt and sense of unworthiness began to nag her again and often she cried herself to sleep fearing she would spend her life as a frustrated virgin.

One night after her dance, when a year had passed and she moved to sit at his feet, the Pharaoh stood and boldly took Mwa into his arms. He kissed her cheeks, her nose and her mouth, and caressed her until her skin was aflame with desire. When she was ready to be taken, he held her by the shoulders and looked deeply into those eyes that had taken him a year before. "The gods have revealed to me that you are to be my bride if you are willing to accept. What is your answer, Mwa?"

Her answer was the dance of the eagle, followed by the dance of the hummingbird which brought her to his face to sip nectar from his mouth. "Never could a thing make me happier in life than to be your chosen bride."

Giving silent thanks to the Great God, creator of all lesser gods, Pharaoh rang for a servant to escort Mwa to a luxurious room that had been prepared for her. He kissed her softly, saying, "Tomorrow, in the evening, I will make my announcement. The whole city will celebrate; then within a week we will marry."

Although it was believed that the Pharaohs were descendants of the gods, appointed as Egypt's leader by their mythical gods, and infallible in all their actions, still many murmured against his decision to marry the white-haired peasant girl.

Gossip was rampant by the time the wedding occurred, and there was a weakening of the loyalty his subjects once had held for him; but the Pharaoh was not moved.

He gave a public address from his balcony, saying, "The gods told me how to proceed and they have put it in her heart to say yes. Who are these subjects of mine to question the ways of the gods?"

In order to win back some of their support, he announced, "Our first-born son will be the wisest and most benevolent ruler that Egypt has ever known."

The crowd cheered.

After two years, when still no pregnancy had occurred, the Pharaoh began to express great anger toward Mwa.

"You shame me in front of all the people." He groaned. "The very proof that a king is the direct descendant of one of the gods is by the birth of a son who can succeed him when his reign is over. I am in danger of losing my credibility with the people."

Another year passed, and the Pharaoh began to fall into terrible rages of depression, fear, and anger. "You have betrayed both me and the gods by shutting up your womb to a son the gods would gladly give me," he shouted.

After agonizing over it for another month, he came to the decision that, no matter how great his affection for her, he must put her away in order to show his loyalty to the gods. He was permitted to divorce her only if she would submit to entering a convent.

Mwa's sense of guilt and unworthiness was unbearable, and she readily agreed.

Life in the convent was stark compared to her palace life but comfortable compared to her early years. It was a place of prayer and devotional attention to the Great God and to His lesser gods. There was a stark deprivation of common luxuries. Three types of work were available within the convent: domestic labor, gardening and helping to educate the male children of wealthy citizens. Mwa chose to work with the laundry. She wanted nothing to do with children, and she had no experience with cleaning, cooking or gardening.

The Pharaoh had returned to his former lifestyle and buried his grief in pleasures of the flesh with his many concubines, making it known that he was searching for a new bride. The people were very pleased with him, and his popularity grew rapidly. He felt that his new popularity was a reward from the Great God for his putting Mwa away, and he searched the land for a suitable bride with broad hips who could give him sons.

After several months of self-condemning guilt for her inability to have a child, compounded by episodes of self-pity, agonizing depression and petitions to the gods, Mwa settled into the silent gazing of her childhood. For a time, the emptiness of mind seemed to bring her peace, but soon she began to feel outbursts of anger toward the Pharaoh.

The anger grew like a fiery furnace in her heart as she dwelled on the Pharaoh's heartless treatment of her, and she took on an angry attitude about everything. Soon she began to experience conflicts with the other women of the convent.

Seething with fury during her silent times, she thought, "I was very content being a silent, dancing beggar with my friends of the street before he took me away and spoiled me with pleasures of the flesh, pleasures of the mind and the pleasure of loving and being loved. He had no right to take all that away, just because I am barren. He is heartless and evil."

Eventually Mwa became accustomed to her anger, and she focused on it every night at bedtime. But during the day, she shifted her attention from her husband to the women around her. She delighted in spreading gossip about the way they smelled and ridiculing those who were homely. But when she found herself making fun of an elderly woman who had no teeth and yet smiled all the time, it was as if a mirror had been held up to reflect her cruel behavior. Shame at her own pettiness revived her buried sense of guilt until it overwhelmed her. She cried in agony for two days, begging the gods for forgiveness, then fell into an exhausted sleep.

After that she began to use her silent times to wish that the gods would speak to her and tell her how to be content in this place. She wanted to return to the harmony she had felt with the beggars of her childhood or to return to the joy she had felt with her husband during that first two years. "But those pleasures are of the past, and here I have nothing to do but think and be angry."

Within a few months her anger became milder, more like a smoldering fire than a raging furnace. It seemed to have a life of its own and was directed at no one, just a thing that lived heavily and quietly inside of her. As much as anything else, she was angry at her own inability to find a solution, because no matter how much thinking she did she could find no suitable answers to her questions, "Why does the Great God give life?

Why do all the gods give misery? Why do they give pleasure and then take it away again? If I could have anything at all, I would ask for understanding, to ease my tormented mind."

She began to wonder what the children who were educated in the convent were learning. Were they learning some answers to what life is about? Mwa longed to be a young boy so that she could attend classes and learn; then she wished that she knew something worth teaching the children.

One night, just before she fell asleep, a memory flooded her consciousness, and she attributed it to the gods as an answer to her prayers. She remembered the uniqueness of her dancing and the happiness it had brought to her and the people who had seen her dance. Perhaps the convent Mothers would let her teach the children how to dance.

Their answer was yes! "But that is not enough to fill the time requirement of four hours daily for a teacher," said her superiors.

"I also could teach the children to pray and to meditate upon the gods."

"That makes three," said the Mothers. "Is there one more thing you could offer?"

Mwa could not think of anything else that she knew to teach but begged for a day to consider it. The time was granted.

Pondering the question that night, she began to remember how still and silent and empty she had felt inside before hearing the music notes of the beggar's flute. She wondered what it was that had stimulated her to dance. "Is there something in a sound that stirs up the blood to make the mind sing and the body sway?"

She tried different sounds with her voice and detected that she sensed each sound in a slightly different way. Some sounds made her feel sad; some made her feel happy; some gave her pleasure and others were annoying to her. Mwa was intensely excited about her discovery. Giving vent to her creative ideas, she developed a system of sounds that could be used for stimulating harmony in various areas of her body and mind.

"I will teach the children this," she said to the deaf walls of her room.

It was morning before she drifted off to sleep, but the sleepless night produced great rewards. When she met with the Mothers that afternoon, Mwa demonstrated her sound system to them. "I can teach this to the children and encourage them to use their own voices to make themselves or others feel good with nothing but intonations. It produces such a feeling of harmony and contentment that I feel sure it must even be good for the health!"

The Mothers unanimously agreed, and she was accepted as a teacher to start at the beginning of the following week. Mwa was overjoyed and eager to make some plans. It was the month of her nineteenth birthday, and although she had never known the day of her birth, she felt this must be it because she seemed to be awake for the first time in her life.

"This is another prayer that the gods have answered," she thought. "My understanding has been granted. If I want to be happy, I must have a purpose. It doesn't matter what the purpose is as long as it is something that I am passionate about. When I danced for the beggar that was my purpose. When I was wife to my husband that was my purpose. Now I will put away the old purposes and stand on my new one. I am a teacher of children. This is my new passion, the best one of all."

Mwa whispered a prayer of gratitude to the gods, and she felt great love for the God of Light behind the sun.

For the next 12 years, Mwa was content most of the time, with intermittent bursts of happiness, and an ongoing passion for teaching the harmonic sounds. Her anger seemed to be something of the past. She found herself looking forward to seeing the children every day and to meeting new children.

When Mwa heard that the Pharaoh had married an Egyptian woman, she was not dismayed. Even when she heard that the woman had produced a son, she felt only fleeting moments of envy but was able to bury them with her work. But upon hearing that the Egyptian Queen's son was benevolent and wise at a very young age, thoughts and feelings of jealousy, hostility, and rage arose from where they had been sleeping in her heart. They came to plague her often, but then she would quiet the rising tide of emotions by toning her sounds.

In her daydreams she fanned the flame of hatred by imagining that the joys she had given her husband surpassed any pleasure that he could have with another. She conjured up images of the Pharaoh feeling tormented with lust for her as the years went by. She fantasized that someday he would be so overcome with desire for everything about her that he would send a servant into the convent to bring her secretly to his quarters. She would meet his eyes with a smile. He would stroke her hair as he had done so long ago; she would dance for him; and they would satisfy their passion for being with one another. She would then be a secret concubine to him by night and live in the convent by day. This, along with her teaching of the children, would keep her happy for the rest of her life.

But her day-dream always ended with deep self-pity and greater jealousy in admitting to herself that she was only fantasizing.

"He probably never thinks of me at all," she would whisper to her namesake, the God of Air. Then she would run to her pillow and position herself to sit for hours, intoning sounds that promoted a temporary harmony in her mind. Sometimes this helped her forget about the Pharaoh for weeks before the next episode of depression would arise.

One day a great clarity of new understanding seemed to come to her out of nowhere. While searching her mind to sort out all the stories she had heard about the gods and the idea that some were even saying there is only one God, she thought to herself, "Love seems to be what everyone wants. Perhaps it is the greatest power of all, yet it is said that God is the greatest power. Are love and God the same thing? Surely if love were to fill the world there would not be so much sorrow."

Mwa was convinced that God is Love and Love is God. No wonder people were willing to sacrifice everything for God. There seemed not enough love in the world to keep the tears at bay. With this self-designed concept in mind, Mwa spent the next many years trying to be an agent of love. Giving love to the other residents and to the children added a new dimension to her purpose, and it seemed to make them, as well as herself, more content. Still, her deep desire and dream of being adored again by the Pharaoh came to torment her often in sleep.

The pain drove her to wrestle again with the question of God's identity.

"I loved my Pharaoh as much as anyone can love another. If God is love, then the love I spent on my husband would be the only power needed to keep us together. It was not love that was missing, for he loved me as well. It was understanding that I lacked. If I had understood his cause, I would have suggested that he take a second wife and produce a son with her, while still holding me as wife number one. Oh, with understanding I would still have my place in the palace and in his bed. Is God knowledge? Or perhaps God is the giver of knowledge? Would I rather have knowledge or love? Love without knowledge takes one into false beliefs, and knowledge without love is cold. God is neither. God is the giver of both, and we do with them what we will. That is the belief that I will hold in my mind and heart. God is the giver of knowledge and love, and we do with them what we will."

Mwa was delighted with her new revelation but still not quite convinced. She decided to test her theory and prove it to herself, one way or the other. Even so, at times when news of the royal family circulated through the convent, the old feelings of envy, guilt and self-pity would come as predictably as the darkness of night.

When she was 52, having lived in the convent for nearly 35 years, Mwa heard that the Pharaoh's son, encouraged by his mother, had ordered his father's assassination. The rumors could not be proven, and the only fact was that the Pharaoh had been killed by assassins and now his son was in power.

Mwa prayed it was not true and that her husband had not been betrayed, for she felt that betrayal by someone you trust is one of the worst things that can happen to anyone. She was consumed with sympathy for the Pharaoh and the unfulfilled hopes for which he had sacrificed their love.

In her sadness, Mwa cried out to her secret God, "If his son has done this thing, he was certainly not benevolent and wise at all but a charlatan to his people. Why are people cruel to one another, and why do bad things happen to people?"

Her anger rekindled, Mwa felt she could never really feel peace again until she knew the answer to those questions. "This talk of the gods in the sky being in charge of the world feeds my anger. Do these gods so enjoy their power that they are oblivious to the suffering and dreams and needs of the tiny human beings below them? Is there no mercy in them at all? This day I vow to never appeal to the planetary gods for mercy again. If they are real, then they are devoid of mercy and I will suffer anyway, along with everyone else in the world, so of what good is a God? Only someone else to disappoint me!"

Mwa began to spend even more time in contemplation of the idea of God, and her thoughts circled around and around in her mind. "If the gods are not real, then we are all stupidly assigning our own thoughts and actions to the gods. They're not doing anything to us or for us. We are doing it to each other and to ourselves. It is not logical to believe the stars and the sun and moon are gods. God has to be something else and not the statues or the stars or the wind or the sea or even the sun. He has to be something a person can know, but not see. But why would he hide so that everyone seems to sense his existence but no one can find him? Wouldn't a God want to be found by his people?"

With all this questioning, Mwa always went full circle back to her conclusion of years before, "God must be the giver of love and knowledge. The mercy I have wanted from God is mercy that I have inside of me. I can give it or withhold it, but it is there for me to use."

Then she realized that she had given it to the Pharaoh through her compassionate forgiveness. She added forgiveness to her mental list of the powers that God gives his children to use. It did not occur to her that she could also give it to herself and even to the Pharaoh's son. In order to have done that she would have to will it so. She did not will it. Self-condemnation and condemnation of evil felt like necessary feelings that would encourage one to fight the evil inside and fight the evil of others.

Eventually Mwa's mind grew weary of trying to reconcile all her conclusions about God. She thought she would rescue herself from further disillusionment by avoiding human relations altogether; this was the closest she could come to forgiving herself for whatever was causing the unexplained guilt with which she was born.

Chanting was the only thing that quieted her heart full of tears. With her eyes closed and attention fixed upon the empty space between her eyes, she found the familiar light. Like the incoming tide of the sea, it seemed to spread the vibrations of her chanting, producing wave upon wave of harmony in her mind and body. She was content to be mindless and at peace.

Within a few months Mwa had stopped showing up for classes, and someone else took over the training of her students. She was not even aware that it had happened.

This escape from her emotions and the pain of life and people was the fulfillment of one of her desires. Her only other desire was to escape her thoughts and be conscious of nothing except existing in this internal sea of peace.

Even so, in the depths of silence her thoughts often took her to contemplation of a common belief of her Egyptian culture. Most of the people believed in a judgment day, when all dead people who had pleased the Great God and his lesser gods would rise to enjoy eternal life on earth. Mwa could not accept this ludicrous idea. She shuddered at the idea of living eternally on earth. She had a nagging belief in reincarnation, but she could not find its origin or find a purpose for it. She hoped fervently that it was not true. All she wanted after this life of struggle was to experience either oblivion or an eternal life far away from this world.

Eventually her thoughts became so disturbing that she began to willfully force her mind to stay fixed in rapt attention upon the light between her eyes. With her will she held the light still and forgot that she had a body or a mind.

As the meditations grew longer, Mwa lost her appetite for food and drink, and at age 55 she died of malnutrition and dehydration. It was the same ending as her former incarnation, but of this she was totally unaware.

Just before her final breath, a friend had tried to give her water, lifting her head so that she might drink. Mwa turned her face away, saying, "I will not breathe again until I become a messenger of God. I will be one who acts the way I have wanted God to act. I will destroy ignorance and anger from the minds of every man, woman and child that I meet."

"You told me once that you believe God is love. Why then would we need knowledge?" asked her friend.

Mwa gathered her thoughts and said dreamily, "I am dying now. With knowledge I could have made better choices in my life. It is by our choices that we are brought into the places of our new experience. If I do not reincarnate, I will be in a place of empty peace with nothing to do and no one to love. If I do reincarnate, I choose now to be a messenger of the kind of God that I want, giving knowledge from one hand and love from the other. That will be my purpose in life."

Even in her compassion, the friend was concerned for Mwa's confusion, "Mwa, you cannot know any purpose at all while you are sleeping in your tomb. At this moment you are all that you will ever be. Love is the cause of all ignorance and pain as well as the cause of pleasure. It is the perpetuator of ignorance and not the healer of it. And knowledge is the cause of evil power being used against those who have no knowledge. Poor Mwa, you need to ask the Gods to forgive you for trying to understand their ways. They will surely punish you on judgment day for denying that they are in control of the world and everyone in it."

Mwa sighed with a deep shutter, almost a sob, and said, "God gave me the power of forgiveness to do with as I will. My will is to forgive myself." Then she exhaled sharply and stopped breathing.

Chapter 4

AARON 1671 B.C.

An interior region bordering Egypt. 30 miles inland, near the Mediterranean coast

> **Journal Entry #3**
>
> *I believe the greatest spiritual progress that I made in my incarnation as Mwa was to increase my power of forgiveness and self-acceptance. I am grateful for that although it seems I still was plagued by jealousy and struggling between self-righteousness. That brought on a secret desire for vengeance toward my offenders and strong self-punishment that produced bouts of depression.*

In viewing the Akashic Records concerning this next incarnation, I see a family of many siblings dedicated to hard work through farming and the raising of sheep.

They live about 30 miles into the desert land near Egypt. Their religious culture is a way of life, and they are a part of the Hebrew tribe. They believe in a God named Yahweh, an invisible God of power who is in control of everything, even the thoughts and feelings of his subjects. This God is very demanding; much like a cruel father who says he wants what is best for his children yet treats them with severe punishment when they disappoint him. He also is believed to treat them with lavish rewards when he is pleased.

The legend of these people, passed on by word of mouth, is that Yahweh had first claimed the Semites as his people when they were in possession of a great dynasty. When Yahweh had become angry with their way of life, he had warned them of the consequences by permitting invaders to take their land. They had become hunters and wandering nomads, ever in search of food along the Mediterranean Coast and its interior regions. Even after the invasion and finding themselves homeless, they had trusted Yahweh to provide for them, but Yahweh tested their faith. After many years of finding no respite from their homeless poverty, they began to speak out against Yahweh and wish for a different God. But one of their members, a man named Abram, clung to his faith. Yahweh, feeling betrayed by the others, decided to abandon the Semites and become the God of Abram and his family.

According to the story, Abram changed his name to Abraham and reported to his family that Yahweh had come to him in a dream with a message to take his tribe into a formidable land called Babylon. If they did so, Yahweh would reward them with a fertile, productive parcel of land that they could claim as their own. Abraham obeyed, and eventually a fearful King that Abraham had deceived gave the land of Hebron to in order to avoid his own God's punishment for believing what Abraham had told him.

Abraham gave thanks to Yahweh for the outcome and proclaimed that Hebron was the land that Yahweh had promised to give his people. In return for Abraham's faithfulness, Yahweh promised Abraham that all of his future descendants would forever be Yahweh's chosen people. Within a few generations, Yahweh had become disappointed with the people of Abraham and had asked one of their descendants, Jacob, to lead his relatives, wives, concubines and servants out of Hebron and into a land that Yahweh would give them. Aaron's father was the son of one of Jacob's many brothers and a nephew to Jacob.

Aaron was born near Egypt as the youngest son of nine siblings. His father, a younger brother to Jacob who now was known as

"Israel", had followed Jacob out of Hebron away from Abraham's people into this fertile area where the Israelis were prospering.

When Aaron was old enough to speak, his training in the legends of his people and their religion began. He found great excitement in the stories of old and concluded that jealousy and deception were the theme of many of these legendary stories. He also perceived that the desire for approval, land, and favoritism was always shown as the motivation for these attitudes. As a young boy, Aaron decided that he would guard against jealousy and deception while being grateful for any approval that he did receive. "I do not need to worry about how to deal with favoritism," he thought with amusement. "Sometimes I think that I am invisible or more like a work animal than a pet to anyone. But I am content to do as I am told and try to stay out of trouble with my father, for his hand is heavy when his children fail to do our part. He says that stern discipline is God's way, and if it is good enough for God's children it is good enough for his."

Israel's followers were told that the reason they were hated by other people of the world was because they were the chosen people of the most powerful God, Yahweh; and others were jealous of his favoritism to them.

"Jealousy and a struggle for favoritism again even though Abraham lost Yahweh's favor!" thought Aaron smugly. "Seeking favoritism seems the cause of much evil."

To Aaron, all these stories just pointed out that people crave love and security, and he secretly rejected the jealous and demanding Yahweh as his God while enjoying the stories of the Hebrew people. He had a firm belief that there is only one God, not numbers of tribal gods such as Yahweh. But he had no real concept of what or who or where that one God might be. It was just a knowing that rested gently within his consciousness but was not pressing upon his mind. To speak of a personal awareness of God would be blasphemy to the Israelis, so he kept it to himself and eagerly did as he was told. There was a sort of peace in serving the demands of others without thinking, and he truly enjoyed working both with the animals and in the fields.

When Aaron was 10 years old, he and his cousin, Joseph, began secretly sharing ideas about an inborn skill that each seemed to possess; it was the ability to sense things before they happened. There were many families of Israel's followers now living in various parts of this interior land, and all were thriving. Aaron's father, Daniel, was a secondary leader in their large multi-family group, and he dutifully supported the dictates of his older brother who was the primary leader.

"Why can't you be the leader?" Aaron once inquired of his father. "Your brother is old and unsteady of limb."

"May Yahweh forgive your ignorance," said Daniel hurriedly. "Do you not yet know our history? God favored Jacob as the new leader of the Hebrews when the other descendants of Abraham failed. He brought my brother, Jacob, and his brothers with their wives and children and servants and sheep to the interior. Yahweh gave Jacob a new name by which we must all be known in order to honor Yahweh for leading us to this fertile valley. Jacob's new name is Israel, and the name of our families and servants and their servants is Israel after his appointment to leadership. Israel has assigned the eldest male as leader for each smaller tribe but Israel is leader of all. It is not for me to choose. You must avoid displaying jealousy of my brother and become a spokesman for Yahweh in reverence to Israel."

Aaron couldn't bring himself to break his father's heart by sharing his doubts about Yahweh, but he knew inside himself that he would never be a spokesman for a God who threatened and punished people in order to force their obedience.

He enjoyed playing and working with his many cousins. Traditionally the eldest son would inherit the father's position, and Aaron felt relieved that such a task would not fall to him unless his older brothers were to be deceased or outcast. For a year now, Aaron had been serving as an apprentice shepherd, being trained by his cousin, Joseph, who was the youngest of Israel's sons and only four years older than he. Joseph confided with embarrassment to Aaron that even though he was the youngest of twelve sons, his father was secretly coaching him in leadership qualities that he might someday need. Aaron felt the courage, then, to tell Joseph his secret. "I must confess, but only to you, that I cannot accept Yahweh as the highest God, for he is demanding and cruel and punishes his people harshly without teaching us how to please him. He has no mercy in him."

Joseph slapped his young cousin jovially on the shoulder. "Ah, but listen while we are confessing. I believe Yahweh is the Great God but that neither the followers of Abraham nor the people of Israel really understand him. I believe that Yahweh is good and kind and that he is the God not only of Israel but of all people everywhere."

With a puzzled look, Aaron scratched his head. "Then why did he favor the Hebrews, and why does he now favor Israel and his people?"

Joseph got a faraway look in his eyes as his face softened and he said, dreamily, "Perhaps they only believed they were special to Yahweh because they wanted to be the favorite and were hungry for a land of their own. We boast that we are the favorite of God, and other nations hate us for it. My father boasts that I am his favorite son, and my brothers hate me for it. There is no merit in being the favorite. It is sometimes a burden that is painful to bear."

One morning while he was still nine and Joseph was thirteen, Aaron awoke with terrible stomach cramps and a pounding headache. "May I linger at home?" he begged of his father. "Joseph can watch the sheep without me for one day. He often makes me sit far away from him anyway so that he might be alone to think."

Lifting an eyebrow in doubt, Daniel sent Aaron to his mother. "Let your mother decide. It is not for me to say whether you be worthy to watch the sheep today. Perhaps Yahweh is punishing you and making of you a girl with this illness."

Undaunted by his father's insult, Aaron reported to his mother as he was directed and was promptly put into bed with a poultice of herbs to warm his aching stomach.

Snuggling down under the coverlet, he enjoyed his day of rest.

That evening the news came that Joseph had been devoured by wild animals while watching the sheep. Aaron was consumed by an agonizing sense of guilt, sorrow, remorse and shame. "I am cursed!" He cried. "I took too much pleasure in shirking my work today, and Yahweh has shown me the evil of indulging in pleasure. How cruel is my punishment. How even more cruel is the heartless Yahweh!"

Every night for a full week, Aaron would go to his knees at bedtime in supplication to Yahweh for relief from his guilt and grief over his cousin's misfortune. Then one night he had a dream.

In the dream, Joseph was alive and well. He had a new name and a mother who was like an angel, providing for his every need, yet he was a prisoner without liberty to return home.

When Aaron told his father about the dream, Daniel accused him of trying to deny his own guilt in the matter by pretending that Joseph was still alive. "We will hear no more of your dreams. Your punishment is to tend the sheep alone and pray Yahweh does not send the wild animals after you."

Aaron kept the dreams to himself, yet every night for an entire cycle of the moon, the dreams of Joseph came. It was as if Joseph was sending him messages, and he began to look forward to them.

The dreams stopped as abruptly as they had begun, but because of them Aaron had been healed from his sorrow over Joseph's death and filled with hope.

"I am convinced he is not dead but living a good life in a foreign land where he was taken against his will," thought Aaron. "Since no one wants me to be free from grief and guilt I will not tell them what I know. It is enough that Yahweh knows, Joseph knows and I know. I give thanks to Yahweh that Joseph lives and that somehow he has arranged a way for me to know."

During the next five years a great famine came to the interior region. The rains had stopped entirely, the streams had dried up; and all but one of the Israelis' wells had turned to dust. No crops would grow. The people of Israel put all that was left of their meager supplies into a common storage to share with one another and pleaded with Yahweh to tell them why they were being punished so harshly. Many had starved to death.

Rumors came that the Pharaoh of nearby Egypt had been warned of this event by a dream seer and that because of the warning he had stored more food than the Egyptians could ever need. The aging Israel, now ailing and near starvation, requested that two of his bravest sons go to Egypt and beg supplies for the starving Israelis.

"Please, may I go too?" begged Aaron. I am young and strong and I could be of help."

In his heart he knew that his real interest was to see the opulent land of Egypt and perhaps to find work as a servant so that he might stay there, away from the hardships of his current life and the cruelty of Yahweh.

As if having read his mind, Israel waved a finger at him. "Nay, my boy. These are my people, and I am Israel. It is Yahweh's wish that I and my sons provide for our people and see to their welfare as long as they are under Yahweh's domain. My sons have the welfare of all Israeli people as their responsibility in life. Yahweh does not require that of you. Yahweh requires that you stay where you are and do all that you can for your father and his family until our rescue comes."

Weeks passed. Aaron was curious and eager to hear about his cousins' trip to Egypt, but there seemed to be some kind of secret meetings going on that only the elders could attend. He saw the elders of Israel, including his own father, growing weaker and huddling together to whisper now and then. Soon Israel's sons returned from Egypt bringing supplies, and Aaron knew something else had happened but he could not find out what it was. Only the elders knew.

At last, the news rang out. Joseph was alive, and he had appealed to the Pharaoh to help the people of Israel. Joseph had been the dream seer who had warned Pharaoh of the impending drought. To show his gratitude, Pharaoh had given a huge parcel of the most fertile Egyptian land to Joseph for his people to inhabit and use as their own.

It was great cause for celebration among the Israelis, and as weak as they were with the ravages of hunger and thirst, they could not suppress their joy. They danced that night and sang praises to Yahweh for forgiving them the sin of whatever they had done to offend him. Now he was giving them yet another new land that they could own as a people.

Early the next morning, having done his part to prepare for the trip to Egypt, Aaron ran to the hillside where he had spent so much time with Joseph. "I knew you were alive, my cousin!" he shouted. As the echo came back again and again, he cried with joy and appreciation for Yahweh, not the Yahweh celebrated by his father, but the Yahweh that Joseph believed in and the Yahweh who was merciful after all.

Life was good for Aaron and the Israeli people after their migration to Egypt. The land they were given was indeed fertile, and it was vast enough for each family to have an ample plot for themselves and their descendants to come. Soon after they had settled, Aaron's father gave him a parcel of land and a few sheep along with seeds to plant. Although Aaron had hoped to resume his role of confidante and friend to Joseph, he soon accepted that it was not to be. Joseph was an important man in Egypt and busy with his own life day and night, and Aaron saw him only once after the move. But it was a meeting to remember.

Joseph had visited Aaron in his small but comfortable home. Patting Aaron's shoulder as in days of old when they were shepherds together, Joseph asked, "Did you know that I was alive, Aaron?"

"Yes! I had dreams for many nights," said Aaron with excitement. "I knew you were alive and well cared for."

Joseph smiled, "I could feel your shame, and I did not want you to feel guilt or sorrow while I was receiving the finest education and great opportunities here. Yahweh was taking good care of me."

"You are truly a prince, my cousin," said Aaron.

"We are princes one and all, and Yahweh is my King," shouted Joseph.

"The Yahweh that Joseph knows is also my King," said Aaron. They drank a toast to Yahweh as they understood him, and in that moment, Yahweh seemed to come alive for Aaron.

"Come," said Joseph. I must take you to meet the lovely Egyptian woman who purchased me from the slave traders when I first arrived here. Her name is Iliana.

"I have asked Iliana to teach you the healing arts with herbs and teas so that you might become a healer among our people."

When Joseph had left them alone, Iliana rang for her servant, a young Israeli girl whom Joseph had placed with her soon after the Israelite migration.

"Pour us some wine, Ruth, and cut the bread and cheese."

Aaron and the girl caught each other's glance, and both blushed as she poured the wine silently.

When Ruth had left, Iliana said, "The wine is good, is it not?" "I cannot tell, madam, as I have not tasted wine before."

Iliana laughed. "Well, you shall have wine every day that you visit me for the lessons your cousin has ordered, and if you desire a courtship with my servant girl, that might also be arranged."

They laughed, and he loved both Iliana and her servant girl, Ruth, from the start. His visits to Iliana's home were frequent. Aaron seemed to have natural healing abilities and a deep understanding of the lessons. "You are the quickest student that I have ever had," said Iliana with delight.

Aaron's healing talent grew, along with his love for Ruth. Within a year he asked for her hand in marriage, and she accepted through tears of happiness. The following day, Ruth was accidentally trampled by a runaway horse and buggy. All the healing abilities of both Iliana and Aaron proved powerless against her injuries. When she died, Aaron sobbed publicly. The driver of the runaway carriage approached him with an apology, and Aaron said through his tears, "It is true, my life would have been different if not for her death.

But please carry no guilt on my account. Yahweh tells me that I am a healer. Henceforth I live not for love but to be a healer as Yahweh wishes."

Aaron became the most popular healer of his time among the Israelis. He was loved for his knowledge of healing, his forgiving ways and for his stories of the dreams that he had enjoyed when everyone else thought that Joseph was dead.

In his later years he gave up direct healing to become a teacher of healing arts. The people said he was like a god, filled with knowledge and love and power to heal.

Aaron had given his parcel of land to his brother and was content to live in his brother's house with a quiet room all to himself. He never married, and sometimes he would have a strange dream about a sad little woman in a convent who believed she would be happy if only she could be adored as a giver of knowledge, forgiveness, and love.

Then he would chuckle to himself with irony, saying to the woman in the dream, "I am adored as a giver of knowledge, forgiveness and love. Yet I am not happy, merely content. Dear woman of my dreams, you hunger for happiness, but to be honored as a giver of knowledge, forgiveness and love is not the answer."

Then his relentless mind would be swept away with pondering the question, "What does produce happiness? I was happy for a time when I was learning from Joseph as a boy. What was the key? I was happy for a time when I learned Joseph was alive. What was the key? I was happy for a time when I was serving as a physician for my people, but then I wanted a change. What was the key? I was happy for a time as a teacher of physicians, but now I am restless again. What is the key to finding a purpose that offers sustained happiness? Is it even possible or merely a wish?"

With all his knowledge, he could find no answer. Eventually he said, "I know only how to heal, but I want to know so much more. Why is it that my soul cannot rest from searching for answers to questions that have no practical use?"

He lived out the rest of his life with that question on his mind.

Aaron was loved by everyone who knew him. When he was 41 years old, he died suddenly from an accident when he was on his way to teach at the Israeli school for physicians. The mourners wailed that he had been a gift sent by Yahweh for their healing and now Yahweh was taking him away to punish them for their sins.

Chapter 5

THUSYDYAS

Athens, Greece Around 390 B.C.

Journal Entry #4

I am happy to know that my reasoning ability was revived in the former incarnation as Aaron and that my question about the true nature of God was still a driving force for me. I seem to have been as much in need of admiration as I was in need of answers.

This next incarnation is again in the Mediterranean region but across the sea in magnificent Greece. Athens is a wealthy, thriving metropolis in a democratic society where free-speech is supposed to be a right. However, those who dare to speak out against the methods of this democratic society are considered enemies of the state and promptly arrested. It is in the time of Plato, whose ideas of an ideal society do not promote democratic rule. His concept of an ideal society is that it be governed by a small group of the most benevolent and wise men available. These men would swear to uphold specific principles, and require that the people live by those principles or lose their citizenship and be deported from Greece.

Thusydyas was born into an extremely literate family. His father and uncles shared a profitable family business that promised to provide wealth for all their future generations. As merchants, dealing in foreign treasures such as silks, gold, incense, exotic perfumes and carvings of ivory, jade and unusual woods; each man would proudly assign his own male children to be apprentices to himself so that he could train them in the art of trading, sailing and salesmanship. Thusydyas' mother was a well-bred, gentle lady who wrote poetry to share with her ladies' group. She was an accomplished harpist and singer who entertained friends frequently at gatherings in their home and a dabbler in artistic sketching of anything that caught her eye. Thusydyas, an only child and his father's only heir, was called Syd.

Business, social engagements, family life, entertaining, and artistic pursuits were the topic of all conversation within the family. They shared a philosophical belief in the importance of education and the application of knowledge to one's position in life. These were considered to be the very purpose for living, while contributing to the happiness of people in one's circle of influence was considered the mark of a noble person. There was no belief in religion or life after death or reincarnation or any kind of deity. Every person in Thusydyas' family was taught that to be a noble person adds to one's own sense of joy in living.

On any given evening of the week small groups of wise men with a ravenous hunger for philosophical discourse would gather in small groups in the center of the city in what we might think of today as a huge city square. A leader would be arbitrarily appointed to begin the inquiry into ideas, and the intellectual fun would begin.

As a small boy of five, Syd was awarded the privilege of accompanying his father to these group discourses. Often his father was appointed as facilitator of the group, and on rare occasions he would even ask Syd a question, just to demonstrate that even a child with no worldly experience had some knowledge stored inside his mind. Frequently the boy's responses would bring peals of laughter from the men and the other boys of their circle, but that was part of the fun; Syd laughed just as heartily as they did. At times, however, they would nod their heads and make philosophical comments about what he had said.

When this occurred, Syd would feel very proud, then listen intently to hear any ideas that might sound important to him.

On the boy's seventh birthday, his grandfather, three uncles and their children were invited to a celebration at his father's home. Syd was looking forward to seeing his cousins, but the one he liked most was Perisophoclies. She was just a few months older than he and an only child like himself. They both enjoyed making up rhymes and little songs that they would share with each other. They loved telling each other their dreams and speculating on the question of who placed all those dream stories inside their heads, and when and why? Was it just to entertain them while they slept, or did it have some purpose? There was no end to the abstract ideas they enjoyed discussing and the sense of rapport that they felt with one another. Often Syd had found himself wishing that Peri (as he called her) were his sister so they could be together every day.

Now he learned that on the way to his birthday celebration, the carriage of Peri's family overturned, crushing her parents to death and knocking the girl unconscious. A physician's carriage delivered her to their door along with the tragic news.

Peri recovered from her physical injury almost immediately, but her grief was so pronounced that she became almost silent with everyone except Syd. It was decided that she would leave her grandfather's home where she had been staying and take up permanent residence with Syd's family. The physician said this was her only hope of ever recovering from the experience of her parents dying right before her eyes.

Syd's mother was very glad to take the girl into their home. She had been barren after her son's birth and had always carried a secret sadness because she would have liked to have a daughter. Syd had mixed emotions. He still wanted to be with Peri every day, but he felt guilty, and a nagging question tormented him: "I wanted her for my sister. Could my wish have been the cause of her parent's death?"

As he struggled with this guilt, about which he told no one, a deepened sense of responsibility for her happiness arose within him. This was the first secret he had ever kept from Peri.

A tutor came to the house every other day to give lessons to the two children. On the alternate days they were encouraged to think about what they had learned and try to find some use for it and to get plenty of exercise and fresh air.

On the evenings that Syd accompanied his father to the discourses, Peri would spend time with her new mother learning the art of rhyming and reading and playing the harp. The evenings that they were not so engaged they would spend with each other, telling what they had learned in their activities. The sharing of it seemed to increase their enjoyment ten-fold. Secretly Syd learned from Peri how to play the harp and the art of rhyming, and Peri learned the art of philosophical discourse from him. The fact that it was secret made it even more exciting and fun for them.

When Syd was 14, his father announced that it was now time for him to learn the art of bargaining, purchasing and sales so that he could become a productive member of the family business by the time he was 16. Although Syd had no interest in the business at all, he was willing to perform his duty. But on his first voyage at sea, Syd became seasick, and it was obvious he would not be able to perform the purchasing tasks. When they returned, he was told that he must learn the value of all the merchandise: where it came from and why it was special. He must learn more about calculations and numbers for the activity of sales, and he must learn how to interest the buyers in his merchandise. This all sounded like a deceptive game of trickery to Syd, and everything inside of him rebelled at the thought of spending his life doing this sort of thing. He only wanted to sing and play the harp and recite poetry and talk with Peri and sit with the philosophers in the square but he disciplined himself to do his duty. His father was very aware of Syd's lack of aptitude for this kind of work, but he was convinced that it was because of the influence of spending so much time with his mother and Peri.

"The girl is totally over her grief by now," he said to his wife. "It has been quite a sacrifice for me to permit my only son to spend evenings with a girl while I should have been exposing him to the world of business. Much damage has been done, but I know just how to undo it. His sixteenth birthday is coming soon. I will deliver a birthday surprise that will shame him and require him to become a man instead of a dreamy boy."

When the day came, his father announced in a harsh, commanding voice, "Syd, my son, the greatest philosopher in all of Greece opened a school for young men a few years back. On many occasions I sat with him in the square, and we exchanged ideas. He remembers me from those days and thinks highly of me, and because of this he has agreed to admit you into his Academy. You will study astronomy, politics, mathematics, and philosophy. It will cost me a grand amount each year to help fund his Academy, but by the stars you will not come out until you have become a man. When you are ready to take your place in the family business, tell me face to face; until then you will live at the Academy in the most sparse environment and never see a harp or a woman again as long as you live."

For Syd it was a dream come true, except for the unbearable idea that he would never see Peri or his mother again. But he brushed that thought away in disbelief. Surely, he would be brought home on occasion for some special events. He would see them both again. But to study at the Academy—the thought was so overwhelming that he leapt from his chair and embraced his father, kissing him on both cheeks. Then he began to sing and dance, whirling Peri and his mother around as if they were feathers in a breeze. Laughter would not stop pouring from the deepest parts of his belly, tickling his torso all the way up.

"Stop it!" shouted Peri. "I shall die if I never see you again. Go to the Academy and then come back a business man so that I will have my grief bearer once again.

When you marry, I shall be your spinster sister to live in your household all the days of my life. I cannot bear to be separated from your spirit of goodness and your mind that flies with mine."

"Never fear, sweet cousin," he said, "I will have much to teach you when we meet again.

His father was stunned; but convinced that Syd would tire of the Academy and take his place in the family business, he continued with his plan.

Within a week Syd was taken to the Academy. He saw his father talking with the Master Plato himself and was overcome with a sense of awe and appreciation that this could be happening to him. After he was settled in his 8x8 boxlike room, he reported to the dining room for his evening meal at the time instructed. A plate of cold, nondescript food was set for him on a bare wood table and he was surprised that no one else was there. As he finished his last bite, a man about his father's age entered the room. It was the Master Plato. Syd was struck speechless with admiration.

"Rise," said the Master, "and walk with me, Thusydyas."

Every night for a month this routine occurred. He was not invited or assigned to any classes; just left to wander about after breakfast until dinner time, then the walk with the Master. During their walk, the Master would ask him a theoretical question, and to every response he would probe a bit deeper. The boy was accustomed to group discourses and private discourses with Peri but not to such intense and perfect reasoning as this man was displaying. It was so beautiful to him that tears often came to his eyes, and he felt glad for the darkness of the night. The silent moon was the only witness to Syd's tears of gratitude.

On the thirty-first day of Syd's residence at the Academy, Master Plato did not come. Another man appeared and sat with him at the table. He said, "You have passed the interview, now your place in the school of instruction has been determined. You will wake every morning at four and sit upon your chair to contemplate all the events and ideas you have experienced on the previous day. You will not let your mind stray to former days or future days or other ideas, but concentrate it upon the events and ideas of just that single day. When you have finished, you will report to the cook for a breakfast plate and take it to your room to eat in solitude. You will not speak before your second meal of the day.

After your first meal you will enter the rooms of all the row one Academy students and empty their waste pots in the common toilets. You will wash their pots at the pump and return them clean to their bedsides. After that you will bathe and dress in a clean robe and smooth your hair. You will then wash the robe you took off and hang it to dry. After that you will report to the cook for your second meal of the day which you will eat in solitude in the dining room, neither meeting no one's eye nor touching another.

After the second meal you will wait in your room until a comrade comes to get you. You will walk with the comrade to your classroom in silence. Once you are in the classroom, you may take a seat and interact with the comrades and the instructor there in whatever manner you please. Do you have any questions to ask me?"

"Yes. What will I study first?"

"Each day of five will be a study of one of these five topics: Astronomy, politics, mathematics, philosophy and poetry."

"Poetry? What a joy! But does my father know I will be studying poetry?" "The Master has determined your courses of study. Poetry is but a language of symbols, rhythm, and perfect order. The Master considers poetry to be the language of Real Ideas and necessary for a man who wishes to know more of the Truth."

"The Truth about what?"

"The Truth about Truth," smiled his companion. Then rising, he turned and walked out the door without a word of dismissal or farewell.

Syd practiced this routine without deviation for two years. With two days each week to simply meander on his own around the Academy grounds, he found it a great pleasure to wake at four each morning and keep silence until after his second meal. He enjoyed being a creature of habit by morning and a creature of discovery after noon. On the two days of no classes, all students who chose to participate would gather in the afternoon and form work parties to do maintenance and cleaning work on the latrines, the grounds, the crude furniture and the buildings. Then after the evening meal those who desired it would walk together and hold discourses and laugh. They never talked about their families or what they might do when they left the Academy. They were interested only in knowledge. Sometimes after he had gone to bed, Syd thought about Peri and wondered whether she had married. He remembered his mother fondly and wished her well. He would have liked to see them but not if it meant leaving this place.

Toward the end of his third year at the Academy, an interesting phenomenon occurred: Syd found himself discoursing with himself. He would inquire of himself, then something inside him would answer. His answering "self" told his questioning "self" that life goes on and that no one ever really dies. It told him that there is a deity but did not offer any firm concept of how to define that deity.

He wished with all his heart that he could find some kind of confirmation for these ideas, but talk of God was forbidden at the Academy. Plato taught that ideas are the grand element in the Universe and that intelligence is the greatest element in a human being. He taught that, through questioning, the intelligence unites with the ideas that float in the air. In that way knowledge is produced in the person. He said that people are free to use their personal intelligence or squander it, but the ideas are always there.

People could learn and apply the knowledge for the pleasure of learning and applying knowledge, or they could remain ignorant and search for pleasure in activities they could not control or repeat. He insisted that, regardless of their choice whether to live in wisdom or in ignorance, they die, and the intelligence in them dies too--like a flame going out when snuffing a candle.

Thusydyas secretly knew beyond a shadow of a doubt that this was not all there was to the Truth because his intelligence had revealed it to him. "My intelligence has united with ideas about the Deity, assuring me of such a reality," he mused. "It has brought to me the idea that I have lived before and will live again. Using my intelligence and developing ideas is not a wasted effort or an end in itself. I have an idea that the knowledge I gain in this lifetime will stay with me in the next and be used for some purpose."

When he thought this way, giving questions and answers to himself, it caused him to laugh aloud with pleasure; and his comrades teased him about having a secret playmate inside his robe.

In the springtime of his fourth year at the Academy, Syd was bitten by a poisonous snake while he was rolling joyously in a bed of wild flowers. As he lay dying, he asked himself, "Will my intelligence go with me, or will it depart?" He answered himself, "This is your lucky day. Today you will know the answer to that question."

Chapter 6

MIRIAM

Roman Territory 14 A.D.

Miriam was born in Nazareth, 17 years before the crucifixion of her brother, Jesus. Miriam's parents were of the working class with a thriving carpentry and furniture-making business that was begun by Miriam's grandfather and passed on to her father and his brothers.

The family had a modest but roomy and comfortable home, with lovely carved furnishings and ornate doors hand-crafted by her father, Joseph, and her own brothers. The family's religious group was the mainstream Jewish sect, but they were more active in the mystical sect of Judaism called the "Essenes". Miriam was the baby of the family, with one sister and five brothers. Her oldest brother, Jesus, had worked with their father until he was 16 but had been given liberty to travel and study in the Far East beginning the same year that Miriam was born. Consequently, she seldom saw him, and as she grew old enough to ask questions about why he was with them only during certain seasons and gone for months at a time during the other seasons, her parents would always say, "When you are old enough to understand, we will tell you the family history and the family secret."

Eventually she stopped inquiring and just learned to enjoy him when he was there.

Miriam adored all of her siblings who spoiled her completely, but Jesus seemed to have a quality of his own that fascinated her. She loved his gentle sense of humor, his affectionate ways with her, his exciting stories about the various cultures he encountered, and his extreme kindness to everyone. She especially loved the wise things that he said, even though she understood very little about their meaning. With each visit he brought a few small gifts from the exotic worlds of his travels and distributed them to selected family members. On the occasions when she was the recipient of one of his gifts, she felt so full of gratitude and curiosity she thought she would burst.

Through her religious studies and conversations that she overheard at home; Miriam learned the history of the Essene community.

Originally the Order had served the purpose of seclusion from the larger society of Jews, and only men were permitted to join. They were required to leave family, friends, home and lifestyle and take on the role of prayer as celibate monks. They believed that through their collective and continuous prayer they could open a channel between earth and heaven through which the prophesized Wisdom Teacher could come. This Wisdom Teacher would possess the greatest possible Spiritual wisdom. He would teach the Jews who were willing to listen and would lead all Jews into peace and freedom. The Essene Monks had practiced silence when it was not their turn to join in the prayer vigil. Eventually some of these holy men had desired to leave the commune but had no sense of affiliation with the literalist views of the mainstream Jews. A change in policy was then made, permitting these men to maintain their membership. They were encouraged to attend certain meetings, to set up groups for meetings among themselves, and to teach their wives the Essene concepts. Still others who wished to stay in the commune felt restless with a desire to do something other than pray and take care of daily routine chores.

They had appealed to their leaders that they might start a school for the children of the Essenes. Their reasoning had been that if the Wisdom Teacher should choose to use the channel of natural birth, there would have to be a pure and holy virgin involved in the prayer activities, not only men. Then, since they did not know which virgin might be chosen, should that be his way of entry, it would be important for them to train many virgins in the responsibilities of parenting him. They argued further that they did not know when this might occur, so to have a school would assure that both boys and girls were uncontaminated by the worldly conditions or the teachings of the Pharisees or other Jewish sects. The school was begun about 40 years before Miriam's birth.

"That is the very school that I am attending," said 10-year-old Miriam to her mother as they conversed about the school.

"Yes, my dear. And I will tell you why some of your brothers did not attend this school. To qualify for education in the School of Jewish Mysticism, the Essene parents must have a strong reason to believe that the child is already a Mystic of some degree. After reviewing an application for admission, a group of examiners question both parents and child in order to determine more specifically whether there seemed to be Mystical qualities in the child. Acceptance usually comes within six weeks after application.

There is no charge for the education itself, but if the parents wish the child to live in the commune, a fee is charged for lodging and food. Two of your brothers have lived in the commune, as did your sister, and now you are here with us only during the holidays. I, myself, lived in the commune for most of the years of my childhood.

Essene girls are betrothed at age 13 by the Monks to marry at 15 when their education is complete. The match is made to a male Essene of 17 years or older who has attended the school, completed an apprenticeship for his life's work, and elected the path of family life.

"At age 15", Miriam's mother continued, "when the boys complete their mystery studies, they are assigned to a two-year apprenticeship with a businessman near their home or within their own family business. Some trades take longer to learn than others, and those young Mystics are required to wait until their apprenticeship is complete before a match can be made for them."

"Were you betrothed to my father by the Monks?" asked Miriam.

"Yes," said her mother. "I was accepted into the Wisdom School at age six because of my gentle disposition and my natural tendency to meditate upon the nature of God. It is the same reason that you were accepted into the school four years ago. Now you are old enough to be told the family history and the family secret."

A thrill raced through Miriam's body, and she shivered with delight. At last, she was to know the mystery surrounding her brother.

"Both your father and I attended the Essene School and lived among the Essenes for several years," her mother said.

"I was 13 when I was betrothed to Joseph, and he was 21. He had just completed a six-year apprenticeship in his own father's business of furniture making and carpentry. We were both very happy with the match, and Joseph spent the next 18 months at his father's home, working along with his father and brothers. He built a workshop for himself and a house for me. With all humility I will tell you that I had been ranked among the highest of the female Mystics at the school and was one of four who were daily being offered to God in prayer as the pure and chaste vehicle through which the expected Wisdom Teacher would come. Four months before my fifteenth birthday, the angel Gabriel came to me by night. He said that I had been selected to give birth to the Wisdom Teacher. I slept then, and when I awoke, I pondered it in my heart. Being not fully convinced, I decided to wait until some proof had come before telling the Monks. When I realized that I indeed was with child, I asked to meet with the Monks to share the good news that their prayers had worked. But they were divided in their willingness to believe me."

Miriam could feel the emotion rising in her mother and squeezed her hand in support.

"I insisted that I had experienced no relations with a man but even those who had not blamed me seemed in doubt.

"Yes, we've been praying for it, but we did not imagine it would happen this way," they said.

When I asked what they had imagined would occur, they said they had not been able to imagine how it would happen. Some of them even accused one another of having molested me during the night and posing as an angel to hide their guilt.

Eventually, since no other agreement could be met, they agreed to let my betrothed decide. If he chose to marry me, they would accept my story and permit us to marry right away. If Yahweh did not put it into his heart to marry me, they would take that as a sign that I was lying. They would then send me home to my parents in shame, to do with me as they wished.

Your father was stunned and saddened when he heard the news. A man of the Essenes always remains celibate until he takes his betrothed in marriage. It is the tradition of the Mystics. Joseph's reasoning was that he, himself, had prayed for God to send the Messiah of the Jewish people through one of the waiting virgins, so it would be a lack of faith if he should show doubt that I had been chosen. But he did have a doubt.

Prayer was the only answer. After petitioning God to send a messenger with the truth about the matter, Joseph slept. An angel came to him that night with a message to take me as his wife. Then he knew without a doubt that my first-born would be the Wisdom Teacher. He felt only joy in the prospect of helping to nurture the boy in his early years."

"That was Jesus, my own brother Jesus," said Miriam with great excitement.

Her mother nodded, "We were married. There were some frightening times, but your father's carpentry business prospered, and every year for four more years we produced another baby boy until there were five. "So many heirs you are giving me!" your father said. "How will I be able to feed them all?"

Miriam felt the tension lift from her mother's heart. "And what did you answer to that?

"You feed them now and teach them your trade then they will feed you in your old age," that is what I said. Nearly two years passed, then when our first girl was born. Joseph said, "It is enough. God has run out of carpenters for me to train. We will call our family complete. "How could we know that God had yet one more daughter to send us?"

Just then, Joseph entered the room saying that he was relieved to know this was the last family member with whom they would have to share their story. Now everyone would know. He continued the story, "Jesus, along with your brother nearest him in age, was accepted into the Mystery School when he reached the age of six years. The other boys were not Mystics, and your mother and I were pleased to teach them the Essene philosophy at home. Your sister was also accepted into the school at age six, ten years before you were born, just as you were accepted at age six.

"In the meantime, the Monks were still divided as to whether your brother is the Wisdom Teacher. They argued about what they might recommend for him once he reached 15. They reasoned that if he is the expected one, then he would need to be exposed not only to the Jewish Mystery Teachings but to all the Mystery Schools of the world, which were predominantly in the Far East and Egypt.

If he is not the Avatar, then he would need to have a trade. The Monks unanimously agreed that Jesus was to complete only two years apprenticeship in my carpentry business to learn the basics of the trade, then he would be sent by the Monks to study with Mystery Schools in foreign lands until such time as he is called into service by God, or until he realizes that he is just another carpenter.

"So that is why he travels. The plan is that, in order to prepare him for whichever of these futures he might experience, he must spend half the year working with me and your brothers, saving every penny he makes to help fund his travels. Then the Monks arrange for him to spend the other half of the year traveling and studying the wisdom of other world religions under the tutorage of various Mystery Schools. The Monks decreed that I am to provide lodging, clothing and food for him when he is at home, with no requirement of him to help support the family.

Of course, there will be no betrothal for him. He must remain celibate as a Monk unless he should choose to live his life as a carpenter instead of as the expected Wisdom Teacher."

To conclude their story of the family history, Miriam's mother gave her a hug and said, "I am a seer of auras, you know, and when you were born after so long without a baby in the house, I saw your colors and I said to your father--God has sent another Mystic to bless our home.

Miriam beamed with pleasure and the wonder of it all. She had never thought of herself as a Mystic, but she enjoyed the idea tremendously.

In her reflection upon what she had been told, Miriam realized now why her brothers seemed jealous of Jesus at times. With a shudder of horror, she recalled a memory of four years before, when she had been almost six.

A feast was being prepared to celebrate two great events. It was the homecoming of her brother, Jesus, from a trip to one of the Far Eastern lands, and it was also his twenty-first birthday.

A bitter argument arose between her father and her brother, James. She could not remember the words that were spoken before James kicked a chair; then he picked up a vial of anointing oil and threw it across the room. The vial landed in a vessel of fermented fruit punch that had been prepared for the party. Oil rose to the top of the wooden punch barrel as James watched in a panic.

Encouraged to greater defiance by his father's mild response, James shouted, "He wears the white robe and his hands are soft, while his father and brothers work day after day, year after year, never traveling more than 20 miles from home. He is just a bastard, growing fat and lazy under our mother's pretense that he is a great Avatar sent from God!" Then he spat in Joseph's face.

Miriam had never witnessed such things in her life, and she was afraid of what her father might do. She began to tremble. Joseph did not move, except to wipe the spittle from his face with the sleeve of his gray robe.

James became even more enraged at the silence.

"Why is he so special?" James demanded. "I went to the Mystery School as well. I am also in communion with God. The work is hard, and Jesus is free to sit at the feet of teachers throughout the world and then come home to comfort and admiration when he is weary. Now even more of the family funds are spent to celebrate this year of his emancipation. Will you give him a purse to match mine, even though he has not earned half as much as I?"

Miriam was sitting huddled in a corner on the floor, hugging her knees to her chest, trembling uncontrollably now, but Joseph seemed undisturbed. Calmly he poured a ladle of water into a bowl and splashed it onto his face, drying it on the hem of his robe.

Then he spoke loudly and firmly, yet not without sensitivity to James's emotions. "You have had your say and shared your concerns. It is my turn to speak. Life seems unfair at times, my son. We all pass through rooms that seem full of demons and injustice. But once we are safely in the next room of our life we can look back and see that if not for that room of difficulty that made us stop to think, we would have taken a different path. I will explain it to you once more, now that your age of emancipation is not far away.

Jesus is not betrothed as you are. He will never know the pleasure of a wife, nor build a house of his own. His Mother has sworn to God that we will prepare Jesus for a special mission that is to benefit all our people. Once he is called into service, he will be outside the protection of the Essene Brothers, outside the protection of the Jews, outside the protection of the Romans, outside the protection of this family. He will not be a carpenter as you will be, but an outcast hated by many. Now he travels to prepare for his work. Later he will travel in order to accomplish his work, with no purse and never a home of his own. Until he has completed his preparation, he will have the protection and comfort of my house. In return for that he will carpenter with me half of every year.

When a man is born, he brings with him a gift with which to bless the world.

Sometimes many are blessed, sometimes few, but a man is happy when he is giving his gift. Your gift is the masterful furniture work that you do. I see how your face smiles and your eyes shine when you are working your craft. Now would you trade your purse that you have earned, your Essene bride to be, your greater knowledge of your trade, your friends and comrades in the town, the shelter you are building to house your bride?

Would you trade all of that for what his life is and will be?"

James sat limply on a chair. "How do you know his life will be as you described?"

Joseph answered, "Are you a Mystic who has been through the Mystery School of the Essenes and do not know what the scriptures say about the Messenger from God?"

James laid his head on the table and wept. "Forgive me, Father, I am an envious man. I do not deserve the comfort that I have. Let me take my purse now and go prematurely into my own house so that my brother will not see my anger as a breach between us when he arrives."

Joseph went straightway and brought out a large soft bag tied at the neck with rope. Bells were attached to the ends of the rope and they jingled as he moved. Placing it in a small cart on wheels, he offered the handle to James and embraced him saying, "You are right to hide your anger until it has cooled. Go quickly now, and I will tell your Mother that you have requested emancipation. She will pack your belongings, and you can see her in three days."

They were both weeping when James's left. Miriam had cried too but at the same time her father's words kept playing in her mind as if they had special meaning to her: "A man is happy when he is giving his gift." That seemed to be the answer to something she had long wanted to know.

Within 15 minutes her brother Jesus had arrived. The sound of loving greetings and excitement filled the room as family gathered around to welcome him home. His beard and hair were flecked with gold from the sun, and his robe was so white it hurt her eyes to look at it. His face was glowing with a beautiful smile as he hugged each one with a whispered greeting just for them. When he got to her he just stood back and laughed, "My littlest sister, how serious you look. Has some terrible thing happened to you?"

"James threw oil into the punch barrel," she blurted out.

Putting a finger into the punch, Jesus pulled it out and licked the juice with an appreciative grin. "Look, the oil has disappeared. Now will you smile at me?"

Miriam forced a timid smile then hugged his knees as if she would never let go. "Where is James?" Jesus asked, looking around the room.

"I'll tell, let me tell," Miriam shouted, "He said you are a bastard with soft hands and he took his purse and left our house."

Jesus sat on the floor and gathered her onto his lap. Placing a finger across her lips he said, "You err in reporting one man's feelings to another. This thing is between my brother and me, and you trespass uninvited into the space that divides us. James" anger with me is his rightful secret unless he elects to reveal it to me. If a man reveals his heart to another, he can no longer hide from himself. When he is ready to come out of hiding, he will tell me of his own accord. Until then, little sister, let there be peace between you and me, without my brother between. And let there be peace between my brother and me until he chooses to break it."

Guests were arriving, but still he sat with her on his lap. Miriam was not satisfied. She wanted justice. "But he spat in Father's face. Aren't you going to chastise him for that?"

"This is not your quarrel to settle, nor is it mine," said Jesus. "It is a matter between our father and James, and they have not invited me to intervene. Your peace will be disturbed many times in your life over problems that are not yours to resolve. Do not take such notice of the life situations of others, lest you forget your own. As for me, I am ready for the party to begin!" Kissing her quickly on the cheek, Jesus leapt to his feet with a single movement and began to whirl in dance to the music. She forgot everything except how much she loved him.

During the next six months, Miriam sat at Jesus' feet and followed behind like a shadow when he was in the house. She was fascinated with the stories of people far away. Just being near him made her feel the sweetest contentment she had ever known and the greatest excitement. When it was time for him to leave, she pouted and begged him to take her along. For the second time he sat on the floor with her on his lap, his gaze turned fully upon her.

"Your life is for you to live and mine is for me, little one," he explained. "After your birthday you will attend the Mystery School and prepare for your own way of life. Perhaps someday you will travel; perhaps you will not. As for me, I travel alone for now, and I will see you only when I am in our parents' home."

Tenderly he blotted her tears with his white sleeve, then pulled a shiny cylinder- shaped cloudy white stone out of his pocket. She watched, amazed, as it turned from cloudy to clear in his hand. She could see right through it.

"I once made a trip to the land of the Hindus," he said. "A Mystery teacher there gave me this stone. He could see that I was young and inexperienced with travel, confused with the strangeness of the Hindu people. He said that, in order to feel immediate peace, I should hold it in my hand as I pray. It is filled with my spirit, having spent every day in prayer with me since then."

Miriam's eyes opened wide as he unfolded her fingers and placed the crystal in her palm.

"When you have a burden, you wish to share, or an inquiry you wish to make, hold the crystal in your hand, remember my face and call my name. I will hear you and answer your call," he said.

The following year when Miriam entered the Mystery School, to live in the commune, there had been a great wedding between her sister and a maker of shoes. Her brothers were still in apprenticeship to their father as his business required no less than six years to learn it well. Their purses were growing fat. Only James had left the family business and now had a thriving furniture making business of his own.

Miriam's school years passed quickly and happily as she discovered her own gifts of singing, sewing and complex reasoning. She learned to read and write and play the harp. She studied the symbolic interpretation of scripture and learned esoteric meditation, geometry and number calculations. Much of it seemed easy for her, as if she had learned it before. For exercise the girls practiced stretching like luxuriating cats, social dance, and gymnastics. The boys practiced gymnastics, lifting of weights, running and social dance.

Every year, in honor of the two major Jewish holy-days, she was permitted to visit her family home for an entire week. Jesus was always there for Passover. He always accompanied her on her return trip to the school, engaging in deep conversation while they traveled a full day on foot. Once there, Jesus would spend the night, meeting with the Monks for most of the following day. He would take his evening meal and a walk with her before bedtime and then leave before daybreak on the following day to return to their parents' home. After that, when the time came that he must leave for another trip, he would visit her at the school and, again, meet with the Monks. Miriam was never sure whether it was herself or the Monks he was coming to see, but it didn't really matter. The joy of having him talk with her, and call her little sister in front of everyone was greater than her question.

During Miriam's sixth year of school, prior to her thirteenth birthday, the year of betrothal, her father died from a brief illness. He had written and posted a script when he had fallen ill, appointing Jesus head of his household, according to tradition. Secretly he advised his wife and Miriam of money that he had hidden away in the event of his death. They were to use it sparingly and ask nothing of Jesus. Jesus was to come and go as he pleased. The two youngest sons had continued to work in their father's business after they were emancipated and married. Joseph had promised them ownership after his death, with only three stipulations to which they had readily agreed: They were to manage the business according to the principles Joseph had established. They were to give ten percent of their earnings to their mother for household expenses; and Jesus would work in the business six months each year to earn funds for his travels until God called him into the work for which he was born.

It was a sad year for Miriam and her mother, and they drew closer than ever before in their mutual grief. As her thirteenth birthday drew nearer, Miriam confided to Rose that she wished never to marry. "I think it was no accident that I came as the late sibling to Jesus. I want only to care for you, my Mother, to contribute comfort to his household and, whenever he permits, to follow two steps behind him and cling to his every word. Would it be selfish of me to remain a maiden so that I might spend my years in devotional service to him?"

"You must state your position to the Essene Brethren and let them decide," advised Rose. "Even Jesus was subject to their decisions until he reached the age of emancipation."

"What do you suppose he would have done if they had said he must marry?" Miriam speculated.

Knowing him with as much familiarity as they did made the question seem preposterous and they giggled with amusement at the thought of it. Together, as if it had been rehearsed, they chorused, "He would have prayed God to give them greater wisdom, and the decision would have been reversed!"

Miriam prayed daily after that for the wisdom of the Essene Monks. A week before her birthday she made her appeal to the Monks. "All my siblings are married with families of their own; my father is dead leaving only myself and Jesus to care for my mother. If my brother is indeed the Messiah, I will be needed to run his household and care for our mother as the years progress. I beg to remain a maiden and devote my attention to learning from the Master and serving him."

"We see the wisdom in your request," said the Monks. "Your brother is head of your household now. His wisdom is greater than ours, and if he does not disagree, so shall it be."

When their mother informed Jesus of Miriam's request and the decision of the Monks, he merely nodded, making no comment whatsoever.

In her 13th year, Miriam completed the Essene School and returned to her mother's home. She felt it was no coincidence that Jesus began his ministry that same year. There were rumors about the controversy surrounding her brother's message to the Jews, and Miriam could not understand why people questioned his identity or the wisdom of his words. For a few weeks he stayed at home, as head of their household, teaching in the Synagogue. Then all too soon he began to stay away for long periods at a time, speaking in the open to all who wished to hear.

Occasionally he would return home for a meal, a bed, a change of clothing and a hot bath, bringing his traveling companions with him. After greeting the men, her mother would rush to prepare a meal for them while Miriam would lay out sheets of soft cloth for them to wrap themselves in once they had bathed. She would also spread straw pallets on the covered porch that circled around the entire house. The men would set to drawing water from the well to fill a huge wooden tub for their bath. The tub was covered by a roof on the outer edge of the porch, and had been built by Joseph as a family bath. It was big enough to hold six men. While the first group bathed with Jesus, the other men would rest on the straw pallets. There was a wood plug about twelve inches in diameter tied to the outside of the huge vat. When the first group had finished their bathing, one would kick the plug out with his foot to let the water drain to the ground under the porch. It would make a tremendous popping sound, sufficient to wake the sleeping men. This was their signal to leave the pallets and draw water for their own bath. The fresh-bathed men would wrap in the clean sheeting and take to the pallets for their rest. Not until they were all clean and rested would they hold audience with the women. While they bathed and slept, Miriam would wash their robes and hang them to dry, ready to be worn the following day.

A thrill always rushed to Miriam's throat when the men came out for their meal. She listened to their conversation with fascination as she and her mother silently served the food and wine. After eating, the men would all take a walk while Miriam and her mother cleared the tables. When they returned, the women would sit with them for tea and conversation in which they all participated. The nature of their conversation was always of spiritual and philosophical matters. Occasionally Miriam would offer to anoint their tired feet with oil as they talked.

Once Miriam said to Jesus, while they were in audience with the others, "I do not agree with much of the Jewish religion. Since we know privately that God is the God of all and does not favor one nation over another, what would you say to this: Of all the religions you have seen, which is the most true? Should I pretend to believe Jewish ideas with which I disagree?"

"Do not openly agree or disagree," her brother said. "Obey the laws to show respect for your parents and your culture. Acknowledge that you understand what they believe by practicing tolerance and no-defiance. Be a model citizen to set an example for others to follow, and enjoy the pleasure of inclusion."

"Is that what you do?" challenged Miriam.

"It is what I do when I am here; and when I am in another culture, I respect their laws and rituals. But the day will soon come that I must reveal my greater knowledge to everyone, not just to my family and disciples."

Rose looked troubled, "Won't that bring trouble your way, my son?" "Yes, it will," said Jesus, "but that is why I was born."

"To get in trouble?" asked Miriam.

Jesus chuckled, "No--to tell all the things I know about God. If that brings me trouble, so be it."

"Did you learn all those things from the countries you visited?" she inquired. "No. I only learned their religions, their beliefs and their cultures from them. I learned about God from God."

"Tell me, tell me!" insisted Miriam.

Her brother said, "The true religion for you to practice is inside of you. It changes as you grow, just as your body changes as you grow. Sometimes as it changes, it is hard for you to recognize yourself as the same person, yet the body and the religion are still your own. Only God can reveal the Truth to you. I can but point the way to your discovery and tell you what He has revealed to me."

Miriam's passion to know was like a wild and beautiful animal inside her, while her outer demonstration was one of acceptance and dutiful obedience. One evening as she massaged the oil into his feet, Jesus was in a more talkative mood than usual. The other men and her mother had been sitting quietly at peace while Miriam questioned Jesus with insatiable curiosity.

"Your life with God is a private thing," he said. "The evidence of it can be observed by others, but the experience of it is hidden from the eyes of others, lest they try to wrestle it from you or rush you beyond your capacity to understand."

"Speak more clearly, my brother. I do not understand," pleaded Miriam.

Jesus tried again, "When men establish religions in the world, it is like all the rivers trying to flow into one channel. They argue over the best path to take to the sea, when one looking from above would see that all rivers twist and turn overland and underground to wind their way to the sea. Every river comes from the sea and returns to the sea in a rhythm determined by the stars. But should a river become conscious of the sea, it can determine when to return and when to go out again. No longer will the stars rule its timing. It will catch a higher wave and flow more deeply into the center of the sea. It will dive to the depths and observe the life of things unseen except by the eye of the beholder who has dared to come this far from shore. Some will crest again and flow back to shore, carrying fresh waters through the riverbed. Others will stay in the sea.

Their riverbeds dry up then, until another takes the same path to make its way to the sea." "Are we all like rivers?" Miriam asked.

Jesus said, "Not until he begins to search for the sea does a man transform from a thirsty pit in the wilderness into a spring of flowing water. Like a butterfly is grown from worm to winged beauty, the soul of a person transforms from thirsty pit to flowing river."

"Is that the parable you would like me to consider?" inquired Miriam.

"It is," answered her brother, fondly tousling her hair. Then he stood and stretched with a wide yawn. They all retired for the night.

Occasionally Jesus would look directly into Miriam's eyes as she sat at his feet during his discussions with the disciples, and smile as if they shared an amusing secret. Although she did not know what the secret was, she would return his smile.

As Miriam became more acquainted with her brother's traveling companions, she felt a special closeness to the one called Nathaniel. Talking with him was so warm and comfortable, and although he had not attended the Mystery School, his ideas and reasoning ability were superior to those of many Mystics she had known. When the men were away, she found herself thinking about him as much as she thought of Jesus, but in a very different way. Upon their return, a secret thrill would flood her face with a blush and her heart would change its rhythm. At times when Miriam would entertain the men with songs from the Psalms of David, or soft music on the harp, she would catch Nathaniel's eyes watching her with admiration, and she was pleased.

One day after the others had tired of talking and some had gone to bed for the night, Nathaniel asked Miriam to accompany him for a walk in the garden. As they walked, she stumbled over a fallen limb and he caught her around the waist. His touch sent fire through her veins and she was too embarrassed to look at him, lest he should see the shame of her desire.

With a finger under her chin, Nathaniel lifted her face to the moonlight. They gazed into each other's eyes for what seemed an eternity. Then Nathaniel spoke.

"If I were not committed to serving your brother and traveling with him, I would ask him for your hand. But I know he is the promised Messiah and my soul will not let me forsake him."

"My brother is, indeed the Messiah," said Miriam. "If you were not committed to him, I could not love you so. It is enough for me to know that you feel as I do. I believe that my life is meant for a greater cause than marriage and the rearing of children. How gratifying it is to serve that cause with you."

The following day, Jesus took both of them into the garden with him. He bent to pluck a flower with petals not yet open to the world. Offering it to Nathaniel he said, "This is a symbol of your betrothal to my sister. A traveling man makes a poor husband, and for yet a little while you must stay with me. But the day will come and I will tell you when it is, that you will depart from the other disciples and travel no more with them.

After you have seen without a question that I am not dead but living, then I will assign another in your place as a carrier of my word. Then you will be assigned as the keeper of my sister. On the day of which I speak, you must leave Jerusalem quickly to fetch my sister from this house where she will be packed and waiting for you. You will take her to your family home, telling no one who she is. You will tell them only that she is betrothed to you and that she is in mourning because the head of her household has been cruelly killed and her family scattered abroad. You are to request that she reside under your own mother's care one year before you are wed."

They stood speechless, staring at each other as Jesus briskly turned toward the house. "How did he know?" they echoed each other's voice.

Nathaniel laughed. "Is there anything he does not know? Be careful what you dream about, my sweet."

"And what is he saying? He is the head of my household," said Miriam. "Is he saying that he is to be killed?"

"Certainly not," reasoned Nathaniel, "for he said that he will give me a sign to take you when I have learned that he is not dead but living. Perhaps it is going to appear that he has been killed but then I will learn that he is still alive."

"It is too much to think about," they agreed, shaking their heads in confusion. "The good part is that he has given his blessings for our marriage, and we are betrothed to one another."

On the day of Jesus' crucifixion, when Miriam was nearly 17, she stood helpless and heartbroken at the foot of the cross with her mother. Rose seemed to be in a trance as she kept her eyes on her son's face. There was no evidence of pain in her eyes, only a look of maternal tenderness. Her eyes filled with tears; her mind filled with realization of everything she had ever known about him. Were they tears of sorrow or pride in his strength? Miriam could not tell. Her pain was too deep to care.

Jesus had told them this event would come and had prepared them for it as best he could. But he could not have prepared them for the cruelties that were inflicted upon him.

Miriam sobbed, feeling more alone than she had ever felt in her life. As Nathaniel stepped to her side and placed his arm lightly across her shoulders, Jesus looked at them and nodded. They remembered his instructions that Nathaniel was to take her to his mother's house after learning that Jesus was still alive. Miriam felt a moment of hope, then looked again at his blood-streaked body. Outrage, panic and desperation filled her all at once, and she fainted at the foot of the cross.

Within three weeks after the Crucifixion, Nathaniel had seen the living soul of Jesus on no less than three occasions when he was with some of the other disciples. At the third sighting, the Master had announced to the disciples that Nathaniel would be leaving their company to receive a secret assignment, and that Judas, brother of James, would join their company in his place.

This Judas, brother of James, had been a loyal follower of the Master, traveling and sleeping often in the camp of the 12. All the men knew him and he was well versed in the Kingdom of God teachings. Disappointment and elation fought for supremacy in Nathaniel's heart as he left immediately to go to Miriam and take her to his family home in Cana, a city in Galilee. Once he saw her, he was at peace again. Every assignment from the Master was to be considered a contribution to his work. Nathaniel vowed that he would give his entire being to honoring this assignment and never again dwell on other services he might have performed.

Nathaniel's family was happy to see him. Accepting his explanation without question, they made no reference to his having disappeared for close to three years. Men, women and children of the family worked together in their family business of tentmaking, tent-repair and garment repair. There was plenty of work and plenty of space in the house for both of them.

Miriam shared a room with Nathaniel's widowed sister and her daughter.

Because the tenting material was quite heavy and Miriam was smaller than the other women in the family, she was offered the work of garment repair. She plunged gratefully into her role. The ritualistic work helped to process her grief as she tried to sort out the sight of Jesus' crucifixion and the reports from Nathaniel that he had seen and heard for himself that Jesus was not dead but still alive. Remembering what he had told them on the day of their betrothal restored some degree of peace to her, but still the agony of his suffering was vivid in her memory.

She felt especially glad that sewing was one of her talents so that she could do an excellent job for her new family. Nathaniel did not sleep in the house during that first year but on a hammock in the gardening shed. Because they both were beyond the age of emancipation, they were not chaperoned, but their respect for Jesus and his trust in them kept them chaste until their wedding day.

In honor of Jesus' request, they had kept their affiliation with Jesus and his work a secret from Nathaniel's family. They shared with no one that Miriam was the sister of Jesus, or that Nathaniel had been one of his 12 closest disciples.

The family of Nathaniel was firmly committed to the Pharisee's way, attending Temple services and honoring every requirement of the Jewish Law, as well as the improvised rules of the Pharisees. In order to prevent questions, the betrothed couple participated in all of the family's religious activities. Only in private did they speak of Jesus, the ideas he had shared with them, and their frustration at having to be silent when the family spoke with disgust about those "rebels." The "rebels" they were referring to were the growing number of Jews who claimed that Jesus had been the Messiah. In the family setting when his name came up, or issues related to him, they held their silence and did not participate in the conversation.

To have a little house of their own where they could freely talk and pay tribute to Jesus and live the principles that he had taught them became a passionate goal for Nathaniel and Miriam that went beyond their attraction to each other. They wanted to share not just their love for each other but to openly live a way of life that they both held as ideal.

Rumors about the followers of Jesus were quite disturbing. The Romans were hunting them like criminals and torturing them mercilessly. Bounty hunters, both Roman and Jew, were everywhere--looking to receive a reward for informing the soldiers of their whereabouts.

"This is why Jesus told us to keep my identity and your involvement with him secret. He foresaw that this would happen," said Miriam with sudden insight.

Nathaniel held her and they cried together.

One sunlit day, as they sat in the garden discussing a philosophical point that Jesus had made, a disagreement about his meaning arose between Miriam and Nathaniel.

Miriam fell silent, then reaching into the pocket of her robe she pulled out the crystal that she carried with her constantly. Opening her palm to expose it to the sunlight, she cast a mischievous smile at Nathaniel as he stopped his speech in the middle of a word and stared.

"What is this?" he asked in awe at the dancing colors in the crystal.

"My brother gave it to me when I was a tiny girl," explained Miriam. "It is a crystal from the land of the Hindus. He said that if I hold it in my hand and call his name, he will hear me and answer my question or heal my pain. Shall we see if he will resolve this question for us through the crystal?"

Nathaniel could only nod his agreement. The question had been whether he would want them to leave their comfortable place among friends and family where they posed as traditional Jews in the outer while acting as Jesus' followers in private and in their hearts, or to leave everything behind and join a band of Jesus' followers, living a life of hiding and poverty. It had started with Nathaniel asking her a question, "Are we being cowardly to hide our regard for Jesus?"

Miriam had answered, "Of course not, for if we admit our relationship with him, we will be breaking the promise that he required of us as a condition of his permission to marry."

Nathaniel pursued the question, "But as he gathered disciples to him for service to God's Plan, did he not say to them, "Leave all and follow me"? Even to one who wanted to delay because of family duties he said, "Let the dead bury their dead, follow me."

Placing his hand over hers to cup the crystal between their palms, Nathaniel said quite seriously, "Let us inquire through the crystal, now. Jesus, what is the right thing for us to do? Should we in loyalty take an open stand as your supporters? Or should we live this ordinary life and take our pleasure in safety and comfort while our hearts burn to demonstrate our love for you?"

After posing the question they closed their eyes and became silent, waiting and listening inside themselves until each forgot the other was there.

After some time had passed, by what seemed to be mutual consent, in the same moment they withdrew their hands from each other and Miriam pocketed the crystal.

Nathaniel was the first to speak. "Some idea inside my head gave a message I cannot ignore. I pray that you will agree. When Jesus required the promise of hiding our affiliation with him, it was not without a cause and it was not simply for our safety and comfort in a new life. That no one knows of our love for him will give us opportunity and power to do important work that somehow will contribute to his cause. I do not yet know what the work will be, but through our work of sewing and mending of tents, he will draw to us those who are to be blessed by whatever it is we are to do. Our time has not yet come, and all is as it should be for now."

With tears of gratitude glistening in her eyes, Miriam said, "I too felt a message but it was in pictures as well as thoughts. I saw us talking to someone in secret, a frightened looking man. I greeted him with a warm embrace, gave him tea and a basket of bread, and then moved him through one door into another. Then you were with him on the other side, and in a moment, he was covered with heavy tenting material-moving along the road in a horse drawn cart. You were driving the cart. I could not see where you were taking him."

Suddenly Nathaniel sprang from the bench, laughing in merriment. He picked Miriam up and swung her around and around and around in circles until she was dizzy. Setting her feet on the ground, he kissed her on top of the head. "It is our future service to the cause that you have seen," he said. "Now I must set forth to build us a house with a sewing room for you that opens into a tent-repair shop for me."

Every coin that he earned went into building their house. Miriam saw him only at mealtimes and in Temple for the next six months. The day after her year of mourning was over, Miriam and Nathaniel were married. It was a simple wedding with much dancing and laughter.

She loved sharing a home with him. The freedom of being able to talk openly was uplifting, and Miriam found herself singing the Psalms of David with joy in her heart once more. They had placed the crystal of the Hindus on a small table in Miriam's sewing shop. Every day when they took their midday meal and tea together, they would hold the crystal and talk to Jesus, asking for guidance in their work of tent-making and robe repair, as well as their secret work of helping the persecuted Friends escape from prison and death.

Nathaniel was still in contact with some of the "Friends", as the Jesus followers were called. By way of the underground, he and Miriam had sent word to them that if any should need safe passage in their escape from the bounty hunters, they could come to the garment shop using a secret phrase to identify themselves as "Friends". The pass phrase would be, "My friend has sent me to pay for the work you did on his robe."

Miriam would give them a supply of bread and water and escort them to the door of the tent-repair shop. Nathaniel would then load them into a wagon under tents, and take them to a safe place for hiding. Nathaniel and Miriam were glad to have this opportunity to help the Friends find safety, and they believed Jesus had foreseen this as their role when he placed them together.

After five years of marriage, it was obvious that no children would be born to them. They were disappointed at first, but both of them had always found it easy to reconcile themselves to whatever their circumstances might present. "To have children would surely distract us from our work," they declared with agreement.

Twelve years after Jesus' crucifixion, when Miriam was but 29, she was sewing and singing in her shop one day. A large hairy man came bursting through the door of her shop, his eyes looked wild with fear, and his robe was torn as if it had been cut.

"You poor man," Miriam said as she rushed to his side. "May I get you a drink of water?"

"Yes, yes, my friend," the man gasped as he plunged himself onto a chair.

Miriam decided to cut him a piece of bread as well, and she wondered whether his use of the word "Friend" meant that he was one of Jesus' followers. Perhaps he had not heard of them.

As she came through the curtain back into the room, the man was holding her crystal in his hand and looking at it curiously. He seemed relaxed and no longer afraid.

"That is a crystal from the land of the Hindus," she said. "It was a gift from my brother who is no longer in the world."

The man squinted his eyes to get a better look at her while he wolfed down the bread and water. "I have seen you before," he said. "You are the sister of the man, Jesus, who was crucified for treason some 12 years ago, are you not?"

Cautiously Miriam lowered her eyes. "Why would you think that I am she?"

"I was there," he said, "watching the pitiful sight of them mistreating such a man. After that was done, I joined up with a band of Friends. There are thousands of us about but it's not safe to let ourselves be known. You are his sister, are you not?"

"Give me your robe and wrap yourself in this sheetcloth," said Miriam. "I will tell you about the crystal while I repair the robe."

His eyes grew wide as she told of the many times she had received Jesus' counsel by "calling" him through use of the crystal. "Why this is something that the Friends should have," he said gruffly. "It is not fair for one person to have such a prize when she is safe in a snug, warm house and we run and hide like rats. Give it to me to take to my group, and then we can petition Jesus to keep us safe and to make us strong against our enemies."

"I cannot part with it," said Miriam. "It is like a bond between him and me, his personal gift to me."

"Have you finished my robe yet?" the man asked abruptly, getting up to walk behind her and peer over her shoulder.

Before she could answer, he jerked her head backwards by her hair and slit her throat. Throwing her to the floor he hastily put on his robe and grabbed the crystal. It was a moment of truth for Miriam, who could still see dimly and was still able to breathe. It was an opportunity to choose. She chose forgiveness.

"I forgive you," she whispered hoarsely. "Take the crystal and go."

"How dare you forgive me!" he shouted. "You are the evil one. Hiding this treasure away for all these years, when the Friends could have used it for our protection and to grow in wisdom."

Then he plunged the knife into her solar plexus, pinning her to the floor, and fled.

As his wife's killer ran out the front door, Nathaniel came through the connecting door from his shop. "Miriam," he called, "Let us stop for bread and tea."

Then he saw her in a pool of blood on the floor. She was still alive, trying to tell him something. Blindly he cradled her in his arms and rocked her back and forth. "Who did this? Why would someone hurt my fragile flower? I will use the crystal. Perhaps the great healer can heal you through it."

Nathaniel looked toward the table and saw that the crystal was gone. Frantically he searched on the floor. "Where is it, where is the crystal?" he shouted in desperation. With her last breath, Miriam pointed toward the door.

Nathaniel ran outside and shouted brokenly, engulfed with tears, "Help me! My wife has been slain for a piece of stone."

No one was there.

Hours later, Nathaniel's sister came by to see how Miriam's work had gone for the day. She found Nathaniel holding the blood-soaked body to his chest and whining pitifully like the sound of a puppy who has lost his way.

Nathaniel was in shock until the day of the funeral. When he saw the stone rolled in front of her tomb, rage came rushing again through his veins. He wanted justice more than he had ever wanted anything in his life. The next day he broadcast aloud to everyone he could see that he was offering a reward for the capture of Miriam's killer.

Nathaniel's mother was saddened at his fury. Entering quietly into a room where he was alone, she sat and looked deeply into his eyes. Then she whispered loudly so only he could hear, "You traveled with Jesus for close to three years. Do you remember what he taught?

Surprised, Nathaniel stared at her. "Are you a Friend?" he asked.

"Yes," she said, "I am a Friend, and I have known of your whereabouts from the beginning."

"He taught many things," Nathaniel said. "I remember them all."

"Do you believe that he was a great messenger from God", asked his mother. "Yes, I have no doubt," answered Nathaniel.

His mother continued, "Can you tell me why he would say we must always practice forgiveness, when people do such terrible things to us as this man did to your wife? Why do you think he would not want us to avenge her?"

"Because to return evil for evil is to produce more evil in the invisible world; then the circle never stops but goes round and round and round." said Nathaniel.

Kissing him lightly on the forehead, his mother said, "Thank you, my son, for clearing up this matter for me. Now I understand."

The truth had set him free, for the moment. Nathaniel returned to his home and lay down to sleep. But sleep would not come. Even though the knowledge of forgiveness was in his mind, the urge for justice was burning in his heart.

Accusing Jesus, he thought, "We did as you asked and saved hundreds of Friends from slaughter. Why did you not save Miriam from slaughter in return?"

After wrestling with his question half the night to no avail, Nathaniel sat up in bed and deliberately brought to his mind an image of the crystal. He envisioned the face of Jesus and called out to him, "Master, take this burden from me. Set me free."

A voice spoke inside his mind, "When you loose the killer from your mind, then you are loosed from thoughts of him. Whatever you store up in your mind is held there. Whatever you loose from your mind is gone from it; then your mind is also free. What is there to gain by giving hurt for hurt?"

The voice was not the voice of Jesus, but of Miriam.

Two years later a messenger came to Nathaniel with a package. It contained the crystal. A message that accompanied the package said, "A man has been stoned to death by Friends of Jesus in Nazareth. He had shown them a crystal, saying that it had the magical powers of Jesus captured inside it. They laughed at him; then he boasted about where and how he came to own the crystal. They were outraged by his brutality, and they stoned him until he was unrecognizable, leaving his body for the buzzards to consume."

Nathaniel cried out, "It is my fault. I once wished it so." Guilt engulfed him.

A soft voice came to his mind, "Forgive yourself. The circle of hate is no one's creation. It is a whirlpool of sorrows that we find hard to rise above. Take yourself out of the circle by forgiving yourself as you would forgive any man. Then your part in the sustaining of that pool of vengeance is over."

Nathaniel imaged the crystal again, knowing now that the true Crystal of Communication between himself and wisdom was the power within his own mind. Nathaniel spoke directly to God with the greatest conviction he had ever known, "I am forgiven. My ignorance of mercy is no more."

Immediately a ray of white light flashed through his mind's eye; then it was gone.

For no reason at all that he could think of, Nathaniel felt happy.

After that, when he mended the tents, he sang the Psalms of David that Miriam had sung, and he felt content just knowing that she was alive and well. Until the day he died of a heart attack in his sleep, Nathaniel secretly assisted Friends to escape the bounty hunters. But his true purpose in life was to express all the goodness he knew in everything that he did.

Chapter 7

MILAH

Athens, Greece 350-400 A.D.

In her home life Milah's father was a fisherman who spent many days each month away from home. She lived with her mother and father in a section of small, neat wooden houses that were built in rows. All the floor plans were the same, with a flat front porch close to the ground. Between each pair of houses was a covered archway leading to a utility building that housed cleaning supplies and the "toilet room" where one could bathe or use the toilet in privacy away from the main house. A powdery substance like lye, dumped into the toilet every morning and evening, did a remarkable job of keeping odors under control.

Down every row, the back of each house adjoined the back of the house behind it. The front porch of each house of a row squarely faced the front porch of the house directly in front of it. A neat pathway of cobblestones about ten feet wide served as a divider between the rows of front porches. Their neighbors were friendly, and the children cheerfully played together outside as if they were all one family but they never went inside another's home or utility building. Front porch visiting was common.

Milah's father and mother had a serene, pleasant, quiet relationship when they were together. Although they seldom spoke to one another, there was a tenderness between them and no sense of animosity that five-year old Milah could detect. But there was a distinct lack of common interests as well as an absence of personal interest in one another. It was as if neither was aware that the other had desires, goals, disappointments, plans and dreams. Or, perhaps they were afraid to inquire. Milah would have guessed that they came from entirely different backgrounds, but they never spoke of their past. On the evenings her father was at home, Milah's mother, Anna, would begin preparing the evening meal as soon as she arrived home from the big house where she worked. She would serve her husband a cup of hot or cold liquid while the meal was in progress as he sat watching her cook. If they talked at all it was her father listening and laughing gently or grunting appropriately while Anna entertained him with tales. He was not interested in her activities and personal experiences, but in the family with whom she spent her days. Anna never inquired about his fishing adventures, and he never spoke of them. They always ate in silence, and after the meal her father would kiss Anna on the cheek, praise her for whatever dish he had enjoyed the most, and offer to help with the clean-up. Anna would blush and smile, refusing with a shake of her head, then shoo the two of them outside to visit with the neighbors. On evenings when the weather prohibited outdoor enjoyment, Milah's father would invite the child to recite poetry or recount historical facts that she had learned from her tutor as she grew older. When he was at home, they always went to bed within an hour after Anna had completed her evening chores.

Milah went with Anna every day to her place of employment, where she was incorporated into the group of children as if she were a sibling. She had been an infant when her mother found the position, and she fantasized that she was really a member of the big household. She pretended that Anna simply borrowed her from the big house every evening, and then took her back "home" for the day. It was only on the one day each week that Anna did not go to the big house that Milah accepted her true identity as a child of poverty living among people who were largely illiterate, very uncouth and boring compared to her daytime companions. There were no children in her own neighborhood that Milah particularly enjoyed. They simply did not understand her "educated interests and fancy ways." But she was comfortable being largely shunned and left often to herself in the evenings. After all, with nine loving and happy semi-siblings to play and learn with six days a week, evenings were the only time Milah could claim the solitude that she loved so well.

The children of the master's household thought of Milah as their step-sister, for even though Anna and their father appeared to have no relationship beyond their business arrangement, he insisted they treat Milah's mother with the same respect and obedience as a parent. They all loved Anna very much.

Milah's favorite playmate of the nine was Aramis. He had been born on exactly the same day that she was. His mother had died the day after his birth, and Anna had been hired four months later. Milah and Aramis had shared the same crib and had learned to walk and talk within a month of each other. Of course, they shared all their secrets with each other and nurtured one another through childhood tears. Aramis was very protective of Milah, and they enjoyed the game of telling everyone that they were twins.

Mila's mother took both her job and the idea of formal education very seriously. One of her tasks was to select tutors for the children of the household in which she was employed. She arranged for all the children to have a general education until they were 10 years old, with no differentiation between girls and boys. However, when their tenth birthday arrived, she insisted that they have an aptitude test to determine the course of their future scholastic pursuits; whether their studies would be predominantly in the arts and sciences, or in political and military studies, or in a specific trade of some sort.

Those who had artistic aptitudes of any kind were to spend three of their school days each week with the art tutor and three days weekly studying other subjects. Milah was delighted when both she and Aramis showed an aptitude for arts and sciences. Only three of the 10 children, Milah, Aramis and his 13-year-old sister, Alicia, had been talented enough to be placed with the arts tutor who covered a wide range of artistic subjects with them. Milah and Aramis began with a general education in the arts, while Alicia, who had been studying with the arts tutor for three years, practiced her special talents of dance and singing.

When Milah was 11, her father drowned in a fishing accident. Very little was said about it between her and her mother. His body was never found, and within a week the two of them had moved into the big house, leaving that era of poverty and emptiness behind them.

Two years later, Milah, Aramis and Alicia were showing such scholastic promise that Anna decided they had surpassed their tutor. She requested and gained permission from her employer to send them to an Arts and Sciences Academy in Rome, where they could audition for stage performances and practice their talents with live audiences.

Anna bought each of them a handsome new wardrobe with funds provided by her employer, who paid their arts tutor a tidy sum to accompany them to the Academy for audition. Their auditions were successful, and they were accepted into the Academy.

The difficult part for all of them was in learning that they would be separated.

Socialization was forbidden between boys and girls at the Academy. Boys had a dormitory inaccessible to girls and, in order to prevent distraction from their development, were forbidden to see them except during classes, rehearsals and performances. When they were not studying or practicing, boys were required to use their time off playing sports with other boys or studying war games.

Sixteen-year-old Alicia, considered an adult, was placed in a house with "mature" young ladies. She was permitted to socialize with young men of the Academy during chaperoned group parties or dances.

Milah was placed with girls aged 12 to 15. The Academy did not accept anyone under 12 years old. In their time away from classes, the young ladies were trained in the graces of femininity such as posture, proper walking, sitting, elegant social manners, table manners, conversation, appropriate apparel for different occasions, various table and yard games, board games and sewing of different kinds.

Milah suffered emotionally from the separation. She had been registered as the daughter of Anna's employer, and her life as a fisherman's daughter was not known here. Anna had cautioned her to never reveal it. She would have been refused entry into the school if they had known her true identity.

Milah found that her everyday life was no longer just a pleasant fantasy as it had been before. It was now a make-believe drama that she must live on the stage of life every day from now on. She wanted to live openly, and she longed to be with Aramis and Alicia who knew and loved her for who she really was; but there was never an opportunity for personal conversation between them.

Both Aramis and Alicia, free to be themselves with nothing to hide, adjusted very well and made friends quickly. Milah became withdrawn and guarded and gained a reputation for being mysterious and unapproachable. She reminded herself of her father and wondered how he had come to be so mysterious and silent. But it was too late to ask him. He had been such a non-personality and so uninvolved with her that she had never even thought of him after his burial until now. Perhaps her mother had known his story. So, just as she had lived dual roles before as the only child of a poor fisherman in the row houses and at the same time as one of ten well-educated, perfectly-groomed and financially-spoiled children of a wealthy business man, she was still living a dual role; one as a silent, withdrawn, mysterious and beautiful but unapproachable girl, the other as a top student in the Academy with great popularity as a stage performer who had an uncanny ability to play any part that was assigned to her, whether young or old, male or female, urchin or princess.

When her mother died of a fever the year that she was fourteen, Milah felt a total loss of identity. Philosophy and religion were a part of her education, and she found herself intrigued by the historical accounts of the man, Jesus, whom the Christians said was God. She did not accept the idea that he was God, but he did seem to have been a very wise and holy man with a great message to present. She felt a sense of emotional intimacy toward the stories of him and gratefully embraced portions of the Christian writings that were presented in her studies. Even so, she would not pray to Jesus.

Milah held a secret belief that God would be more likely to honor her prayers if she prayed with her attention fixed on the soft light that she always saw in her forehead when she closed her eyes. She prayed daily to the inner light that God would help her become a real person with an identity of her own.

Pouring herself entirely into the arts of singing, dance and acting, as well as prayer; Milah was soon able to overcome the sense of abandonment that she felt toward life in general. Still, with no one to talk to who knew her background, she longed for a new identity to replace her emotional clinging to childhood associations.

When the loneliness for self would strike, she would tell herself firmly; "That was me as a child. Now this is who I am. I am an excellent student, a model member of the Academy, a very talented and popular performer, and my name is Milah." Through that practice she gradually began to feel a sense of confidence and self-esteem that she had never known before.

When she was 15 and a half, Milah was invited to join the elite troupe of traveling performers from the Academy. This troupe served not only as a popular traveling entertainment group but also as a living advertisement for the quality of education one could receive at the Academy. The Academy Theater Group had been a part of the Roman culture for over 30 years, and anyone who had ever been a part of it was assured of an entertainment career once they reached the age of adulthood, which was 16. The troupe traveled from town square to town square in villages they had never heard of before, soliciting parents with potential students to let their children audition on closing night for admission in the Academy. From those who were accepted, the first year's tuition was collected in advance, and this was how the troupe's travel expenses were paid.

While on the road, all members of the troupe actually sat together at meals and shared conversations, and Milah was thrilled to discover that her beloved Aramis had been a part of the troupe for over a year. She felt comfortable with this small group of boys and girls. It was more like the family of pseudo-siblings she had enjoyed as a child and they all seemed quite compatible with one another. Her new sense of joy showed in her performances, and whether dancing, singing, acting or reciting poetry she was a delight to all who watched. The old depression seemed to have ended.

It was common for a relative or friend of one of the performers to join the troupe for a meal or celebration party after a performance. One evening a friendly young man in his 20s who said his name was Jared joined them for wine and a lavish meal after the show, and it never occurred to anyone to question whose friend or relative he might be.

He seemed to know everyone there and was especially interested in conversing with Aramis and complimenting him on his talents. When Milah joined them with a glass of wine in her hand, Aramis introduced Jared and left the two of them alone, hurrying away to chat with a girl that he had been watching with adoration.

The attraction between Milah and Jared was startling to both of them. Not only were they enamored with the physical magnetism between them but, also intrigued with the thrill of sharing long philosophical discussions about everything from worldly affairs to metaphysics, and they laughed at the same things. Within two months Jared had asked Milah to become his wife.

"Ah, am I not a great matchmaker!" boasted Aramis when he heard the news, and he encouraged her to accept.

During their initial conversations, Milah had learned a great deal about Jared. He had inherited a thriving vineyard in Rome from his father, with a great deal of land, a magnificent house and generations of servants who lived in the house or on the land in smaller houses. It was they who tended the business and the vineyard, while Jared was free to do as he pleased. He had gained great favor with high-ranking political leaders by contributing generous sums of money to those who appealed to him. In return they often invited him to affairs of the State and were quite impressed with his wit and his knowledge of history and political strategy. He loved to boast that his education had been predominantly in oratory, debate, history and politics. He was a great horseman, wrestler and runner. He was fond of saying, "I feel like a king. The gods have favored me."

Jared explained to Milah that, because of his talent for oratory presentation and debate, he now worked only intermittently, contracting to compose political speeches and at times. "I even act as spokesman in a leader's place at times," he bragged.

This "career" had him traveling occasionally but most of his work was in Rome where he lived in a luxurious wing of his house.

"I want you to live there with me, Milah and feel free to pursue your interests in artistic performance as long as you do not travel excessively."

Their courtship was filled with fun and adventure; but other than the information about his life, their only serious conversation had been in philosophical discussions or their heartfelt vows of love for one another. With the exception of Aramis, Milah never saw any of her childhood "siblings" anymore. He was very popular with his own friends, had numerous interests, enjoyed much public recognition, always had a romance going and was still her confidante and dearest friend.

Soon she would be 16 and free to marry if she should desire it. But Milah felt it would be unethical of her to marry Jared without discussing three issues that, to her, were of utmost importance. These were issues that might cause him to change his mind about wanting to marry her, but she felt compelled to take the risk.

When she approached him with a serious look on her face and said they must talk, Jared teased her by saying, "There's nothing in the world serious enough to put such a frown on a happy face. I don't want to talk about anything that might put that serious look upon me."

But Milah would not be teased out of it. "I insist," she said quietly. "I want a marriage in which conversation flows like a river racing downhill, in which nothing is forbidden to ask or to say. I do not want a silent alliance as my parents had. They had love but no interest in each other's thoughts. There was no confirmation of their love except for producing me, and sometimes I wonder if he was actually my father."

Jared sat listening with a sulky face, but Milah had his attention.

She confessed to him her true identity as the only daughter of a poor Greek fisherman. She described the row houses in fisherman's village and the drabness of her home.

Jared laughed and kissed her saying, "That's even more reason for you to marry me since you have no wealth or people of your own upon which to depend. That you love me is more important than any kind of ancestry you might bring to our marriage."

"All is well so far," thought Milah.

Then she told him about a recurrent dream she had been having since moving to Rome at age 13.

"In the dream I am a tired and sun-browned, devout woman of middle age. My skin is weathered, and I wear a dark, shapeless garment. I am sitting on the ground outside a tent; the tent is my home. A handsome man is on his knees pleading with me to return to him. His heart is in agony at my refusal."

Taking his hand, she said, "I believe that I have lived before. You seem familiar to me. Are you the man in this dream? Perhaps it is a memory from another life, or could it be a prophecy of our future?"

Jared laughed loudly. "I too believe that souls are reincarnated. But you can be assured that I would never get on my knees to any woman. So, I cannot be the man in your dream! Neither from times gone by, nor in future time."

Milah decided not to pursue it, but she thought to herself, "Then my heart is torn, because I love the man in the dream as much as I love you, my dear Jared. And if I have lived before, then how many men have I loved?" She held her tongue.

"There is one more thing I must bring to your mind before we marry," said Milah.

Jared was relaxed now, viewing her "issues" as childish, humorous and unimportant.

Milah posed a question: "Do you believe in the Gods or in one God or in no Deity at all, or in nature as the ruler of all life, or in the movement of the stars? We have discussed the general philosophies of life but never religion. Devotion to God is very important to me. I believe in some of the Christian writings, and I pray not to the God of the Christian movement but to the God to whom Jesus prayed, the creator whom he said is all forgiving, all loving and all knowing. I also sit in silent meditation upon the thought of God, and occasionally I feel a sense that I am in the company of God.

He is not speaking but listening to me as I think and feel. Even so, I dislike the Christians and their disrespect for other Gods. I also believe somewhat in the cycles of the moon and the movement of the stars and their influences. And of course, my belief in the many lifetimes is vastly foreign to the Christian teachings. Many worship the psychic powers of the mind as their God, but I believe those to be mundane compared to the true God.

So, tell me, Jared, what do you believe of such matters?"

An angry dark look grew in Jared's eyes like dark storm clouds. He was silent as if afraid of his own anger.

"Why does this anger you?" asked Milah.

"It seems you have asked me this before," said Jared. "Never," said Milah. "We have never spoken of a Deity."

Jared scowled, "Nevertheless whether we have or have not, be forewarned; you will not ask me this again. My relationship with the Deity is a private matter in which I give no other person admission. Suffice it to say that I love my Deity well, and if you knew how much you might be jealous. But let me announce in equal strength that if Isis knew of my love for you, she would be blinded with jealousy at its steadiness and beauty."

"Then Isis is the Deity of your heart?" asked Milah, mildly surprised.

"Nay!" said Jared. "For if it were Isis then she would now know of my love for you, and I would have to choose another God. She is jealous and would not have me unless I love her most of all. I could not love another above you. My revered Deity is another that I will not reveal; so, hush about this for all our time together."

"But, can't you just tell me what you think about the Christian idea?" appealed Milah.

Jared stood up. Speaking slowly and sternly to Milah. As if to command that he not be misunderstood he asserted, "I will not say."

Milah felt frustrated that he did not show more interest in her views of what seemed to her a vastly important consideration of life. She felt frustrated that he forbade her to inquire of his, and she wondered how he could apply the phrase "my Deity" to one he was ashamed to announce. Then she remembered that, until she had told him, no one other than Aramis had known of her secret love for the teachings of Jesus, and she felt a stirring of understanding.

If she married Jared, she would have to permit him a private spiritual life, and she would also have to keep her own spiritual life and beliefs out of her conversation with him. It was tempting to discuss these ideas, yet she valued his right to privacy. She promised him that she would not introduce the topic of religion or the question of the Deity to him again.

Jared sat down and smiled. "Since we are being so serious, and honest, I too have a confession to make," he said. "I am 27 years old, not 20 as I have led you to believe.

That means I am 11 years older than you." Milah gave no response.

"So, will we marry now?" asked Jared with a flirtatious look on his face.

"Yes, we will marry if you promise to never lie to me again," said Milah.

Secretly she still wondered whether he was the man in her dream, regardless of what he might say about it. He kissed her, and she failed to notice that he had not made the promise to never lie to her again.

For all of Jared's lifetime, and certainly all of Milah's, tribes of barbaric German vagrants called "Huns" had been gradually migrating to Rome, pitching tents here and there, and begging or stealing for survival. The land of the Huns was impoverished, and the people were starving. It was not strange that they should want to live in Rome, the wealthiest and most tolerant nation on earth. The "civilized" people of Rome tossed them a coin now and then, while the lower-class citizens of Rome simply ignored the Huns as if they didn't exist. A few of the benevolent wealthy, including Jared, had invited a clan of them to pitch a circle of tents at a far corner of their property and would send bread and meat daily by one of the home-owner's servants. In return the Huns who lived on their property would become a part of the work force during harvest season, sharing in the work and the feasting when harvest was over. Jared had received reports from his servants over the past two years that the number of Hun tents on his property had multiplied alarmingly. They were becoming too many mouths to feed daily.

Their wedding was arranged by Jared. It was a private affair, attended only by the household servants. Milah wore a lovely white dress that he had purchased for her and she felt like a princess as she said her vows.

A week after their marriage, Jared took Milah on a lengthy all-day carriage ride and picnic to show her his land. He wanted her to see the Huns so that she would be comfortable with the fact that some of them lived nearby. Jared said confidently, "If left alone with a belly full of food, they are as harmless as sleeping wild animals." He carried with them a freshly butchered calf to present to the vagrants.

The Huns' shouts of welcome to Jared and a hearty exchange of slaps on the back were unnerving to Milah. Sitting on a fallen tree near a campfire, she and Jared shared a drink of some foul-tasting beverage offered by the Huns. Milah felt the hair stand up on the back of her neck every time one of them would get behind her. After only a few minutes, she gasped with a sense of choking, and felt faint.

"What is wrong, my dear?" asked Jared in alarm.

Milah could barely whisper, "It must be the bitterness of the beverage, I am not accustomed to its taste."

Jared apologized quickly to the Huns for the briefness of their visit while lifting Milah and placing her in the carriage.

As they raced toward the house, she said, "Slow down, Love. I feel fine now. It was only a temporary spell. Why do you let them poach on your land? Don't you know about the uprisings they have been staging in the past few months?"

"I'm not interested in the character of the other Huns. These are mine. I told you I have tamed them. And it's cheap labor for the harvest," he explained with annoyance at her questioning his decision.

Milah shuttered, "I felt sure that big ugly brute with the scar across his forehead would sneak up behind me and cut my throat before we could leave."

Jared laughed, amused at her fearful imagination.

One year later, on their first anniversary, Jared said, "I have been saving a surprise for you, my Dear. I, also, was born in Greece near the seashore, as the only son of a horse rancher. My mother was a Roman. When I was eight years old and my parents" marriage became too unpleasant for both of them, my mother returned to her family home here, in Rome, with me. She soon was remarried to the man from whom I inherited my Roman vineyard and home. Up until I was 16, I spent six months of every year in Rome with my mother and the other six months in Greece with my father. He taught me the horse ranching business, and I love horseback riding as much as anything I can think of. I am eager to ride with you across my father's horse ranch that will someday be mine. As a gift to you for our anniversary, we are to leave tomorrow to visit my father in Greece for a full month. A carriage will take us to the seashore where we will travel by ferry to the nearest point in Greece. That will put us on my father's land. There a carriage will be waiting to take us to his house. I have already sent word that we are coming."

Milah brushed aside her inclination to point out that Jared had kept this from her for so long and it was akin to deception. She allowed herself to feel excitement as she thought about their trip.

Soon they were on their way and the carriage trip went fast with Jared filling every moment with stories of his experiences on the ranch and his wonderful white stallion. His enthusiasm was contagious and Milah could hardly wait to meet his father. Her heart swelled with expectation as they approached Jared's childhood home.

For two weeks they had a glorious time on the ranch while Milah practiced riding every day. Household servants lived in the main house along with Jared's father. At least a dozen families lived in small houses that his father had built on the property to accommodate his hired help. Jared's father was very congenial, and he explained to her that after his heart attack two years previously, he had placed a foreman in charge of virtually all the operations and decisions. "I had begged Jared to leave Rome and take over the ranch for me, but Jared loved the big city and his vineyard more than the ranch and he refused to relocate. We parted two years ago in anger, and Jared has not come to see me since that day. Even so, the animosity between us was resolved through messengers and now I am just happy to have my boy home for a visit and to meet his charming young wife. If only I had chosen my own mate so well."

At the beginning of the third week of their visit, a rider came to the ranch carrying news from Rome.

"All of the Huns in the city have banded together to kill every Roman they encounter. They go boldly into the homes to loot and to burn what they do not want to steal. They are ransacking everything. The Huns on your property are among these looters," the messenger reported with excitement. "They have killed all of your servants and taken over your house."

"Ungrateful animals!" shouted Jared, then turned to his father. "I am leaving immediately. Milah will stay in Greece with you for her safety. I will ride to the shore and take my horse with me on the ferry in case there is a shortage of mounts in the city."

"No!" protested Milah. Fear gripped at her insides as he mounted his stallion. "I will go, too. Surely I would be safe with you."

"Not so, my wife. I have no idea what I will find or how long I will be gone, only that it will be gruesome, and a woman is better to be left out of it."

Leaning from his horse's back, Jared lifted Milah in one arm to kiss her good-bye. "Promise to wait right here for me," he whispered gruffly. "If it takes a year, or 10, or the rest of my life, I will come back for you." "I promise," she said through her tears.

Jared rode swiftly away without looking back.

News of fighting in Rome was frequently brought to Milah and her father-in-law during that first year. At the end of the second year, they sent a workman to Rome in search of Jared or news of him. The workman never returned.

The fighting was still going on, and Rome would never be the same. Only the working class, the artists and the entertainers were safe from attack. They were considered harmless and powerless as they possessed no land. Other Romans soon became second class, working class, or homeless citizens. Many were imprisoned.

During the third year that Jared was away, his father had a heart attack from which he did not recover. Prior to his death he called Milah, his foreman Gath, and all the household servants to his bedside. "I fear that Jared is dead," he said weakly. So, I am leaving the ranch to his widow. You are my witnesses."

Addressing Milah with great dignity through his pain, he continued, "Promise me that all my workmen and servants and their families who are currently on the ranch will remain in your employ and be permitted to live on the property as long as they desire.

And my wish is that you now invite Gath to move into the main house to provide safety and companionship for you. He is a trustworthy foreman and a confirmed bachelor of 45, with no bad habits to speak of."

A flood of tears filled her throat and belly. "How can God take away my only link to Jared!" her heart shouted. But she held back the tears, touched his cheek tenderly and whispered, "I promise."

Milah did not share her father-in-law's belief that Jared was dead. Obsessed with her feeling that he was still alive, she never left the ranch for a moment, lest he should return and find her gone. She sent a fourth person to Rome in search of news about Jared. When some time had elapsed and none of the four ever returned, she stopped sending inquirers and resigned herself to waiting.

At first there were suitors who had been friends of Jared and were eager to take care of his widow. But eventually they stopped coming to call, accepting the fact that she was committed to waiting at the ranch for Jared even if it took all of her life.

The love of poetry, Christian writings, history, and stories about foreign lands filled her hours with reading in inclimate weather. At night she loved to sing and dance or recite poetry and relive her performances at the Academy. Often, she would cry out, "Jared, my love, are you still on the earth with me? If you should call my name, surely, I would hear. If I knew the name of your God, I would pray to that God to send me news of you."

To ease her pain, she often reminisced about how Jared's personality was such an exciting contrast to the serenity of her own. She created a poem about Jared and set it to music with a simple tune that she could use as a Mantra, to send her love across the water and through the air to find his listening heart.

With Gath's help, she designed and developed a lovely garden that was a sanctuary for birds and small, harmless creatures. On warm beautiful days she would spend virtually all the daylight hours gardening, hiking, swimming, horse-back riding or just sitting in her garden.

Occasionally, she felt a boiling sense of rage rise from the pit of her stomach and her mind played with terrifying thoughts. "If Jared is alive, surely he could have gotten word to me by now. How dare he treat me with such disregard? If he is dead or imprisoned, surely someone would have known about his home in Greece and would have notified me. What if he is still alive and free and living happily without me? What if he has decided that traveling and serving the politicians is more pleasing to him than marriage. Perhaps he hopes that I will think him dead. Oh! Forgive me God for thinking such evil of my husband. What if he is a prisoner, caged in his own house without adequate food or water or facilities for cleanliness?"

Her imagination would build one fearful thought upon another to torture her mind during those times of fear and rage. Nothing would make it stop except to sing her song to Jared, then fall asleep with his name on her lips. Milah knew that her self-pity and sense of powerlessness were based only on the limitations she had placed on herself through holding to her promise, yet she would not release herself from the promise she had made to wait there for Jared. She would rather make this ranch her prison than to freely roam the world without Jared if there was any chance at all that he would return.

Upon receiving her letter that Jared's father had died, her old friend, Aramis had paid her one short visit during that third year after Jared's departure. Before receiving that message, he had not known where she and Jared had gone and had believed her to be dead. She had been so consumed with her own grief that it had not occurred to her that someone might be grieving over her. After comforting her in his arms, Aramis told her, "I saw Jared three years ago, just after the plundering started. I was performing on the stage of the town square when everyone turned to look as he came riding into the square on a magnificent white horse. We were at a distance from one another, and I was not aware of who he was at the time. Soon, I began to lose my audience to a speaker on the opposite side of the square and when I curtailed my music performance to investigate, I was surprised to see Jared making a speech. He was asking for information about the uprising and asking men to band together and wait for him in the square. He said he had business to attend to and that he would return before nightfall to lead them in a battle against the Huns in the city.

I waited with the other men until far into the night. Jared did not return. It was rumored that he was seen riding with a band of men toward the countryside. I did not know what to think. The following day I hired a coach with guards and rode out to the vineyard by day, but when I arrived at the gate of the stone wall, we were warned by the Huns to turn back or be killed. I inquired about you and Jared, but the Huns merely laughed and began to beat on the gates, scaring our horses into a frenzy."

Although the report gripped her heart with fear, she was even more certain that Jared was alive. Somehow, she felt a bit of easement from her grief just to have some news of his activity after he had left her.

Another three years passed, and Aramis made a second visit.

"Things are increasingly worse in Rome, and you are fortunate to be in Greece.

There is still no sign of Jared," he reported, "only rumors."

Before she could inquire about the rumors, a twinkle danced in Aramis' eyes, and he returned to his playful nature, "I was delighted to receive your message with an appeal to visit, even though it is only to comfort you in your grief. I was hoping that you had realized you have always been passionately in love with me," he teased, managing to draw a singular moment of laughter from her.

Further attempts of Aramis' to cheer her up had failed. She clung to her broodings if they were now her only link to Jared and refused to respond to Aramis' efforts.

One year later, Aramis sent word that even artists and entertainers were not safe from the Huns these days. He wanted to come for a lengthy visit. His father had died and his siblings were either dead or scattered. His sister, Alicia, had been raped and killed by the Huns.

"I would rather be with Milah than to hide out of harm's way, if you will permit it," his message said.

Milah had sent him an invitation to come. While waiting for his arrival, she mourned the dear Alicia and planted a lovely tree in honor of her memory.

When Aramis arrived, Milah felt a part of herself awaken, a part that had been dormant for a very long time. It was akin to joy. They were thrilled to be together again, and she wanted to know all about his adventures for the past year. Aramis reported that he had never married. He had become a celebrated actor and musician and was quite popular with the ladies. After he had rested and had a meal, they took a walk and Milah inquired about the vineyard.

Aramis looked uncomfortable, "I am sorry to tell you, my sister in spirit, that the Vineyard is still in the possession of Huns." His eyes shifted to look away from her as he murmured, "I have heard nothing of Jared, even though I have diligently and frequently inquired."

She sensed that he knew something about Jared that he was not telling her, but she was afraid to inquire. A month went by, then two and three. Aramis was enjoying the stability of being in one place and the safety of being out of Rome. He loved riding, and the garden and the vastness of the ranch. He was an expert horseman, and this was the first time he had been on a horse since he and Milah had attended the Academy in Rome.

"Riding here reminds me of our childhood," he said dreamily one evening as he and Milah lay on their backs, gazing up at the stars. "Father owned three fine riding horses, you might recall, and when I was small, he would always take me out riding on the first day after he returned from a business trip. I would sit behind him and hold on tightly to his waist while we rode a lengthy trail down to a winding creek. The creek looked so far down when seen through the eyes of a small boy, and I had felt certain that if I fell, I would surely die. Father would always stop to let the horse drink water from the stream before turning back to climb the trail back to the house. There was a special tree nearby where we would sit and have talks about the responsibilities of manhood, and he would inquire about my activities and interests. Later, after I learned to ride and had a horse of my own, the ritual continued with him riding ahead of me. Even now at 24, I miss the strengthening and predictable quality of my father's love."

"My love for you is strong and predictable too," protested Milah.

"It is a fair replacement," answered Aramis, slipping his arm under her head for a pillow. Aramis' presence at the ranch was good for Milah. He arranged campfire parties at least once a week for all the people on the ranch. They cooked, danced and played musical instruments and sang. Often, he staged a humorous skit to amuse her. Milah joined in the fun, and for a few hours at a time she could forget her sorrow but it was obvious to him that she would never see him as a potential replacement for Jared.

Within the next nine months, Aramis had won the heart of a workman's daughter and they began to discuss marriage. Milah was overjoyed. She hoped that they would live in the big house with her and the servants and Gath, but Aramis missed the stage and Rome. News had been brought to them that things had settled down in Rome, and as long as everyone kept their place, there was relatively little danger.

"We will marry and stay on for another six months," Aramis agreed. "But then we must return to Rome for my work, lest my public forget me entirely and I would have no way to earn a living for my wife. I have no desire to return to my father's house here in Greece, though it is still intact and occupied by two of my brothers. I do love Rome."

That year was a turning point in Milah's life. Before Aramis left, she asked him and Gath to help her build a monument to Jared. With the war finally over, she felt certain he would return if he had survived. The monument was simply a large boulder that she had them smooth down on one side. She had it placed so that she could clearly see the shoreline from a bench that the men placed in front of the boulder. For additional shelter she planted an evergreen tree on each side of the bench.

"This is where I will go to think about Jared. Because he has been gone for eight years now, I refuse to give myself permission to think about him in any other place or time. There are other things and people to think about. I am not so certain anymore that Jared lives, yet, neither am I certain that he is dead. Whichever is true, I have no desire to ever marry again or to venture from this ranch."

Aramis felt relieved that she had repented from her tenacious hold on the belief that Jared was alive.

After she was alone on the ranch again with the workmen and their families, Milah settled into a time of contentment. Routinely, she sat at the monument twice a day until eventually it felt like a cozy, warm, friendly shelter. She came to believe that when she sat in that place, the spirit of Jared came to join her in silent, loving communion, whether from the spirit world or the form world she could not tell.

Aramis had reminded her of how to create happy times, and now every day was filled with delightful pleasures that she orchestrated. Through Aramis' efforts, she had made friends with the workmen's families and all the servants. She now had friends, beauty, wonderful things to do, and luxury. What more could she ever want? She was content to wait for Jared with dignity and peace.

Aramis and his wife seemed happy together. Their lifestyle was one of traveling frequently with a troupe of performers. Aramis' wife worked with stage props and costumes and was thrilled to be a useful part of his life's work. Even so, they paid annual visits to Milah, begging her to visit them at their villa in Rome.

But she would not go. "What if Jared should return and find me gone and no one to welcome him home? I will keep my promise to wait."

With each visit to her ranch, Aramis would report uncomfortably to Milah that he still had heard nothing about Jared. The Huns were still at the Vineyard. "If you come to Rome for a visit with us, you could go there yourself and inquire of Jared."

Her response was always the same, "He is wherever he is, and I am where I said I would be. I know not where to find him, but he knows where to find me."

Milah remained healthy and active for the rest of her life. During her forty-ninth year, while singing his song on the bench in front of Jared's monument, Milah simply stopped breathing and slipped to the ground. When she did not return for dinner, the old foreman went to find her. He had her body wrapped in coarse brown cloths and buried under the bench.

It took two weeks for the news of her death to reach Aramis and his wife in their travels. The message said, "Milah went into her final sleep while singing to Jared. Her body is buried next to the stone that you helped me place near the shore. If you should see Jared, tell him she waited and did not leave the ranch for 32 years. As you know, my nephew has been maintaining the ranch for these past 10 years while I have simply been watching after Milah. I am old, but you can trust my nephew to continue with his duties as long as you want him to do so. Milah has said that you are her twin brother, and her only kinsman. That means the ranch is now rightfully yours. Come soon and give us some direction."

Chapter 8

LEE-SI-YAN

Southeastern China, near the Yangtze River 1136 A.D.

Journal Entry #7

Living a life of long-suffering, self-sacrifice, righteousness toward others and service through one's talents is not all there is to the spiritual life. As I witness these former incarnations it seems that co-dependency and clinging to the past life after life are the bonds that keep me from self-actualization. I see that, as Milah, I still wrestled with rage at the thought of what others should be doing and I was still feeding on self- pity. I also used my imagination to build images of what I did not want, instead of what I did want. The hunger for human love seems to often result in a tendency for me to run away from life. Perhaps in this next incarnation as Lee-Si-Yan I will begin to overcome the fear of being alone and the craving for acceptance and belonging.

The Akashic Records reveal to me an overview of the social conditions of this time and place. They are quite remarkable. Every citizen of the village who can afford the time for schooling is encouraged to pursue a free basic education. The age that one begins formal education is not fixed but can be at any time. The basic education, provided by the government, consists of language usage, simple mathematics, appreciation of the arts, local laws and expectations of the society, the history of China and the study of Confucianism as an idealistic perception of government and human relations.

The poorer class of citizens is not so fortunate. They work day and night, requiring their children to begin earning wages as soon as they are able to learn any sort of labor. The offspring are given no time to indulge in education although it is available to them. The average citizens usually send their children to classes only long enough to learn simple arithmetic, arts, history and social customs and laws. Reading and writing are considered arts in themselves and are not studied by the average citizen because of their complexity. It takes many years to learn the art of writing.

Following a three-to-five-year education the average young man or woman must apprenticeship with a business owner. Their goal is to become employed by that business owner once their apprenticeship is over, or to be placed with the owner of a similar business based on the trainer's recommendation.

Every able-bodied citizen over 15 years of age, regardless of their social or financial standing, is required to be in an apprenticeship, or gainfully employed. Females also have the potential to act as a household member providing direct domestic services to their own household, or to earn wages as a direct domestic servant in another household.

The only exemption to the law pertaining to work is for mentally-impaired persons. They are either provided for by their families or placed in an institution if their families determined that is best for them. In the institutions for the mentally impaired, residents are kept in a sheltered environment with simple routine activities that include a vegetarian diet, sleeping to the sound of stringed musical instruments, acupuncture treatments, herbal treatments, group walking and group exercises similar to tai-chi-only more like dancing face to face in a line with a partner. All these disciplines, done on a daily basis, are thought to be calming and health-producing to both mind and body for the mentally impaired.

The sheltered ones who were capable of concentrating on simple tasks are permitted to work in the vegetable garden, the herb garden, or the decorative landscaped gardens with supervision by an employee of the institution. They are not permitted to have visitors because it is believed this might alter the routine activities and possibly upset the residents. They are, however, permitted to leave with a relative or friend for several days at a time with prearrangement. It is believed that avoidance of unexpected changes is necessary to sustain the inner peace of the residents.

I am Lee-Si Yan. Her family lives in a small village deep in a valley, surrounded by mountains. The climate there is semi-tropical with lush foliage and cool nights. Her affluent parents own a huge, ornate house with several wings under multi-level roofing. It was inherited from my grandparents by her father, who is the oldest son.

This multi-generational household includes Lee-Si Yan's maternal grandparents, many siblings older and younger, three cousins, and two uncles with their wives. Each family lives in a separate wing of the house.

It is a family tradition to provide every child, male and female, with an excellent primary education. At age 13 each child of this family meets with the three brothers who are business partners. They receive a "sales pitch" from each in an effort to persuade the young family member to train in their aspect of the family business. Once the choice is made, that child continues with four years of formal education in skills required for that vocational choice. The four years of formal education are followed by a three-year apprenticeship to the selected business. Upon completion of the apprenticeship, he or she is awarded a partnership in that business with full responsibilities.

Any female of the family who chooses not to go into business automatically becomes a Household Manager or Household assistant, helping to manage household affairs, supervising the kitchen help, gardeners, and housekeepers, and giving direct care and supervision to the children. Males of the family have no such option. They are required to select one of the businesses to enter. I see little of my early childhood as Lee-Si.

She was a slender dark girl with deep, dark eyes that never seemed to focus on anything, nor did they dart around like that of a nervous person might. Instead, they appeared to be downward cast and fixed on something that no one else could see. The girl seemed to be in a mental world of her own, and it was impossible for anyone to hold her interest on a practical topic for very long. She accomplished her basic education with great difficulty because of her inability to concentrate on subjects being presented. Lee-Si's mind drifted regularly to day-dreaming, mentally chanting a song that had no words, meditating on beauty, or fanaticizing about far-away lands instead of applying her attention to practical matters or the environment and people around her.

At the close of her basic education at age 13, her instructors reported, "The girl seems to be in a mental world of her own and it is impossible for anyone to hold her interest on a practical topic for more than a few seconds. We regret to report that she seems to be mentally impaired."

Fear for their daughter grabbed at the hearts of her parents. They implored her uncles to meet with her for assignment of apprenticeship, regardless of what the instructors said. After the interviews and efforts to persuade her to their interests, her uncles threw up their hands in disgust.

"She is not fit for business and cannot listen long enough to answer our simplest questions," they reported to her father. "She might be fit for household service but would never qualify as a Household Manager. We recommend the institute for the mentally- impaired."

Her protective mother was saddened. Convincing herself that the girl was simply slow to mature, she called a meeting of the four Household Managers of their large family dwelling to interview Lee-Si for placement under their supervision. After an hour of efforts to converse with Lee-Si about her placement, they agreed with embarrassment that she was fit only for kitchen service with full supervision.

Lee-Si was content with their decision and showed no resistance or concern, but the kitchen servant under whom she was placed was not so compliant. She complained daily to her own manager that, although Lee-Si could perform a task well, she had to be reminded every moment of the next chore that was hers to do. The girl's parents fretted daily over the embarrassing potential that their daughter might end up in a group home for the mentally impaired.

After two years in the kitchen Lee-Si was still morose with no signs of change in her lack of enthusiasm for life. In fact, she was becoming even more withdrawn.

"No one understands me," she thought and would sink into that thought for hours. On her 15th birthday, after her traditional birthday celebration, her household agreed on a final effort to prevent the inevitable. Lee-Si would meet with the elder eldest brother, whom she enjoyed more than any other person, to discuss her future.

The disinterested girl, still childlike in appearance, arrived on time for their meeting, bowed politely to her uncle, and then sat sipping tea with a far-away look in her eyes.

"What are you thinking about?" her uncle asked in order to get her attention. "I'm not thinking," she said softly, "simply enjoying."

"What are you enjoying?" he pursued.

"I'm enjoying silence," she answered.

Her uncle shook her by the shoulders in frustration, and turned her to face him.

Startled, she looked into his eyes.

"Here is something I want you to think about, then answer me clearly and precisely," he said firmly. "Your time of responsibility to the society has come. Your basic education has long since been accomplished and you must into training for your vocation, what will it be? Will you train for the healing work with me? Will you train for the raising and preparation of herbs with your other uncle? Will you study landscaping with your father? Or will you train to be a Household Manager like your mother and work as a happy household servant? You seem to have no real interest in any of these, but choose you must. Choose now, and let's get on with your training for vocation."

"Oh, I will not do any of those things, Uncle," she replied. "As you have said, I have no real interest in such occupations. I have learned in my classes on other cultures that there is a religion of Yogis who believe that they can, by emptying their minds of thought, become so enraptured with the peace of an empty mind that they swoon with delight and become oblivious to pain, or emotions or desires. That means they never experience illness or anger or disappointment or sorrow. That's what I want to do."

Frustrated, her uncle replied, "Certainly if one has no desires, it would be impossible to experience disappointment, but without desire it would also be impossible to experience fulfillment of desire, now, wouldn't it?"

"I don't know exactly what it is they feel," said Lee-si, "but I want to know. It is the only thing that interests or intrigues me. You ask what I want to become and what kind of training I wish to pursue. I will tell you. I want to become a Yogi. I want to spend my life training under a Yogi Master. Will you ask the family to find one for me and send me to him as soon as he will receive me?"

"First you must convince me that this is a better choice for you than the home for mentally-impaired citizens. You would have the same freedom from responsibility there and a structured life-style of minimal change."

Lee-si took a full minute to think before she decided to share her secret with him: "Uncle, I have never told anyone this before because I thought I could find the answer and eliminate my shame. Since my earliest memory of being, I have felt a great sorrow and anger in my heart, as if I am waiting for something that will not come. I have searched my soul to find the cause, but it will not reveal itself to me. Both the sorrow and the mystery remain. I am weary of seeking its source. I want only to find the source of joy. Perhaps training to be a Yogi is what I have been waiting for. I think it is what I was born for."

Her Uncle was stunned. It was clear to him now that she was not mentally impaired, yet deeply saddened by something no one could name. He had known her since her birth, and he recalled that she was only two-years-old when this silent sadness had come upon her. She would hide in the garden, and it would take the entire household to find her. She was always found sitting on the ground humming a little tune over and over as if it meant something to her. Sometimes there would be tears running down her cheeks, and their conclusion had been that she was afraid of not being found.

As a man of honor, he had no alternative. To respect the trust of his family he must tell them her response, and to honor her request of him he must do the same.

When the family heard of her response, some laughed, some were outraged, but each of them felt it was a ridiculous request. Not one of the elders could think of anything at all unpleasant that had happened to her before the onset of this madness.

But, the more they tried to reason with the situation, the more they arrived at the same conclusion: there were only two possibilities for Lee-si's future. She must either be placed in the home of mentally-impaired citizens or be granted her wish. She would never be good for anything else. Unanimously they voted to grant her wish to avoid the scandal. Each family business owner would be responsible for one-third of the expense. Her father knew many people who traveled frequently and who possessed great knowledge of the world. Surely one of them would be able to help with the placement. He accepted the responsibility of finding a Yogi Master for Lee-Si.

The girl was told nothing. She waited in a sense of shame, feeling she had betrayed herself by revealing the sadness that lived inside her.

After three months' time, when a Yogi Master still had not been found, her father was almost ready to give up and opt for the second possibility when one of his friends introduced him to a traveler from Tibet. His friend had known the man for over 20 years and swore that he was trustworthy. After several conversations Lee-Si's father learned that the man from Tibet had a family and a home, and that he knew many people who believed in the Yoga Philosophy and practiced the disciplines.

"How does one get started in the Yoga training?" he inquired. "Is there a certain school or a certain teacher with whom they must begin? Is certain preparation required before being accepted as a student?"

The Tibetan laughed, "Every Yogi who has passed a certain point in his development is an Adept, and qualified to be a Guru. An Adept can explain the disciplines and guide a novice stage by stage. This is something that could take a lifetime to master; once on the path, a person seldom finds interest in anything else. Do you wish to become a Yogi?"

"And what if I did?" asked Lee-Si's father. "How much would I have to pay a Guru? Where would I live, and how would I eat?"

"If you are sincere," the Tibetan said, "you could travel with me to Tibet. It would cost you nothing except the necessary expenses of travel. Once we were there you could stay in my home free of charge until I find a Guru to accept you. Few Adepts are willing to serve as teachers; those who do are very selective about who might qualify for this gift of their time and attention. A Guru would accept no payment, but he would require you to purchase a tent in which you would live alone near him and close to a stream of water. You would be permitted very little involvement with any other persons. Food would be delivered to you by a traveler, and you would pay for whatever you wish to eat. Your way of life would be solitude and silence. Soon you would be eating very little and never experiencing hunger."

"I have no interest in such a life, but will you take my daughter with you," Lee- Si's father asked. "She wants nothing in the world except to become a Yogi."

"It might take considerably longer to find a Guru who is willing to accept a female disciple," the Tibetan said. "It is a life of frugality and deprivation that few women would choose. Some Yogis who seem to have great knowledge of the Truth about life even discourage women from taking up the path. They claim that a female cannot become a Yogi because of the tendency to be more emotional. They believe that one must wait for a male incarnation if one intends to become a Yogi, but not all of them believe this way."

"I insist that you accept payment for her lodging while she is waiting," said the father. "If she has not been placed within a year, please send me a message, and I will come personally to bring her back home. If you do find a Guru for her, let me know and I will send money that you can use to pay for her food. If she is to do this, I do not want her to be distracted by matters of money."

The two men bowed and nodded in agreement with the proposal. That evening Lee-Si's mother told her of the arrangement while they packed two carpet bags with her belongings. For the first time in Lee-Si's life, her mother saw her excited, and she knew in her heart that this was right for her daughter. Perhaps it really was the life for which she had been born.

While Lee-Si's mother helped with her bath, washing her back and her long black hair, Lee-Si could not stop talking. In her attempt to paint a verbal picture of idealistic serenity and beauty as the Yogi experience, she told what she knew of the disciplines involved. This only served to increase her mother's compassion and concern for her daughter. It would be difficult indeed.

Once Lee-Si was tucked under the covers, her mother began to stroke her hair and to sing to her as she had done when Lee-Si was an infant. As a toddler, before the hiding and sadness had become so severe, Lee-Si enjoyed pretending to prescribe herbal tonics and mix them for her "patients". Her make-believe patients had been anyone who was willing to play the part and drink the water with her make-believe herbs. Her mother had hoped that she would take up the healing profession.

A tear of both regret and relief slipped from her cheek as she bent to kiss her daughter's cheek. "I will not see you again before you leave, my daughter. A carriage will stop for you at dawn."

She would never see Lee-Si again.

The trip took much longer than Lee-Si had expected. Because of Lee-si's disinterest in the environment and its inhabitants, it also seemed quite uneventful. She found the family of the Tibetan man very warm and friendly.

Their house was large with rooms set up for travelers, homeless people and migrants. She saw beautiful orchards of exotic fruits, and they explained to Lee-Si that they made their living from the orchards. They charged the travelers for room and board, but the homeless and migrants were kept free of charge in exchange for help with harvesting the fruits. Their house was full of gold artifacts.

Lee-Si was given a small room with a window through which she could see the sun each morning. It was very pleasant, and nothing at all was required of her. For many days she was free to roam about as she pleased, and no one ever searched for her, even if she missed a meal or stayed out after nightfall.

When she had been there a full week a very thin traveler, with long beard and mustache and hair down to his waist, stopped for the night. He joined the family and guests for dinner and studied Lee-Si closely. Lee-Si was not told anything about him other than that he was a Yogi and his name was Usun.

Usun ate very little; in fact, Lee-si did not see him eat even a bite, yet the food disappeared from his plate.

Hours later one of the children of the house knocked on her door. "The Yogi is requesting your presence in his room right away."

A thrill raced up Lee-Si's back, and she shivered with anticipation. Was Usun to be her Guru? Lee-Si's heart was beating out of control and a rush of joy rippled through her throat like the wings of a butterfly, silent and beautiful. Lee-Si bowed formally as she approached the Yogi. A white turban covered his long hair. He was seated on the floor in a cross-legged position, his back straight and his eyes closed, just as she had seen in the drawings. Without opening his eyes, he made a sweeping motion with his arm as if inviting her to sit. She duplicated his pose to the best of her ability, and he smiled as if he were seeing her awkward efforts.

She closed her eyes and they sat in silence for an hour. Finally, he took a long deep breath and exhaled sharply as if to get her attention. She opened her eyes in surprise.

"Let us walk," he said.

With arms folded he walked slowly looking at the ground. "So, you wish to become a Yogi?"

"Yes," Lee-Si said, "More than I want to breathe."

"And when did this desire come upon you?" the Yogi asked.

"The very first time I saw a drawing of a Yogi I felt that all tranquility of spirit would be mine if I could become like him."

"Is tranquility of spirit your greatest goal?" asked the Yogi. Lee-Si thought for a moment before deciding to share her secret. With embarrassment, she described her secret untouchable sorrow. After a silent pause, she continued, "My knowledge of the world is sufficient for me. I know much about the secrets of nature and its treasures; I know the cause of desires and sorrows in people; wars and sickness have the same cause. Why would I seek more knowledge of such things when my purpose is not of the world? I sense that I have touched the Bliss of which you speak, but certainly not in this life; perhaps it was in a former or only in my imagination. Yet whether it was real or not real before, I know it can be real if I become a Yogi."

"Are you prepared for the sacrifices you would be required to make?"

"The only sacrifice that would give me pain would be to sacrifice my hope of becoming a Yogi."

"Are you prepared to practice the disciplines required for progress?" "A discipline becomes an enjoyment when it is practiced for spiritual enlightenment," answered Lee-Si. "Every discipline will be an enjoyment to me."

"Very well," said the Yogi. "I will be your Guru as long as you hold true to the words you have spoken to me this day. We leave tomorrow for the mountains. Pack lightly. You will require very little."

Her heart rose to merge with her mind in an image of her new life.

After many discussions about attitude and ideals, ethics and morals, her Guru, was gratified to learn that Lee-Si could forego the first-stage development disciplines and go on to the next. She seemed to possess a remarkably harmless character both in idealism and in practice. Reports that he received from her family and her school masters confirmed this for him.

In keeping with his promise to Lee-Si's father, her host purchased a tent for her and arranged for a vendor to deliver food supplies weekly to the girl's tent. This was to continue for the rest of Lee-Si's life or until she left the region.

Within a year she was reciting the Vedic Hymns and practicing the art of permitting all things in the environment to come and go without applying her will to the mundane. The repetition of the hymns reminded her of the melody she had practiced since childhood, and the result of the recitations was the same: moving her mind into a point of non-thought and non-feeling, with a sensation of deep freedom and peace. At other times, her mind produced lovely images of perfection, while it floated on the sound of her chanting.

But these were things she had experienced to some degree since her earliest memory, and Lee-Si began to feel disappointed. "Is this all there is to hope for?" she thought.

But she dared not confess her feeling of disappointment to Usun. She set a new goal for herself: "I will gradually release the expectation of a grand experience. That will eliminate the potential for feeling disappointed."

Within six months she had achieved that goal. She could sit for hours in perfect contentment with no expectation, no goal, no hope, silently being in absolute peace. At the end of her fourth year in the mountains, Usun gave her a gentle nod of approval. "Now you are ready to learn the Postures."

She found the Postures interesting and pleasant, and her mind was stimulated to a bit of curiosity. "Will this produce enlightenment for me?" she thought. But immediately she felt both shame and disappointment in herself. "I must have no expectations," she repeated over and over even as she practiced the body stretching contortions.

After another two years she was taught how to control her breathing while practicing the Postures. At last, she felt she had no goals of her own. The only goals she entertained were those assigned by Usun for learning and practicing new disciplines as they were given. She was content to let Usun tell her what was important and what was not.

By the time one year had passed, Lee-si had developed the habit of controlled breathing through meditation upon the work of raising her Kundalini power. She could suspend her breathing for a full three minutes or more while concentrating upon a selected chakra.

She began to lose her desire for food. Everything tasted exactly the same, and often her food would sit untouched for days at a time. She fed on the vibrating energy that she sensed night and day.

Lee-Si fell naturally into the withdrawal of her mind from all outer sensations and began to develop a total concentration of mind that would prevent her from being aware of anything at all except her own mind focused into itself, unmoving, uncaring and unaware of anything else at all. Even her mental habit of the Vedic Hymns was silenced in this deep place of peace. It was a stillness like none she had ever known before. She likened herself to a butterfly, immersed in its cocoon, alert to the inside of the cocoon but unaware of anything outside the cocoon. It was lovely and she never wanted to come out, yet there was still a sensitivity to the discomforts of the body that prompted elimination and sleep. She wondered if she would ever become as unaware of those desires as she was of the desire for food, and she had to discipline herself to avoid wishing for that as it would signify impatience.

One day Usun announced to her that the final discipline was to be given, ending his commitment to her as a teacher.

"Nine years have gone by," he said, and you are ready for instruction in the final discipline. Once it is given, there is no further relationship between us. Your progress has been rapid, and it pleases me to set you free."

"You are now released from the former assignment, to blank your mind by concentration upon the emptiness therein. From this day forth you must concentrate upon nothing but the essence and meaning of Brahma until you reach Nirvana, the ultimate state of consciousness; conscious oneness with God.

For the next four years Lee-Si spoke to no one. She left her tent only every three days to bathe in a nearby stream, eliminate wastes from her body, and carry drinking water from the small waterfall back to her tent. She was oblivious to the passing of time, seeking the Light that the Guru said she would see and experiencing only emptiness in response to her efforts. She ate less and less and felt pleased when she had lost her desire for water. At first, she forced herself to eat a morsel and take a sip of water several times a day, but eventually she decided not to question her freedom from the desires to eat and drink.

One morning during her meditation upon Brahma, holding her exhalation far longer than the usual three minutes, Lee-Si simply felt no desire to inhale. With the deprivation of oxygen, water and food, her soul found no channel of vital energy in the body to which it could attach. She turned her attention toward the highest point of her meditation and saw a tunnel of Light that she followed with her mind.

Her Guru paid the food vendor to take the uninhabited body away in his wagon saying, "Inform Lee-Si's family that she is longer in the earth and they can stop sending the supplies."

Chapter 9

SHI-GE SHU

Southeastern China near the Yangtze River 1168 A.D. to 1210 A.D.

Journal Entry #8

I must say that the past incarnation certainly explains the great power of concentration with which I was born into my current life. It is obvious that the plate of my subconscious was full of past experiences that required processing; and I was seeking a time out for reflection. It seems that, in seeking a balance between creative living and resting from creativity. I wonder when I will see a conscious realization of the need for balance. This next incarnation is just a short time later in the same village that was my home as Lee-Si-Yan.

The new name is Shi-Ge-Shu. She was Born 1168 A.D. and had no conscious memory of having been born in this same village as Lee-Si just 32 years before.

The villagers enjoy a warm climate with lush vegetation, and She-Ge's parents are hard-working people who own orchards on sprawling miles of land with a variety of different fruits. Twelve boys have already been born to them, the last only a year before, and her parents have been praying for a girl.

"She sets my soul to dancing," said her father upon seeing the beautiful daughter his wife had produced. "We will name her Shi-Ge. It means "poetry set to music".

The role of the older boys was to help their mother and father and a hired work force with the harvesting, sorting, and taking wagon loads of fruit to the market place to sell to the merchants. Materially the family was very comfortable, though not wealthy.

Their large, impressive house was very ornate and made of wood with high ceilings. Its architecture was interesting as well as functional, with a bedroom wing on each side and a central area for welcoming guests. There were four bedrooms to each wing. Toilet rooms were on a small hilltop, one behind each wing of the house. A small four-room cookhouse stood behind the big house with a long, narrow, covered roof connecting the back veranda of the house to the front covered porch of the "cookhouse". There were also several barn-like structures throughout the orchard property and one near the big house.

On one side of the cookhouse porch was a well from which all the family's water came. Two buckets hung from the side of the well so that two people might draw water at the same time.

As a young child, one of Shi-Ge's favorite activities was to visit the cookhouse.

The cook was a small, cheerful, energetic man who made his home in the cookhouse, and she loved nothing better than watching him at work. She knew him only as "Cook".

Shi-Ge found comfort in the small rooms of the cookhouse. Other than Cook's personal room there were three others. One room was a pantry with storage for utensils and goods related to cooking or bathing. Another was the cooking room, for preparation of meals. The third was a bathing room, with two large wooden vats large enough for three or four people each.

An entire wall of the cooking room was lined with shelving and set up for drying herbs and the preparation of teas. Cook enjoyed the child for her quiet serenity, and often he would go to the big house to fetch her for companionship. As she sat on a tabletop watching him at work, he would share ancient teachings of the ancestors about the health- promoting benefits of various teas and herbs. Through this influence, she became fascinated with the history of her people and began to want, more than anything else, to learn to read.

Although it was not the same in every part of China, this land area was home to a prosperous, benevolent, and peaceful society. People were free, with very little in the way of taxation or government control. Taxes were used for funding free education for any child who had an aptitude for learning and whose family was willing to consent.

Taxes were also used for free health care for all who chose to use it, payment of salaries to members of the military forces who guarded their borders, moderate salaries for their political leaders, and housing and food for orphans and homeless people who were unable to work due to physical or mental handicaps. No proof of citizenship was required for any of these government programs. The only taxation was of property owners, who were taxed by the amount of acreage they owned. If they could not pay their taxes, they merely forfeited the portion of land upon which they could not pay taxes and it was sold to someone who could use it to produce an income.

The religion practiced by all was what we might now call "Neo-Confucianism". It was not thought of as a religion but as a way of life for the people, and it emphasized the ideal of the Chinese people as "all one family". Neo-Confucianism was supported by leaders of the society and was founded in the ideals of self-discipline, ethics, and harmless action as "right human behavior". It emphasized service as a requirement for all inhabitants, from children in service to their parents, women in service to their families or their community, and men in service to their community and their families.

Cooperative contribution toward services was perceived to be the path to economic prosperity for individuals, families, and the nation; and it was revered as the whole purpose for human living.

A dual achievement of education and piety were viewed as the fulfillment of balanced perfection for an individual, whether the education be formal or informal. In this culture free choice was greatly lauded as the birthright of every inhabitant, along with rightful consequence for one's choices.

Shi-Ge had been a quiet infant and toddler, prone to obedience and a need for suggestion of what to do. It seemed as if she couldn't think for herself. At first, she showed very little curiosity or interest in things around her other than her visits to the cookhouse, but when she was eight years old, she suddenly began to beg for liberty to go to reading classes.

"You are the only girl," her mother said in protest. "Who would manage the household if I should die? My desire is that you train to be a Household Manager. Why else would I have permitted you to spend so much time in the cookhouse? Has Cook not whetted your appetite for domestic management? What use would you have for reading? I must discuss this with your father."

Upon hearing of her desire, Shi-Ge's father felt torn between the two. "Few people in our society know how to read. It would be a valuable thing. But of course, she could live the life that we have planned for her without it. No one else in our family has ever needed to learn reading. To work with numbers is all that is required. All the boys, from the oldest to the youngest, have been content- -if not overjoyed--to support our work in the orchards. They have shown no interest in education beyond the basics, and that which apprenticeship with their father and his foremen can provide for them. They dream of having their own homes one day in one of the orchard fields, and of being the foreman of that field in service to their father and his legacy to them. And I dream of the same, to help relieve me of the taxes. I will talk to the girl."

Shi-Ge could not be dissuaded. "Do you not believe in free choice, my Father? It seems that my mind is a vast empty vessel; but it delights me when Cook tells me about the history of our family and our village. I know about the piety of our way of life, but I feel incomplete. There is so much that I do not know, and my mind is craving knowledge."

Her parents discussed their reluctance far into the night. She had not yet completed her basic education and these additional lessons would mean staying at the school for three months at a time, then home for a month and back again. It would take at least five years for even a bright student to become a skilled reader. Her parents were proud of her social politeness and excellent conduct, and she was the joy of their lives. Yet their belief in the wisdom of Confucius would not permit them to refuse her.

Within a week, lest they weaken and try to interfere with her desire, Shi-Ge's parents hired a driver to take them and their daughter to the school for a preliminary visit. Secretly they wished that her quiet nature would render fear of the strange setting and change her mind, but the opposite effect occurred. Her pre-entry testing showed a keen aptitude for learning and a talent for interpretation of meanings when she was exposed to readings from one of the Chinese Classics. A sense of de-ja-vu swelled so strongly in Shi-Ge as to render her dizzy at the thought of developing her mind. Her parents applied for residency and it was granted to their only daughter before they left for home. She was to begin classes the following month, as soon as a room-mate could be found for her.

During the four years of her training in reading and the classic literature of China, Shi-Ge became fascinated with both the history of Confucianism and of China. While the poetry and myths were lovely to think about, she was more compelled by the philosophy of life and the controversy of beliefs, not only among religions but also within the same religion. She found it fascinating to learn that Confucianism had been established as a protest against the worship of mythical gods. Its emphasis was on the importance of people honoring people and simply obeying the behaviors of respect and service toward one another. Confucianism had later been blended with the religion of Taoism, because the mystical elements were missing from it and it had not been fulfilling to those seeking answers to their spiritual quest.

Even now, in the modern times of the year 1181, there was still a protest between two schools of thought in her society.

One popular theory was that, in order to become a "Sage"--the agreed upon "goal" of spirituality--one must admit that the mind is crude and should be arrested from all thinking. One should live as a responsive being rather than a creative being. This theory suggested that only two things are needed for purification from all thinking. One was to accept everything without protest or resistance. The other was to practice cooperative responses to others, performing any kind of service that was asked. That theory stated, "To be in harmony with life is the purpose for our existence. Life is a thing in itself, and in order to live in harmony with it we need only permit it to have its way with us and with others. Acceptance is the key to spiritual fulfillment and the key to becoming a Sage. A Sage knows that the laws of the universe produce every appearance and every experience. The mind is nothing and when it stops wrestling with trying to understand the law and life rather than just cooperate with its products, that mind will find its permanent peace and know itself as a Sage."

Just hearing this theory made Shi-Ge feel an uneasiness that started at the pit of her stomach and felt very much like a nausea brought on by knawing hunger. "Somehow, I feel that I have already learned this is not the way," she thought.

The other theory she was introduced to stated that mind is all there is: "The Deity is Mind with its power of Intelligence". The Creator of the Universe consciously used imagination and will, which are powers in the mind. We should do the same. Everything that is aware of its own existence is conscious. Consciousness is in mind and is to be used for applying the knowledge that is in one's mind."

This theory proposed that universal laws and all other laws are in the mind and that, because of the mind acting on the laws when it moves thought, "knowledge" is formed in the mind. To develop intuitive knowledge or "inner knowing" through meditative contemplation was lauded as the goal of human life. This theory stated that wisdom is merely the application of that intuitive knowledge to one's everyday life in a creative and harmless manner.

This ideal was very appealing to Shi-Ge and she decided to accept it as the working model of her belief, until she proved its validity or encountered a more reasonable one.

After her fourth year of classes at the school, having learned all that she could in that setting, Shi-Ge appealed to her parents to set her free from both the family legacy and their expectation that she would marry and produce a family. She begged permission to enter a university for studies in the branch of the Confucian School for Study of the Mind.

Although her parents were saddened at the prospect of not having her as a frequent associate, they were also proud of her decisiveness and her intelligence. But it was her youngest brother who showed the most resistance. His goal was to become a Sage through mindlessness, and he was offended by her acceptance of the opposite viewpoint. When he protested loudly and demanded to know what was driving her to this lifetime devoted to study instead of the role that her heritage had provided for her, she said, "My brother, it is because mind **is** all there is. My goal is to know the mind of the Creator and not be told of it by someone else. Before I can know the mind of the Creator, I must develop the mind that I know--my own mind. Then I will find the mind of the Creator beyond my own."

"How can you know that mind is all there is?" he demanded.

"Consciousness is in my mind and if I have no mind, I have no consciousness. If I have no consciousness, then it matters not whether I pursue that which intrigues me or whether I release my efforts. I know that mind is all there is because I have a mind, I am a mind." she answered calmly.

"I know the opposite," he said. "I know that mind is a trickster and the cause of sorrow. To perceive that life is as it is and to forfeit all knowledge is to render oneself to the flow of becoming a Sage, which is the goal of life."

"Without mind, how can you know that?" asked Shi-Ge. "And if you forfeit all knowledge, would you not also forfeit knowledge of Being; and if you forfeit knowledge of Being, then how is Being different from Non-Being?"

Throwing up his hands in surrender to her stubborn insistence, her brother voted yes to her path of education, making it unanimous among all the family members.

In order to formally forfeit the traditional role of domestic life as a help-mate to a husband and bearer of children or as a companion to her mother in her father's household, Shi-Ge was required to offer her devotion to the university itself as her "mate" and to serve that institution with whatever knowledge, talents or skills she possessed in order to assure its maintenance and success. The ideal was to "serve" that which is serving you. Men who elected the path of study and chose to make the university their home instead of establishing a family household of their own were under the same obligation. Males and females of the university campus mingled for classes, meals and work activities. There was no lack of companionship for exciting conversation, sharing of studies or walking together on the grounds. They never left the university for any purpose except an occasional visit to their parental homes, and with this arrangement they were utterly content.

Shi-Ge opted to work as a practitioner in the health clinic of the university and also in the kitchen. For both areas she used her knowledge of herbs and teas, for healing effects in one case and for health and nutrition effects in the other. In addition to the elementary knowledge that her childhood friend, the family cook, had given her, Shi-Ge mentally devoured everything she could find to read about the ancient art of health maintenance through the use of herbs and teas. She could not know that the talent and enjoyment of this art had arisen from her subconscious memory of many lifetimes ago in Atlantis, prior to her first enlightenment stage, when she had been a practitioner using herbs and teas for healing and exotic applications. Nor could she know that her interest in it had been recovered in nearly every one of her incarnations since then.

Shi-Ge's activities of life were quite uneventful, structured and regulated. Her daily routine was fixed. It was only her mind that stretched and searched and grew and changed, delighting in research and new discoveries while applying its reasoning power and contemplative meditations to questions that led to one stimulating discovery after another. And, again, she did not consciously recall that in a previous life, studying under a great mind by the name of Plato, she had enjoyed this grand adventure of developing her mind; she only knew that life was meant for more than just watching the days and the seasons go by with no purpose beyond socialization, service to others, physical comforts and work. The instinctive life of living for survival, companionship and comfort was the way of the animals, and she knew that her intelligence was for something more. She decided that her next lifetime would be the time to apply more perfectly all that she was learning in this one, but for now she was content to learn for the joy of learning. A frequent thought of hers was, "Pursuing all that I wish to learn about is my purpose in life and I gladly perform the healing services that I am expected to give in return."

Soon Shi-Ge began to feel a greater attachment to her friends, instructors and associates at the university than to her birth family, and they became the family of her heart and mind. Even so, she continued to make annual visits to the orchards to honor her parents and brothers for their contribution to her freedom, her freedom to be Shi-Ge and to live in service to her own purpose.

When Shi-Ge was 42 years old, only a few of her brothers still lived and her parents had long since passed. On a beautiful day during one of her rare visits to the family home, Shi-Ge fell and struck her head on a rock while chasing a butterfly. As she was falling into a semi-consciousness state, she contemplated the cause of her fall, "With my mind fully on the butterfly, I did not have presence of mind to consider the potential of a stone in my path. I must remember that in my next life."

Her youngest brother found her nearly lifeless. He sat on the ground and held her head on his lap. "How can all your learning help you now?" he sobbed.

She answered dreamily, taunting her brother, "My mind is not lost, only my body.

But for what reason does the Mindless Sage cry? Does he not know that the law responded to my carelessness and produced my death? Does his mind dare to desire other than what is?"

Her brother laughed through his tears. "Obviously, I am not yet a Sage," he said, "But you have reached your goal. You have developed your mind. Surely it is the law that drew you to the Path of Knowledge."

Raising her hand to wipe away his tears, Shi-Ge whispered, "There is hope for you yet, my brother."

She died with a smile on her face.

Chapter 10

NISHA

India and Tibet 1490 A.D. to 1570 A.D.

Nisha was born of an unwed mother in 1490 A.D. and abandoned in a Yogi camp in the Himalayan Mountain region near Western Tibet. Her Hindu mother returned to Southern India alone.

The girl had no concept of parents, or family and therefore, she did not miss them. Although she did see travelers now and then, the only people she actually knew were the Yogi men of her small camp who took turns feeding her daily and keeping her clean.

They taught her to abide in silence as much as possible, to respect nature and to obey her elders without question. Before she could sit alone, the men who had accepted this awesome responsibility of raising an abandoned child held her on their laps for hours at a time. With folded legs, they would hold her nestled in front of their solar plexus in the circle of their arms, fold her legs in a meditative pose, and ignore any sounds that she made. In this way she learned to meditate upon the third eye, which seemed very natural to her, and to wait for the Light of Nirvana. "When you are ready," she was told by her hermit friends, "you will be taught the breathing techniques, the poses and the philosophy of Yoga as it is practiced in this place."

She had no female role models at all, nor were there other children. It was easy for Nisha to attain an altered state of consciousness when she sat in meditation, and the Yogis said that she would surely reach Nirvana before them.

But as the years progressed with this limited activity, Nisha became restless. She had accepted and learned and practiced her lessons well, but the desire to see what kind of lives other people lived was like a fire in her solar plexus day and night. It felt like loneliness, like hunger, like anger, like grief. She felt desperate to escape this life of emptiness, where there was hope only for an increase of the emptiness if Nirvana ever came. She did not desire Nirvana. She desired all the things the Yogis prided themselves in no longer desiring. But more than the taste of sense desires and fulfillment, Nisha wanted to satisfy her mind's burning desire for knowledge. She was full of questions that no one was willing to hear, and she felt that she had some kind of secret knowledge for which she had no outlet here.

Justifying her emotions, she would say to herself, "Perhaps after I have filled myself with some of those experiences I, too, will want to return to non-desire, but for now, my desire is the only beauty and the only pain that I know. I love it for the sense of beauty and hope that it awakens in me and, for me, the knowledge of that beauty is worth the pain of waiting."

Her Yogi family did not count years and time, so she was not aware of her age when the Sikhs came to their camp. When she was not yet a woman, she suddenly came into the monthly habit of women; a habit that one of her benefactors explained to her as a karmic punishment for reincarnating in female form. By the time the habit had repeated itself monthly for at least two dozen times, and she was quite accustomed to it. She knew how to keep herself comfortable and clean during that time, and it was not as bothersome as it had seemed at first. Her breasts had blossomed into small, lovely mounds, and she enjoyed secretly observing her nude form in the lake when she went to bathe.

She found herself watching the men when she was supposed to be in meditation and feeling her body spring to life with desire as she fixed her gaze upon one or the other. It seemed that it was not the man who stimulated her desire but the act of her concentration upon the man. She also discovered that if she held her passionate gaze upon a man for a very long period of time, eventually the man would feel her gaze and open his eyes to meet hers with a chastising look. Then she would close her eyes quickly and feel embarrassed at having been caught desiring something.

She was not sure of what it was she was desiring. It seemed that just to be close enough to touch a man would somehow meet her need, and she had developed a habit of fantasizing. In her fantasy a young, handsome man would return her passionate gaze.

They would be drawn together through their gaze until their bodies touched. He would wrap her in his arms the way the Yogis had done when she was an infant, only this time it would be face to face.

"What an incredibly wonderful experience that would be," she thought. "Then perhaps we might even speak of matters that do not pertain to sacrifice, but to indulgence. Perhaps we would practice indulgences together and tell each other of our pleasure in the fulfillment of desires."

While this kind of thinking seemed harmless to Nisha, she knew it to be the cause of her restlessness. But the fantasy was lovelier to her than the thought of Nirvana so she indulged herself. "After all," she thought with a silent giggle, "what effect could it have other than to postpone Nirvana, and I want to postpone that as long as I can."

One day when the sun was high, three men arrived at their camp. They wore animal skins and looked very tired and thirsty as they approached. Nisha greeted them with a wordless nod, then escorted them to the lake and watched from behind a tree as they drank of the water. Spellbound, she observed them as they stripped naked and dived into the lake with shouts of joy and laughter. Nisha had never heard laughter before, nor had she seen any display of emotion. The only thing she knew of emotion was that which was inside herself.

Their laughter intoxicated her mind, and she found herself gazing at the youngest of the three. He was like the man in her fantasy. Ashamed of her thoughts, she ran back to the camp and started a fire to warm her trembling body. Two of the Yogis joined her for a drink of hot tea made from herbs found on the hillsides. They had not noticed the strangers before and were startled when the three approached their campfire.

Nisha spoke quickly, lest they be turned away, "These are friendly visitors who wish to sleep in our camp tonight. They have refreshed themselves in the lake and are now ready to tell us about their travels and why they have come."

Turning to the strangers hopefully, she begged, "Please tell us who you are. Are you seeking a camp to join?"

The oldest of the three men spoke, "I am Nanak. We have traveled long and far.

Our homes are in various parts of India. These two are my traveling companions and disciples. They are Hassum and Mandana."

Nanak was taller than most other men, with velvety light brown skin, a long, handsome beard and a massive build. Mandana carried a small drum slung over one shoulder with a strap of animal skin. He was smaller than Nanak and with a heavier physique than the typical East Indian travelers that Nisha had met. His body and Nanak's looked like that of meat-eaters rather than the slender form of vegetarians.

Mandana had the gentlest eyes that Nisha had ever seen and a soft, deep voice.

Hassum was an energetic young man, an inch or two shorter than Mandana with the typical form of an East Indian. Nisha thought he was quite handsome with an enthusiastic personality. He moved like a rippling breeze as he walked, and his eyes sparkled with excitement. He had volumes of black hair on his head and face, and Nisha hungered to be near him. He sat across from Nisha with the fire between them, and she could feel his energy pressing upon her skin as if he were touching her. It almost took her breath away. To distract herself, she made tea for them while Nanak explained why they were traveling in this area.

"We are Sikhs. I am walking through many lands to spread a new idea that will liberate men from the bondage to religion while enriching their Spiritual experience in life. As I walk to serve my mission, Hassum drives the wagon with our supplies. We usually sleep under the wagon, but since we have been obligated to climb in order to find you, we had no recourse but to leave our wagon unattended in the foothills at the end of yonder trail. Mandana travels with us to show the rhythm of our chants."

Nodding, the men encouraged Nanak to continue.

"There is too much confusion and discord caused by the large number of religions that try to exist together. And now in the Hindu religion, we are seeing more and more divisions of thought that weaken rather than strengthen the truth. There is only one God, and God loves all the same whether Muslim, Buddhist, Hindu, or Yogi. I have been assigned by God to deliver this key of liberation to all Hindus, Yogis, Buddhists and Muslims. The message is the same for everyone. Ignorance, not desire, is the cause of bondage. To gain knowledge is the goal of life, for with the gaining of true knowledge, all false beliefs are washed away. Then the only desire we have when we are filled with true knowledge is the desire to serve God and do whatever God wills us to do."

As Nanak spoke, the other Yogis of the camp left their meditations and gathered around the campfire. They argued with Nanak. Their collective argument can be summarized most precisely in this phrase: "It is knowledge that stirs up the soul and tempts it to desire. Therefore, knowledge is that which the Yogi must find relief from, not that which he must pursue. Liberation is freedom from karma, which produces freedom from transmigration, which produces freedom from form, which produces freedom from awareness of form, which eventually produces freedom from awareness of anything except blissful existence. That is Nirvana: absorption back into the Sea from which we came. There is no God who is conscious of us; there is only Existence, only Being. Everything else is but Illusion. Liberation from desire produces freedom from karma, and by fixing our minds at a single point of stillness we find the mind does not move; therefore, it does not think; therefore, it does not desire. To gain knowledge is to produce thought; to produce thought is to produce desire."

Standing all at once they bowed politely to Nanak: "We reject your offer of the key to liberation. You have our pity for your ignorance. Stay the night in our camp if you must, but leave by mid-day tomorrow and consult with us no more. Goodnight."

Each of the men retreated in silence to his own cave or tent, but Nisha did not.

She stayed by the fire, whispering questions to Nanak. She felt her heart would leap out of her breast with joy at the things he had said.

"What is life in India? How do the people act? What kind of things do they believe? Do they act on their desires? Do they sit and talk together? Do they laugh and speak aloud? The Yogis say that my mother was a Hindu from India and that she stayed with them only long enough to give birth to me. Do you think I could find her if I were to go to India?"

Nanak laughed gently, "India is a very large place, dear girl. Unless you knew the village and the name of your mother's family, you could not find her except by accident. People in India have a number of different beliefs about life. Some are Hindus, but there are several different sects of Hindus. Some are Yogis with a different way of living and believing. It is similar to yours, yet they do not promote departing from all society. Some are Buddhist with similar beliefs to those of your camp, yet different in other important ways. Some are Muslims with a vastly different way of believing. All of them follow their greatest desires; even those of your camp who pretend they have no desires are following their desires to seek Nirvana by withdrawing from all other desires but the one. No one forces them to do it. They do it because they passionately desire to do it. The Muslims are taking advantage of the Buddhists, Hindus and Yogis by playing on their belief in acceptance without thought. They have overrun many of the cities and much of the land, stealing material goods from others. So, yes, girl, they all do follow their desires. Some desires are pure and harmless to others. Other desires are destructive and against the will of God. We advocate serving desires that are harmless to others and to ourselves while doing something that is useful in the society."

Nisha spoke timidly, almost embarrassed to ask, but she had to know, "I know of a secret place where I can go and talk to the Light inside my mind. The Light tells me about a God who desires my company. Is this the God of whom you speak?"

A surprised look came into Nanak's eyes. "Yes, yes," he said with excitement. "The Light you speak of is what I have named the **Guru.** It is the medium between your mind and the Mind of God. There is only one God. God is the giver of the Guru inside you, but there are many beliefs about God. Some are true; some are partly true; and some are vastly untrue; but they have all been conceived as a result of people seeking to understand, to know, to communicate with and receive pleasure from God. Our true purpose in life is to give pleasure to God."

"How can we give pleasure to God?" asked Nisha.

"By being like God and being unlike the animals and birds who know no God," said Nanak.

"Will you teach me a chant?" begged Nisha.

"I dare not," said Nanak. "Your friends trust me not to disturb them again, and they have been kind to me. When I deliver a chant and my drummer keeps the rhythm, God and everyone within a mile will hear the vibrations of my voice. My work for God and my service to the society is to inform all individuals who will listen about the importance of practicing their own spiritual knowledge in the world and to let others do the same. I wish people to know that there is only one God who loves every person the same and has no favorites. Now I have told you. Ask your inner Guru, and it will bring down a chant into your mind sent directly from God."

Holding her face in his hands, Nanak lifted Nisha's chin to look into her eyes; then he kissed her in the middle of her forehead.

Nisha almost swooned with the sweetness of it. She had never been kissed before, and the pleasure of it was as mysterious as it was delightful. Now she wished that Hassum would kiss her, and she was determined to learn more about Nanak's philosophy of life.

After the three men had found a comfortable spot near the fire and fallen asleep, Nisha lay near Hassum. Her face was so close to his that she could feel the warmth of his breath. She felt pleasantly dizzy and reached out to bury her hand in his thick hair.

Immediately he sat up, ready to fight a wild animal. When he saw it was Nisha, he laughed, covering his mouth to prevent making a sound. She laughed silently with him; and taking his hand, she placed it on her breast so that he could feel how fast her heart was beating. He placed her hand on his racing heart as well. They both got the message of passion, and together they walked to the edge of the lake where Nisha learned what the fulfillment of this desire was all about.

After they had made love and were falling asleep wrapped in an embrace, Nisha asked lazily, "Exactly where is this wagon that Nanak said you drive?"

In great detail Hassum told her which trail would lead to it and that it was just three hours away.

After Hassum fell asleep, Nisha lit a torch at the campfire and silently made her way down the trail to Nanak's wagon. She found it exactly as Hassum had described. Hiding inside the wagon under coarse fabrics that she found, the exhausted but happy girl fell asleep dreaming about wagons and escape.

Hours later she awoke when the wagon ran roughly over a rock. She was in motion, and her plan was working. She smiled and slept again.

Late in the afternoon, when the wagon stopped and the men were preparing to eat, Nisha stepped onto the ground. A stern look of disapproval shadowed Nanak's face, but he spoke gently to her. "Explain yourself, Girl. Why have you deceived us into taking you into our travels?"

"I had no escape from the emptiness of living for the purpose of destroying my knowledge. Yet I do have knowledge that the inner Guru has given me. I have knowledge that is not of memory but of knowing. God sent you to convert me. You said so yourself. Now I am converted and no longer a Yogi. Therefore, I cannot stay with the Yogis. I must stay with the Sikhs."

Hassum applauded. The drummer started a rhythm. The three men began to chant, and Nisha could feel the vibrations of their voices from the top of her head to the bottom of her feet. At last, she felt alive!

The little band of Sikhs traveled from point to point searching out the Yogi hermits to deliver their message. A few accepted Nanak's ideas and began to travel with him, or, return to their native lands to practice and teach the philosophy of the Sikhs as they understood it. Nanak accepted every convert as a gift from God and as God's confirmation that his work was assigned by God. He celebrated the wisdom of each new Sikh member.

As they traveled, Nanak often would sit near Nisha in the wagon while followers tried to keep up by foot. He told her that there were already many small study groups who met with their members regularly to sing the chants and discuss their worldly situations and possible uses of their new ideas in their individual lives. This pleased him greatly. Nisha loved Nanak with an admiration and respect that she had never felt for another person.

Nanak took time to answer her questions, and occasionally they touched on personal conversation to a degree. At times when Nanak walked, the drummer would take his place beside her, teaching her the chants and entering into interesting conversations with her about his native land and the family he had left behind. Nisha continued her exciting physical involvement with Hassum, but she felt a greater emotional affinity for Nanak and Mandana because of her passion for spiritual talk. At night she found herself thinking that if Nanak were younger, she might easily fall in love with him, but he was at least three times her age. Nanak had guessed her to be 16 or 17 years old. As for Mandana she loved him like a caring friend with whom she could share laughter and her deepest secrets. He was her confidante while Nanak was her charismatic, grandfatherly teacher, and advisor. Hassum was her exciting lover who shared her understanding of Nanak's teachings, but did not seem to be in touch with his inner guru. With the three of them she felt she had all the love she would ever need.

One evening, sitting under the stars with Nanak after all the others had gone to sleep, Nisha confessed her fantasy to him." "I think I could be in love with you if you were not so old and so insistent that God is all you want and all you need."

Looking at the sky as was his habit when speaking to another person, suggesting that eye contact was too intimate a thing for anyone to expect from him, Nanak responded, "Yes, I was perhaps

35 years old when you were but an infant. I have a wife who was chosen for me by my family, and we have brought two children into this world. I was not born to enjoy the entrapments or charms of family life. They hold no interest for me. I was born to bring a new message into the lives of my people, to offer them freedom from fear of karma and freedom from an existence with no purpose. I would not make an attentive mate to any woman, no matter what my age. My soul is the bride of the Guru within, and how can the bride ever be the groom?"

Nisha was fascinated with his words. "Explain to me this idea of a man being a bride to the Guru."

"The Guru is that part of my being that knows God as intimately as I know the Guru. The Guru is mated to God as I am mated to the Guru. The Guru approaches God and opens itself to receive the seed of knowledge from God. I approach the Guru and open my mind to receive the seed of knowledge from him," explained Nanak.

"I do not understand," said Nisha. "Is the Guru male or female?"

"The Guru is female in relation to God and male in relation to me. I am female in relation to the Guru and male in relation to you," said Nanak.

Nisha tugged at his beard and turned his head until his eyes met hers. "Such strange pictures you make with your words," she said. "But as you speak, I feel the Truth in you for I, too, have a loved one inside; it is the Light, and the Light reveals his knowledge of God to me. Yet while I love the Light, I can also love a man. Perhaps in our next incarnation you will be born of my generation and we can be lovers then."

Nanak stood and helped her to her feet, then bowed to say goodnight. "If you are a woman who needs a man, then I am sure that will not be the case. But if you are a woman who wants a man yet needs no one other than God, then perhaps your fire will be met by mine someday in a future life."

Nisha slept better that night than she had in weeks.

After six months more of serving as a missionary in the Himalayan regions, Nanak and his friends traveled to Tibet and began discussing their plans to return to India. A thrill of mystery and anticipation raced through Nisha's body, and she shivered with delight. Perhaps she might by some miracle find her mother there. But in the next instant her stomach began to churn as if she had swallowed a dreadful poison. After the wave of sickness had passed and she was resting in the wagon, Nanak came to sit beside her.

He looked toward the sky.

"When did you last experience the condition that only women must endure?" he asked with deepest respect.

"It has been at least three months," said Nisha happily. "I am hoping the cessation is permanent. It is a disturbance to me every time."

"You have grown a bit bigger around your middle. Do your breasts feel tender and uncomfortable at times?" inquired Nanak.

"My breasts are tender as they were when they first began to sprout, but now they seem more firm than soft. They seem to be growing again," said Nisha." How big do you think they will get?"

Nanak could not contain his amusement at her ignorance. He laughed as if he would never stop. His laughter was so contagious that eventually all four of them were whooping and holding their bellies with the ache of their merriment.

Finally, Nisha and the two younger men were able to restrain their giggles long enough to ask, "What is so humorous as to have set such wild laughter upon us?"

Nanak frowned soberly. "Nisha is with child," he said. "It is funny only that she has no knowledge of such things that every woman learns from her own society. But it is not funny because now we must either return her to her Yogi camp or marry her to Hassum.

Hassum rushed to Nisha's side. "She carries my child," he said. "She will marry me."

"I will not travel with a child," said Nanak. "You will need to provide her with a home in India if you marry her."

"That I will do," announced Hassum, putting his arm around Nisha's waist possessively.

Turning to her he whispered with love in his voice, "And you, Nisha, what do you say. Will we marry, or will you return to the yogi's camp?"

Nisha's mind was made up in less than a minute. She was determined not to repeat her mother's act of being an unwed mother and abandoning her child to be raised by Yogis. She loved Hassum well enough and felt safe with him, and she enjoyed him as a lover. She also knew that if she gave birth to a child at the Yogi camp, she would not be able to discipline herself to stay; she would run away and leave the child just as her mother had done. Another important consideration was Nanak's belief that once a Soul from the Spirit Worlds had selected parents; those lovers were obligated to prepare a home for the comfort, nurturing, and teaching of the child. He had withdrawn from his own children, but not before he had made them such a home and they were well on their way to adulthood. Their mother had wished to teach them the Hindu philosophy, and he had wished to teach them his. To avoid confusing the children he had chosen his time to depart. He felt that the children and his wife were more at peace than if he had stayed.

Nisha wanted Nanak's approval and respect, and although she would have preferred to continue as a part of the work he was doing, she knew her only acceptable choice was to marry Hassum and become a mother and wife.

"Yes," she whispered to him with an affectionate embrace. "We will let Nanak marry us tomorrow."

Hassum and Nisha departed from Nanak and went to the home of Hassum's parents, where they stayed while a wing was being added to the house for them. He resumed his former profession of being a blacksmith in his father's shop.

Nisha loved Hassum's mother and, from her, Nisha learned not only about the Hindu religion but also about the Hindu culture and family life. Though she was not persuaded to forsake her love for the

Sikh philosophy, Nisha saw the beauty and goodness in Hinduism as well.

Soon after Hassum and Nisha took up residency in their new home, Ana was born to them. Hassum's mother and Nisha spent their days together talking, sharing domestic chores and caring for the child. Nisha paid little attention to Hassum, and soon the passion he had once held for Nisha had transformed into an almost paternal sense of protectiveness, playful affection and a deep respect for her as the mother of his child.

Without the power of that strong attraction to Nisha, Hassum became restless. Ordinary life was not fulfilling to him. Nisha saw his eyes shine with excitement only when they spoke of Nanak, speculating about where the teacher might be in his travels.

Three years passed. Then one day, without advance notice, Nanak and Mandana appeared at their door. Nisha squealed with delight.

"Hassum, come quickly," she shouted. "Our dearest friend is at the door."

The reunion was so charged with love and appreciation among the four of them that they sat up far into the night singing chants and talking. Caught up in their excitement, three-year-old Ana danced and whirled in rhythm with their chanting until she fell exhausted at Nisha's feet and slept the night on the floor.

Nanak and Mandana stayed a week. Even before he asked her blessings, Nisha knew that Hassum would go with them. And how could she blame him? If not for the responsibility of teaching her child, she would have followed them, too.

Before the three men left, Nanak sat by her side and looked toward the ceiling.

She knew he was about to say something personal and important to her.

"You are an exceptional woman to permit your husband's leave with heartfelt blessings. Now I will ask you to do something for me," he said.

"What is it, sir? I will do whatever you ask, for you are the one who brought me into joy when I was in despair and knew no purpose for my being."

Turning to look deeply into her eyes, Nanak said, "From the beginning you were more than a student. You already knew the Guru before we met. But with no experience in life, you knew not how to phrase your knowledge or apply it. Now you have experience, you know the words to use, and best of all you understand the right application of the message I am trying to spread. I want you to open your door to the converts I have made in this village. There are no more than 10 or 12 of them, but I fear without leadership or a group of kindred souls they will forget and return to their former beliefs. I am asking you to be their guide in the Sikh philosophy and discuss the ideas with them. Of all the converts in this place, you have the greatest understanding by far.

More than a disciple, you are now my co-worker in the Mission of spreading this greater Truth if you will accept that place."

A new image of herself arose in Nisha's heart and mind. She hugged her beloved friend exuberantly and said without hesitation, "Tell them to come on the morning of the traditional day of rest. That will be our time to meet, and I will gladly show them the way to their Guru through chanting and meditation. As for setting my husband free to travel with my best wishes for his safety and fulfillment, I must say that I have found romance to be like chasing a beautiful butterfly that leads to tripping and falling over a stone. The butterfly is beautiful, but the end result can be fatal to your cause. I would have preferred to continue my travels with the converters. I have been restless, dear Nanak, but you have again brought a new way of life to me. I vow to be worthy of your trust. I admire you most for your bravery in doing that which your Guru compels you to do, regardless of what others might think you should be doing. I give my husband permission to do the same."

Hugging her sweetly, Nanak said with a twinkle in his eye, "Perhaps I will be your lover in a future life. You are the only kind of woman I could endure in such a close alliance."

Nisha was surprised at her own mind's indifference toward his speculation. She thought, "For me it is the nature of the man, his passion for me, and his passion for our work together in service to God that will bring joy to my life. That man by any name is the lover that my soul embraces."

For the next eight years Nisha kept her vow. She met in her home with her original Sikh group every week. She taught them the chants as they were taught to her. Hassum, Nanak and Mandana returned twice during that time to stay a few weeks before continuing their work.

But it became more difficult and more dangerous for the men. After witnessing a growing element of aggressiveness by the Muslims against Yogis and Hindus and spending some time in prison because of his protests, Nanak retired from his travels and returned to his wife to establish a home in the country. He spent the rest of his life working as a farmer on his land and delivering his message in the safety of his own home to those who sought him out.

Hassum returned home as well and again took up his old profession of blacksmithing and his position as Nisha's husband. He used his spare time to help lead the group, who met in their home, and to spread the message of Sikh philosophy to anyone who would listen. He and Nisha were very happy, and they enjoyed the simplicity of their life style and their work.

Ana was 11 years old by now, and her father enjoyed seeing her practice as a drummer for the chanting in their group. Years later, Hassum and Nisha were overjoyed when Ana married a Sikh leader who took her to travel with him in his missionary work.

The comings and goings of Nanak, Hassum, Mandana and Ana had seemed like a natural part of life to Nisha. She had preferred they stay nearby but had felt no extreme loss when they went their way. But when her mother-in-law died, her heart was broken.

After meeting Hassum's mother Nisha had let go of her passion to find the mother who had abandoned her at birth. This woman had given her the maternal love she had hoped to find.

Two years before her death, this wonderfully caring woman said to Nisha, "I am curious about where you happened to meet Hassum. All you have told me is that you were a convert of Nanak's and your courtship with Hassum occurred during his travels. You have never spoken of your own mother or a family or the culture from which you came. I did not wish to intrude upon your privacy, but now I am an old woman who needs to have her curiosity satisfied. Please tell me about your life before you met my boy."

Nisha had responded with gladness for the opportunity to talk about her past, and a feeling of relief in knowing this woman would not shun her for being a child born out of wedlock.

But before she got past the part about her mother being sent to a Yogi camp to have her child, her mother-in-law began to wail and tear at her hair. Startled, Nisha stopped her tale as shame filled her heart. Was she to be cast out from this woman's love now that the truth of her birth was known?

Looking at the floor, Nisha let the shame wash over her and waited for her mother-in-law to speak.

"My darling first-born," cried Hassum's mother, embracing her, "I was the girl who abandoned you to the Yogis. How can you ever accept me as your friend again? I gave you life and then left you to die so that I might live my life without the shame. I have thought of the infant to whom I gave birth every day of my life since then. And while I was wondering whether she had survived, she was here sharing her life and her love with me. I do not deserve your love. If you abandon me now, I cannot blame you for that revenge. It would be just karma for me."

They cried together as Nisha assured her mother of forgiveness and told the rest of her story. They said a prayer of gratitude that Ana had been born healthy.

It remained a secret between the two women that Hassum was really her half- brother and their daughter was also their niece. The shared secret had brought them even closer, and there was nothing they kept from each other. Now she was gone, and Nisha felt the agony of grief for the first time in her life. Even so, she felt that God had been merciful in prompting her mother's heart to inquire of her past that day. If not for that she would never have known that her mother did love her even more greatly than she had ever hoped.

After a year of mourning, Nisha and Hassum moved into the main part of his parent's house to care for his aging father, a quiet dignified and pious Hindu man. As they set to cleaning the walls and the draperies and arranging furniture according to their whims, they came across an enormous, ornate trunk covered with a heavy tapestry. They had known the trunk was there and had often sat upon it when the house was crowded, but they had never known what was in the trunk. Opening it with a sense of adventure and curiosity, they found a scroll tied with a band of rope. Under the scroll was another tapestry, folded just the size of the trunk. What they read in the scroll changed their lives.

Under the folded tapestry, which was quite valuable in itself, Hassum's father had secretly hidden away an enormous fortune that he had inherited from his parents and they from their parents. The scroll said that the fortune must be used by a family member in a benevolent way that would benefit the community. It must be used in some way that would bring betterment to the society. Until a family member desired to use the fortune in that way, it must remain intact. When they asked Hassum's father about it, he said to his son, "I never had an interest in community affairs, so I have left the fortune as it was when given to me. If you have use for it, then it is yours. As an only child you would have inherited it soon anyway."

With it, Nisha and Hassum were able to change their lifestyle from one of frugal independence to one of generous philanthropy. Nisha suggested that, in her mother-in- law's memory, she would like to use the wing they had formerly occupied as a home for abandoned children. She said enthusiastically, "In the street I see three children who frequently experience hunger and lack. They could live there, and I could be the overseer of their education and activities. We would supply all their needs and erase all their sadness of feeling unloved."

Knowing her history of abandonment, Hassum did not hesitate to give his consent. "If we can give spiritual knowledge and love to these children and raise them as Sikhs, it will be to me like having the opportunity to save you over and over again," he said.

"I could not love you more if you were my own brother," said Nisha with an affectionate hug. And she wished their mother had been there to share the joke.

The home for abandoned children was a great success. Nisha grew old teaching them the chants and watching each generation grow and learn and leave in their turn.

She died peacefully in her sleep one night with a chant of thanksgiving dancing in her mind.

Chapter 11

MARIA

Prussia 1756-1792 A.D.

> ***Journal Entry #10***
>
> *Of course, when there is an over-commitment to cramming the mind full of abstract spiritual ideas, there comes a need to reestablish balance by practicing that knowledge in the practical world. I now see that the philosophy of life and sense of "knowing" with which I came into my current incarnation was stored in my memory from that long ago incarnation as Nisha. What a sweet discovery. This next incarnation appears to be a lifetime of relating spiritual knowledge to practice toward purposeful living in the world. I see the environment and politics surrounding my life as Maria.*

The 18th century is a time of glory and power for Prussia. It consists of aggressive invasions on nearby territories in Europe. Gradually, the Prussians have expanded their territory through extreme military power--sometimes through intimidation, and in other incidences, through acts of war.

All European Nations were under the leadership of kings or emperors during the early part of the century, and Prussia had formed an alliance with the Emperor of the Holy Roman Territory at the beginning of the century. In exchange for military support, the unofficial political and military leader of Prussia was given the title of King of Prussia.

At the time of Maria's birth and during her childhood, the king is the ruling monarch. As long as citizens know his laws, obey them to the letter and swear allegiance to him, to the Holy Roman Emperor, and to the Roman Catholic Church they are left to their own ways. Taxation is heavy, and there are three classes of people other than slaves.

Wealthy aristocrats and royalty make up the influential class. While the king makes the laws, he is not resistant to hearing the views of the influential class, especially if there is a handsome sum of money attached. The middle class is made up of craftsmen with their own small businesses and small parcels of land, as well as any artists and musicians who are property owners. The middle class has no voice in the running of the country and no chance of being heard, but they enjoy the freedom to work at their crafts. The peasant class is made up of non-landowners. Poor artists and musicians who perform just for daily survival wages and the laborers who work for wages and have no property or business of their own are the people of this class. It is from their ranks that most of the military is formed. Because of the prestige and the higher wages of being a soldier, much of the military is made up of volunteers although they do have a draft that can be enacted as needed. Prussian soldiers take pride in their status as the defenders of the citizens and as instruments of expansion toward greater wealth and power for their country.

Maria's parents were of the middle class. Her father was a shoe cobbler for the common folks and a shoemaker for more wealthy clients. Their kitchen and pantry and a wash-room were on the ground floor behind their shop and the second floor was made up of four large rooms. Maria and her twin sister, Alicia, were the joy of their lives. Their favorite social activity was to attend the opera, so no one had been surprised when they named their daughters after great opera stars of the times.

Maria was a quiet, happy child seemingly content to have a family and no other interests in life except singing and the casual companionship of her sister. Both girls sang almost before they could talk, learning songs from their mother, who hummed and sang as she worked. In the evenings the three of them would sing while Maria's father played music upon a stringed instrument that he cradled in his arms like a baby.

Alicia was not so quiet and not so happy. In fact, she was quite belligerent and hyperactive, often striking or biting her sister without provocation. She refused to be cooperative in helping with chores, hated going to classes, and practiced cunning deception with her parents to help meet her insatiable desire for attention and gifts. The only thing she did seem to like was singing with Maria and teasing her.

Between her domestic activities, their mother helped her husband with the polishing of shoes and dealing with customers. Maria often played quietly on the floor of the shoe shop so her parents could watch her as they worked. But Alicia was into everything and had to be kept occupied with "busy" work to do.

Often their parents discussed the great differences in their personalities. "But they are both blessed with such lovely voices for singing," they would say with quiet pride.

When Maria was a girl of nine, the school administrators tested them for aptitude and agreed to recommend Maria for the school for musically-gifted children, explaining that while Alicia had a nice voice it did not have the quality or stability required for professional singing.

"It is not fair that one should be selected over the other," raged their father. "I will not have them separated in school. Alicia merely needs more time; her voice has great potential. Maria will not be permitted to attend the music school unless Alicia is accepted, too!"

He left their mother to take up the quarrel with the school administrator, who reluctantly agreed saying, "It would be such a loss to our society if Maria is prevented from her education. I suppose it can do no harm to accept them both, but you must tell no one that we made this concession."

A carriage appeared at the academic school every afternoon to pick up four "musically-gifted" children and take them directly to the music school for lessons in voice or training in a specific instrument six days each week.

Maria had no friends outside of her daily school activities and felt no need for additional socialization beyond school and family. Developing and expressing her talent meant everything to her, and she never questioned what might be going on outside this small circle of school and home.

She was especially fond of Sundays, a day when the little family of four would enjoy a leisurely breakfast, dress elegantly and attended the Catholic Church. After church she and her mother would share "girl-talk" while preparing a special meal. Alicia detested domestic work and preferred to spend this time with her father, carving animals out of wood or learning how to make the shoes. On Sunday afternoons, the four of them played games or did a project together, ending the day with reading aloud to one another for an hour before bedtime. Maria felt sorry for the peasant children who did not have the privilege of free education as the property owners did. "How can anyone expect their families ever to rise to the middle class if they receive no education?"

"Taxes pay for the education," her father would say. "And they pay no taxes." "How can they pay taxes if they have only enough money to survive and none to purchase property?"

"I suppose they can't, but, even so, I don't want my taxes to increase in order to secure education for the peasant children."

"Couldn't the influential class pay for the extra schools? What else do they have to do with their money but bribe the king and wallow in luxury and greed?"

"Shush! That's enough, child. You can't begin to understand what it takes to maintain a society such as ours. Just be grateful that you are not a peasant and enjoy what life has to offer you."

Then Maria would fall silent, feeling that she had no one to talk to about the important questions of life.

Maria's father was especially interested in political history and kept up with current political events in Europe through association with his customers. When he talked about the constant wars that Prussia was engaged in as if they were just interesting stories, Maria felt outrage in her belly. "How can he be so casual about it?" she thought. "Can't he see that our causes are greedy and cruel?"

She would listen closely as he described the latest events, then send out a prayer for all the people whose countries were being invaded by the Prussian soldiers. She hated war. Alicia, on the other hand, would hang on their father's every word and actually laugh at some of the events he would describe. As they grew older it was more and more obvious that the girls had absolutely nothing in common except their parents and their love for singing.

To complicate matters with their relationship, Alicia became extremely envious of Maria for her opportunities to practice stage performances in local amateur theaters.

Even when Alicia was invited to participate, the applause she received was so weak as to embarrass her. By the time they were 13 Alicia had announced that she was not interested in singing anymore.

"It is a waste of time, and the public is not worthy of my voice or my time," she announced with disdain. "My goal is to marry a wealthy man, have an elegant home and servants, travel throughout the world, and rise to the influential class."

Secretly her father was relieved, knowing she did not have the voice or self- discipline required for professional singing, and now he could rest from defending her rights by helping her achieve her own goals.

"And where will you find this wealthy man to give you such a luxurious life?" teased her mother.

"I will leave school and take care of all the communication with our clients from now on. I will meet the wealthy customers, and they will find me so charming that they will forget that I am merely middle class and want me to meet their sons. If I can charm the fathers, the sons will be easy to draw into my clutches," she laughed, curling her fingers into claws.

"So be it!" said her father. "We have more customers than ever before, and I could use your mother's help in making the shoes."

Even Maria felt relief because she hoped that now Alicia would cease the insulting humor and the envious attitude that she had been subjected to for the last five years. She could concentrate on perfecting her performance without worrying that she was offending her sister.

When Maria's sixteenth birthday arrived and she still had shown no interest in courtship or parties, her parents invited a couple to dinner one evening along with their 17-year-old son. Maria was relaxed and charming throughout the evening, even taking a walk after dinner with the young man. Her parents had hoped this would awaken in her a desire for marriage, children and home. But that was not to be the case.

After their guests had left, Maria asked for an audience with her parents.

"I don't exactly know where to begin," she said quietly but firmly, "Alicia has married well, and I am happy for her. But that is not my desire. The sex act in marriage, and even marriage itself, according to our Priest, are solely for procreation, and I have no interest in raising children or living a domestic life. I believe life is for doing what makes you feel alive, and only three things make me feel alive: Singing, studying and praying.

Everything else holds me back from these three things. Please do not expect me to marry and give up the opportunity to spend my time doing these things that uplift me."

Reluctantly her parents agreed to respect her choice and to never bring it up again. They were very proud of both girls and only wanted them to be happy. Alicia had indeed married a wealthy young man who put her in a fine home with servants, and they were planning to tour Europe as soon as he could get away.

Within the next five years Maria performed many times in six different operas and in three different theaters. Her voice teacher told her parents, "I have been surpassed by my protégé. With your permission, I will recommend her as a student to the best voice and drama teacher in Naples. It will cost a great deal to get her started, but she can live in an inn with other students of the opera and begin accepting engagements right away to help pay her way."

"What else has all our work been for except to see that our girls have what they need to meet their goals in life?" boasted her father. "She will be available just as soon as arrangements can be made."

Maria was filled with gratitude at the generosity of her parents and the encouragement with which they showered her. For a full year, she accepted paid invitations for everything from reading poetry and singing at house parties of the wealthy class to performing in operas at second-rate theaters. Her big break came when she auditioned and was selected to star in a new opera at the finest theater in Naples. From there her career expanded into constant work and travel throughout much of Europe.

She loved earning her own way, independent from her parents, and soon had purchased a small white villa with a tall fence and wonderful flowers growing profusely in front and back. A housekeeper and gardener shared the villa with her, and for the next seven years she felt she was suspended in a seemingly perfect time-frame. It amused her to think that perhaps heaven was not a place to go after death but was the finding of fulfillment of one's dreams without a single desire unmet. The only blemish on her sense of perfection was the hostile attitude that her sister still held toward her.

She had thought it was a thing of the past, but when she became successful Alicia began to show the old signs of envy. She had taken Alicia aside at one point to inquire about her attitude, hoping they could find some way to be comfortable when visiting their parents for holidays.

"You have everything you ever wanted, Alicia. Why are you still so hostile toward me? Is there anything I can do to make peace between us?" asked Maria.

Alicia lashed out at her with eyes full of contempt, "It is not fair that you should have wealth and travel. Those were to be my prizes. You have your "beautiful voice". That should be enough for you. Now I find that you also have a home as luxurious as mine. You have servants, fine clothing, jewels, travel and all without having to endure the idiocy of a man pawing at you."

Maria was stunned at the resentment of her sister. Without comment, she turned and walked silently back into the parlor to join her parents for reading and tea. With this confrontation, Maria now felt a deep revulsion toward Alicia and was ashamed of herself for feeling that way.

She made a silent commitment to herself: "Since she detests me and I feel only revulsion and pity for her, I will simply avoid ever seeing her again."

Maria loved the freedom of being in a place where no one knew her or expected anything of her except to sing. Because of her near perfect soprano voice and her obvious joy in performing, Maria consistently received more invitations to perform with European opera companies than she could accept and more social invitations than she wanted.

During her first visit home at Christmas time her mother greeted her with both laughter and tears. "I'm so glad you decided not to marry. Alicia, I'm afraid, has abandoned us. Her wealthy in-laws have offered her and her husband an indefinite Christmas gift of a vacation to any place of their choice every Christmas season. We will never see her at Christmas again!"

Even as she was consoling her mother, Maria was thinking, "How perfect. I will pay one long visit a year to my parents, at Christmas time. This way I might never have to see Alicia again."

"There, there, my love," she said, consoling her mother. "I will come to be with you and father every Christmas, and we will just make it a very merry time."

She encouraged them to attend her performances at her expense when they were within a day's travel to the theater in which she was performing. At least three times each year, she sent them coach fare and guest tickets to whatever show she was into at the time. But they were still hard-working middle-class people and could seldom find the time to get away. Mostly they were proud of her from a distance.

During her eighth year in Naples, Maria contracted pneumonia and was assigned to bed rest for several weeks. Christmas was approaching, and she did not want to miss the season with her parents. As a Christmas gift, she sent them each a new winter coat and coach fare with an invitation to visit her in Naples from the 18th of December until the 18th of January.

They were thrilled beyond speech. In all this time Maria had asked repeatedly to attend her performances but had never invited them to visit her villa. Of this she had not even been aware, until now.

"We'll be gone for a month," her parents bragged with humor to their customers and friends, "So take care of the shoes you have until we return."

One morning, a few days before Christmas, a stranger from the coach station rapped on Maria's door. There had been an accident. Ice and snow had accumulated rapidly on the roads during an unexpected blizzard. One of their coaches had gone off the side of a steep hill. Four passengers and the coachmen had been killed, among them were her parents.

Maria was in shock to the point of numbness in mind and body. Her own illness seemed of no consequence now. Her heaven on earth was shattered beyond repair.

There was a piece missing. She put on a hat, gloves, boots, and a coat down to her ankles, wrapped a woolen shawl around her head and mouth and walked into the blizzard that had killed her beloved parents who had been her closest friends. Maria walked and cried for hours. She felt guilty, sad, abandoned, scared, confused, helpless, alone and heartbroken. Then, there was nothing to do but walk back the way she came. She cried even harder when she saw her footprints in the snow and knew they had taken her nowhere at all except around in a circle. If only they could take her to her parents' home. She wanted to sit by the open fire, discuss politics with her father again and hear him talk about the wars. She wanted to hear her mother's rich, deep voice reading poetry or the Bible, and feel her goodnight kiss.

Later that day, Maria learned that Alicia and her husband were away on a cruise. It would be up to Maria to make the burial arrangements. Fearfully she told her gardener what had happened and asked advice about what to do concerning the bodies and the burials. He could see that even though she was 29 years old and successful in the eyes of the world, she was like a child when it came to business affairs.

"I know a University Professor from Paris. He is vacationing with his parents for the holidays and is only a few houses away. He will know exactly how to advise you, and I suggest you waste no time in seeing him."

It was difficult for Maria to approach the stranger's house and even more difficult to explain her situation after meeting him. His name was Mark. Sensing her lack of experience in legal and business matters, he gallantly saved her the embarrassment of asking detailed questions by providing for her both the questions and the answers. He told her who to contact about having the bodies claimed and returned back to their home town for burial, how to arrange for a funeral and burial and how to close out the business and sell the property. He even gave her the name of a local attorney to see who could put her in touch with an attorney in her parents'" town.

After it was all done, Maria realized that now she was alone in the world except for Alicia, and she preferred that they remain estranged. Neither of her parents had relatives that she had ever met, even though some had attended the funeral. She left a formal letter with the attorney to be given to Alicia when she returned, along with a request that Alicia not try to contact her again unless she was willing to release her hostility and act as a friend. She never heard from Alicia again.

Maria had no personal friends, and she had not attended church in over two years, nor had she been to confession in more than five years. What seemed to constitute her "life" now was the time she spent practicing or in performances, and she found it difficult to meditate or pray. Everything else seemed like a dream-state and unreal. Suddenly she felt very confused and angry with God for the pain and sorrow that people in the world were subjected to day after day and year after year.

Upon returning to Italy, Maria went straight to the nearest Catholic Church for confession. Once inside the booth, she began to cry and say things that shocked even her. But everything she said pointed her eyes to the insight that while she had cared about her parents, she had cared only for the pleasure she had experienced in their company and the nurturing and encouraging support they had given her. She had not really inquired about how they felt about life or what they wanted from it. Even when she had sent the tickets and invitation, it had been to receive praise from them.

"I have known how to seek being loved but not how to discover the heart and soul of another. I should have gone to visit more often." She moaned. "I should have been able to endure the behaviors of my silly sister and see her attitudes simply as an expression of her own jealous nature. I should have inquired more about my parent's interests. I don't even know how they spent their time when I was not with them. My relationship with them was always in the moment, and our conversation was always about me. I am dreadfully self-centered and always running from conversation about uncomfortable matters. I never think about anything but my own comfort and peace and interests."

In an effort to console her, the priest said, "Now that your parents are gone, there is no recovering the past. What is done is done, my child. As for your sister, it seems to me that your appearance stirs up the evil in her. You did not put the evil there, so you cannot take it away. It seems fair that you would not wish to encounter that evil again. But what is it you want to do with your life from now on? Perhaps more of the same kind of one-focus living, perhaps expansion toward something new. Is this a turning point for you?"

Maria could not answer, but in the following six months she would think about these questions at night and wrestle within her own mind for an answer. "If only I could find a way to stop some of the suffering for some of the people in a way that really makes a difference for them," she thought. "But all I can do is sing. I will sing with more heart and sing only the messages that I wish to promote," she vowed. "Perhaps that will relieve the suffering of a few in some way."

It is often the case that new opportunities come when a change occurs in the way one thinks. That was the case with Maria. Late in the summer, shopping for fresh vegetables and fruits at an open market, Maria placed her hand on a ripe tomato at the same time a masculine hand reached for it. Lifting her eyes to give the man a challenging look, she was surprised to see her neighbor's son, Mark, who had been her advisor in December.

"Maria," he said, "it is fate that we should meet, for no less than an hour ago I was wondering how I might see you again. Did all go well with your parents" burial and the completion of their affairs? How have you been? Have you recovered from your pneumonia and from your grief? May I carry your purchases to your door?"

Maria smiled, "Yes, to all your questions."

As they walked toward her villa, she felt a sense of comfort that she had not felt since last talking with her parents, as if a new friendship was about to begin.

"My priest has helped me enormously with sorting out my feelings. I will always miss my parents and remember the lovely times we shared, but I have gotten over my tendency to wish for the return of time that has gone by," she said with a philosophical flare that surprised even her. "We cannot make a relationship express beyond its potential, nor can we bring back one that is behind us. I realized that if I keep looking back to yesterday, I will miss my opportunity to make the best of my current time."

It was the most personal thing she had said to anyone except her priest since the death of her parents.

"Well said," applauded Mark. "So how shall we make the most of this moment in current time?"

Maria smiled. "As a reward for your kindness, we will let you stay for a cup of tea and tell me all about yourself."

Mark was 32 years old, and he had been married briefly at 25 to a seamstress. She had died from a mysterious fever less than a year after their marriage. He had decided that God relieved him of wife and potential family so that he might focus on his true loves in life: teaching languages and staying abreast of political issues. He was looking for a "cause" to support but, so far, had stayed on the sidelines of political issues, content to discuss them with his many professional friends. After graduating from a university in England, where he had been taught various languages, Mark had moved to Paris to accept his first teaching position. He had loved it so well that he purchased a comfortable villa there with two acres of land. He visited Naples twice every year to see his wealthy parents, his many siblings and their children.

"And what about you?" he inquired. "All I know about you is that you are my parents "neighbor and your parents were from Prussia."

"How refreshing," she thought, realizing for the first time that she had always felt no one was interested in her for herself, only for her music. "He is interested in me, and he doesn't even know that I am a singer."

"I, too, have avoided the responsibility that comes with producing a family in lieu of other interests that are much more rewarding to me," she began.

As she told the highlights about herself, Maria watched Mark's eyes take on a sparkle. She invited him to catch her performance the following weekend, then stood and offered her hand. "Thank you for spending some time with me. It's been delightful."

Mark was in the audience for her next performance and every performance that followed as long as he was in Italy.

On the night before he had to leave, he knocked on her dressing room door. When she opened the door, he swept her into his arms and kissed her warmly on the mouth. Maria was stunned. It was her first kiss and she didn't know whether to slap him, to laugh, or to ask for another. That kiss was the singular most exciting thing that had ever happened to her. She decided to laugh.

"Well, what caused such a display of enthusiasm from you?" she teased. "Tomorrow I leave for France. But I leave with full knowledge that I am madly in love. You have four months to make up your mind. If you agree, then I will meet your priest in December and we will be married in January."

Maria played along, believing he was just being flirtatious, "But what about my career? Will you be moving to Naples?"

"No," Mark said soberly. "That is why you must take the next few months to consider all things related to the marriage. There are opportunities to sing opera in France but not to the degree that you have done in Italy. Your identity would be as the wife of a university professor of languages."

Feeling a strange sense of attraction to that image, Maria asked seriously, "What if I wanted to travel and sing wherever I am invited?"

"As long as you are not away from me too often or too long at a time, we can create a life that pleases us both," Mark said. "If there are children, we can hire a nanny and a cook and a housekeeper. You would decide for yourself how much you wished to travel while our children are growing."

A surge of pure joy rushed from Maria's solar-plexus to her throat. The thought of having the love of such a fine man without sacrificing the freedom to make her own decisions brought overwhelming gratitude to her heart, and she found herself "forgiving God" for all the pain in the world. Laughing at her own absurdity, Maria threw herself into Mark's arms, kissing him with fiery passion. "I shall live for December," she whispered.

"If you change your mind, I lose my will to live," he said.

Their public wedding in Naples was attended by hundreds of fans and dozens of Mark's relatives.

His villa in France was elegant and large. The entrance room was oval in shape, furnished with velvet couches and chairs and a grand piano. Maria was delighted to learn that Mark enjoyed entertaining guests with his limited piano playing and singing of humorous and boisterous songs. They shared many musical evenings, sometimes alone, sometimes entertaining Mark's many political and university friends who became her friends.

Twice each week Mark held open house for a particular group of his friends who discussed politics and current events. They would smoke cigars, drink brandy and get into heated debates about the uprisings that were happening perpetually, not only in Paris but in all of France.

Maria acted as hostess on those evenings as some of the discussions were secretive and not to be shared with the servants. Their talk was about the frequent flare- ups of civil riots, talk of civil war and overthrow of the current government. They were in the midst of the French Revolution.

One evening when they were alone, Mark said quietly and candidly to Maria, "There is killing in the streets every day. Peasants are rioting because they want the vote; aristocrats are fleeing into other nations; others are seizing power in the new Assembly and there is rumor that King Louis will be dethroned. You once asked me to move to Naples. The wars are not contained within the boundaries of France; our warring legislative leaders are moving troops against several nations at once. If you still want us to make a home there, I am willing to do it for your safety."

Tears welled up in Maria's eyes. "There are no longer even any monasteries where the clergy or the peasants can hide," she said. "My own people have joined with Rome to send a warning to France.

They demand that the king's full status be restored. The king is weak and swings his support to whatever faction seems to hold greatest power in the moment. He merely wants to survive. I would like to see our king restored to power. At least we all know our place and our duties in such a society. But I have learned that things do not go back to the way they were. When they are gone, they are gone. We move forward into the future. I cannot tell who is right or wrong here. I only know that France has responded to Prussia's warning by seeking out innocent Prussians in France to kill. I had prayed for a way to make a real difference in the lives of suffering people with the beauty of my song. Now, I am finished with running away from discomfort. Some things are worth at least an effort to change the trend. I hear you debating first one view and then the other. What is your true position in this dispute, my husband?"

"I had no idea you were so aware of the situation," said Mark with admiration. "My friends and I are in sympathy with the movement to restore our government to a monarchy with a limited body of legislative leaders to represent every province. As it is now, every city in France has its own government and laws, and many are in conflict with one another. We believe that peace can be restored if the Legislative Assembly is disassembled. We would like to see a new Constitution created by representatives from each province with the king making the final decision."

By now Maria had completely lost her passion for performing as her primary interest. Her mind was consumed with the important issues of France, the safety needs of Prussians in Paris and the opportunity to make a creative difference. "Foreigners" from Prussia and Germany were being executed in the streets. Mark was glad that he and Maria had never been asked where she was brought up and that her mother had given her an Italian name. All their friends and acquaintances in France assumed she was Italian.

Mark's friends met to consider their responsibility in the matter. They agreed that, as prominent professionals in their community, they could be more effective as undercover agents to assist with the escape of Prussians and Germans who wanted to return to their own countries. The home of Mark and Maria was perfect for such a covert operation. They were known for their frequent parties and their home was known as a place where visitors were welcome day or night. This prevented any attention being given to the number of goings and comings from their home.

The underground "grapevine" carried the news that a "party" would be held on specific evenings twice a week at Mark's home. Visitors in need of assistance for escape were to dress as if for a party and bring only what they could carry in their pockets. They were to watch carefully to see where the butler was standing in front of the pantry door.

When Mark played a certain spirited and very loud piece of music on the piano and everyone began to join in the singing, they were to go immediately to that pantry door and give the password. The password was, "It's a great party, but I have to leave now." They were to avoid approaching the butler if another person were there. Only one at a time could go. The singing would go on for half an hour, getting louder as it went.

Every 5 minutes another person would be shown through the door.

Upon hearing the password phrase, the butler would say, "Here, take this door. It is a short-cut to your carriage." He would open the pantry door to let them out, where they would find another "butler" who would inquire, "May I see you to your carriage?" In order for the agents to be certain that this were indeed a runaway, the escapee must respond, "Your carriage is my carriage, sir."

If they did not give this answer, they would be shown through the door on the left where a "servant" would whisk them quickly away to their own carriage. Those who gave the secret response would be shown through a door on the right where they would follow a tunnel and eventually find themselves in a storm cellar directly under the gazebo. An agent there would give them a packet of water and dried fruits and escort them to a flat-bed wagon with nine wine barrels held on by a double railing. Six of the barrels would be occupied by the escapees; three held wine. Twice each party night this musical escape was orchestrated, which meant that they could rescue two dozen people every week.

The drivers of the wagons were genuine wine-deliverers from one of the most prestigious wineries in Italy. Once a wagon-load of escapees arrived at the border, they were required to stay in an old distribution warehouse full of wine barrels until given the signal to proceed to the winery in Italy. Sometimes it happened within 24 hours; sometimes it took up to five or six days. Once a week half a dozen wagons full of "empty" wine barrels would be driven over the border to the winery to be "refilled" and transported again to the warehouse to be distributed all over Europe. Once inside the winery, the escapees would be freed from the barrels, given a set of peasant clothing and a carpet bag full of food and wine. From there they must fend for themselves and were advised to proceed in groups of no more than six to their homelands by whatever means they could find.

Over a period of three years, Maria and Mark rescued hundreds of German and Prussian citizens and both Maria and Mark discussed the fact that they felt a strange sense of familiarity with what they were doing. Maria stopped performing altogether, lest her fame should bring an investigation of her background. She was consumed with the importance of their rescue mission and with a horror at the insanity of war.

"Life is difficult enough without people deliberately making it more difficult for each other!" she would often say to Mark and his friends.

One evening two non-descriptive men arrived at their party. Strangers were more common than not at these events, so no one questioned their identity but for some reason they looked familiar to Maria. When the boisterous singing began, they approached Maria. "We are your cousins from Prussia," whispered one. "Your uncle is also my uncle on my mother's side. Your sister, Alicia, sent word telling us where we could find you. She said you could help us find safe passage out of France."

Maria recognized that they were indeed her cousins, and she trusted them without question. She was confident that she possessed a "psychic" sensitivity about such things and that she could not be deceived. "Have you not heard the passwords?" she inquired.

"Yes, we surely have, but only once and unfortunately we have drunk so much of your excellent wine that neither of us can remember what to say," they said, hanging their heads in embarrassment.

Maria escorted them to the butler at the pantry door. "It's a great party, but they have to leave now," she said. The "butler" let them into the pantry with Maria following to escort them. The next attendant said, "May I see you to your carriage?"

The two men giggled as if drunk. "Your carriage is their carriage, sir," said Maria.

They were let through the door into the tunnel and Maria returned to the party.

Two weeks later, during one of their parties, soldiers surrounded the home of Mark and Maria. Many attended the party, and when the rescue proceedings got underway arrests were made.

Maria and Mark were imprisoned for only six days. A speedy open air public trial was held. They and all the agents who had been found in their home at the time were found guilty of treason. The next day they were led to the executioner where they knelt side by side in pairs with their heads on the blocks. When Maria was led to the platform with an old friend of theirs, she cried out, "Please let me die with my husband." Laughter rang out among the amused onlookers. One person burst out with song, mimicking Maria's operatic voice.

Her request was granted with condescending, mock bows and more laughter. Holding hands, Maria and Mark requested a priest. More rollicking laughter ensued while the priest delivered their last rites. Her throat nearly paralyzed with emotion; Maria beckoned the priest to lend his ear. She whispered, "After it is over, please tell them our last prayer was that the courage with which we lived might be seen as an example of God's love in action and that the peace with which we died might be seen as an example of God's forgiveness in action."

When the axe fell, they were beheaded simultaneously. There was only an instant of pain before they lost consciousness.

As their bodies were being cleared away for the next beheading, the priest honored Maria's last wish and repeated her message. The crowd laughed.

Chapter 12

TESSIE

Virginia, USA 1804-1847

I see the time period of my next incarnation. The state of Virginia in this new nation is lush and green, with an abundance of water and fertile soil. The citizens are committed to slavery as a way of life and cannot imagine how things would get done without a free workforce for the well to do plantation owners. Desire for freedom was not as much of an issue for most of the slaves as was the desire to avoid the cruelty of heavy-handed slave owners. That type of slave owner was more common than the nurturing kind, who treated their slaves with the same kindness that they extended to their work animals.

The girl was born a slave, one of at least a dozen children who slept where they could find a bare spot on the cabin floor. She was given no name and simply called "girl" along with other girls who lived in the cabin. She did not know which of the adults in the cabin were her own parents, or which of the children were her own brothers and sisters. The philosophy of the slaves on their plantation was that they were simply tools to be used by their white masters, and it was pointless to assign names to their offspring or to become too attached.

At age 10 the girl was said to be too frail for picking cotton and hoeing vegetables, so she was introduced to the woman in charge of the wash house who gave her the name "Tessie". Tessie's regular assignment was to draw water from the well and haul it in large buckets to where it was needed. In addition, she was to wash clothes outdoors in a huge iron pot, hang them to dry, rescue them from the lines when they were dry, then fold or iron every piece and put them away. Her favorite thing to do was the ironing. It was done in the big kitchen with "smoothing irons" which were heated in an open fireplace, then kept warm on top of the iron cook stove. She made it a point to become an expert "presser" so that all the ladies and gentlemen of the house insisted that she be the one to iron their clothing. She felt good about herself, and she enjoyed cooperating with her superiors. Through her many hours spent in the kitchen, she became friendly with the housekeepers and cooks and felt less alone than she had in the cabin or in the wash room.

When she was 14 Tessie was auctioned off as an expert presser and cooperative worker with a sweet, agreeable personality.

"This one is eager to please," said the auctioneer, raising his eyebrows in a suggestive smile, "if you know what I mean. You can train her in whatever household duties you want her to have. She's not very big, but she's well shaped," he concluded. With that remark, he caught her garment at the neck and tore it from her body. Tessie stood shivering from humiliation and fear, her naked body exposed to the onlookers. The bidding began.

Only three plantation owners were interested in buying her. Others were after strong men and women to work in the fields. An argument arose between two of the bidders and the third one stepped up to join in. They began pushing each other, and a fight broke out. The third bidder beat both of the other two unconscious, then made his final bid.

"Sold!" announced the auctioneer, who then escorted her off the platform.

Her new owner had purchased three new slaves at the auction, and during the ride to their plantation he sat beside his driver while she sat huddled in the back of the wagon with the others. She had no idea what to expect, and she missed her friends in the kitchen of the old place.

When they arrived at the plantation, her new owner stepped down from the wagon.

"Everybody out," he said in a loud jovial voice. "This is your new home. I'm your new daddy, and you are my new children. Mind me without question, and I will be good to you. Disobey me, lie to me, trick me or act disrespectful and you will get a beating with no food for 24 hours. If you do it too many times, I will sell you to the meanest plantation owner I can find."

"Tessie, you come with me. The others get back in the wagon and go to the bunkhouses."

Nobody moved. Stepping up to the girl, he grabbed her by the back of the neck and pulled her toward him gently. "You're my Tessie," he said, "And I am Peter Cunningham."

Tessie felt pleased to hear him say her name and she liked him from the start because he left nothing to guesswork. He gave the rules right away and she was eager to receive her list of responsibilities. As she followed Peter Cunningham into his southern mansion, she felt a sense of belonging. He had said, "You are mine."

A house slave let them in with a smile and a warm greeting. "Got you a purty little thing, this time, sir," he said.

Peter Cunningham chuckled.

Tessie enjoyed the compliment and smiled shyly at him. Peter escorted Tessie to the kitchen and introduced her to the head housekeeper, Mindy, who was having a cup of steaming black coffee. "This is Tessie," he said. "She is not a cook or a scrubber. She can do anything in the house that doesn't require a great deal of strength, and she will be the number one presser for the household."

"Shonuf," said Mindy. "It'll be good to have a new presser. Since that last one died, I been havin a hard time keepin up with everything."

Tessie beamed with delight at being assigned something that she knew how to do. "You can stay in the room off the kitchen with me unless Master Peter decides he wants you for one of his women. He keeps them in a fancy room to themselves. They still have to work, but he spoils them something awful with fancy clothes and candies and pretty words. His wife spoils 'em, too. She can't have babies, and she keeps hoping one of his women will have a light-skinned baby so she can raise it in the big house herself."

Tessie made herself comfortable in Mindy's room and began to hope that Master Peter would choose her as one of his women.

After nearly two years had passed with no indication from the Master that she was to be one of his "women", Tessie gave up hope. Even so, she was quite content with her job, her living arrangements, and her new friendships. She and the Mistress Regina, Peter Cunningham's wife, had become quite fond of one another, and when she was not ironing or working with the clothing, she acted as the personal servant to the Mistress.

The mistress, Regina, was quite beautiful, and she loved parties. Tessie felt honored that among all the available house servants, Regina had selected her as confidante and personal attendant. Regina loved her husband with a deep fondness. "But," she confided in Tessie, "it is more like the love of a daughter for a father than that of a wife. I am not at all jealous of his slave women as I have no desire to indulge his sexual appetite more than occasionally. It was not an important issue in my mind."

Tessie, on the other hand, found the Master quite irresistible, and she watched him from a distance with a growing hunger to be in his arms. It was not long before Regina noticed the look of longing in Tessie's eyes when Peter was in their company.

One morning when Tessie was grooming Regina's hair, the Mistress said to her with amusement, "I see on your face that you are lusting after your Master. Has he given you a sign?"

"No ma'am," answered Tessie bashfully.

"Well, you can be at peace about the matter. He truly does have his eye on you as well, but Peter never takes a woman before she is 16, and when he does he insists that it will be a mutual choice. He abhors the idea of bedding a woman against her will, even if she is his property," said Regina.

This gave Tessie new hope, and she took on a glow of enthusiasm that the Master could not help noticing. Just before she was 16, he called her into his study for a private meeting.

"I find you very desirable, Tessie, more desirable than any woman I have ever known," he said. "It has been difficult for me to wait, but now you are full grown.

Would you like to share the room with my favorites and come to my bed when you are called?"

"I would like a room of my own," said Tessie, boldly. "And I would like to be known as your favorite. I would like to be called every night, and I find you very desirable as well."

Peter laughed. "By golly, you've got some spunk, young lady. You shall have a room of your own, and I can hardly wait to introduce you to the fulfillment of your other wishes."

A few days later Tessie moved into an upstairs room with satin sheets and lace curtains and rugs on the floor. When Peter came to her room that night she felt like a bride. The excitement between them was like liquid fire, and she hoped it would never cool.

Regina was happy for her and wanted to hear an account of their affair every morning as Tessie coifed her hair. Just over a year later a baby boy was born to Tessie. His skin was white and his hair straight and dark. He was permitted to stay in the room with Tessie at first, although Peter paid no attention to him at all. After all, this was just one of a dozen children that his women had produced.

The Mistress Regina asked Tessie's permission to request that the child be raised as hers and be treated as a son and heir to Peter. Tessie was delighted, and together they decided to name him David Cunningham.

But when Regina appealed to Peter with their request, he was outraged. "How dare you," he stormed. "You embarrass me enough by not being able to produce a child for me. Now you ask that I accept this slave boy as a son. He is a slave, and he will remain one. When he is five years old, he will go into the bunkhouse with the other slaves and will work as they do. He is nothing to me!"

"But I thought you had a special fondness for his mother," protested Regina, "and God has given him the appearance of a white boy. He even looks like you."

Kicking the door in anger Peter shouted, "I do have a special fondness for his mother. In fact, if she were white enough to pass, I would put you away and marry her. That gives me even more cause to reject your foolish proposal. Why would I want a competitor for her attention? You take up enough of her interest without yet another person coming between us. Furthermore, this boy will not have the name of a white man. He will be called Solomon because he has outwitted me just by being born."

Regina stormed out of the study in tears and rang the bell for Tessie.

When Tessie heard what the Master had said, she was greatly disturbed. She had had no idea that he felt so strongly for her, or that he was jealous of her affection for Regina and Solomon. Although she loved the Master very much and enjoyed their love- making beyond words, she decided to request permission to move into the bunkhouse with Solomon so that he could become accustomed to the others before he got spoiled to life in the big house. She wanted what was best for her son, and her own desires would have to take second place.

For days she and Peter argued about the question behind closed doors, but at last he gave in. His only request was that she come to the big house every morning at daybreak without the boy and stay until sundown. She must also be available to him at night whenever she was called. His sacrifice would be to release the pleasure of sleeping with her and waking with her each morning. Tessie eagerly agreed, and they were at peace again.

Regina spent as much time as she could with little Solomon, secretly visiting the bunkhouse to play with him whenever Peter would go into town. But at age six he was required to begin working in the fields with the other children and was no longer available to her. She loved him as she would have loved her own child, and if it had not been for the reports she received from Tessie she felt sure she would die of a broken heart.

Solomon grew into a strong, intelligent young man. At first the other children had made fun of him because of his fair skin and straight hair but his friendly manner won them over, and eventually they forgot that he was different. He had picked up the habit of singing gospel songs in the fields, and at night he and Tessie would often sing together to celebrate the end of their day of labor and their opportunity to reunite.

One day when Solomon was about 15, he found a book under his mother's bed.

There were no pictures in it, and he grew curious. Reading and books were forbidden to slaves, and he became afraid for Tessie. That evening instead of beginning a song when the lamp was lit, he held the book out to her. "Do you know how to read?"

Tessie was afraid to confess to him, but she was more afraid to put a lie between them. "The Mistress taught me," she said. "She gave me the book. It is a Bible."

"This is the answer to my prayers," Solomon whispered. "Teach me to read. I know I can learn."

"I'm afraid for you. What if you get caught?" asked Tessie. "The Master would beat you and sell you to a wicked man."

"I have a plan," said Solomon. "You teach me to read; then I will tell you my plan. Even if he kills me, I will die knowing how to read."

Every evening Tessie and Solomon worked together on his reading. The others pretended not to see. Tessie was surprised at how quickly he learned. He could mimic the voice and speech of Master Peter perfectly. "If I close my eyes when you read in that voice, it sounds like you're a white man for sure," Tessie said to him proudly.

After three years, Solomon told Tessie his plan: he was waiting for a perfect opportunity to escape. Once he was away from the Virginia, he would use his "white" voice all the time and pass as a white man.

Fear grabbed at Tessie's heart. He had not been inside the big house since he was two years old, and Solomon had never seen how the white men conducted themselves.

He would never be able to pass for white. When she shared her concerns with him, he said with a scowl on his face, "If I can't pass, then I will die trying. I won't be a slave much longer."

Tessie decided it was time they approached his father together. They asked for a meeting, which was scheduled within the week. Upon hearing their request that Peter help Solomon get a new start and pass for white in a new town, Peter laughed at them.

They were prepared for the rejection, and, in fact, it played right into their hands. "Then you could at least give him a job that will permit him a bit of happiness. I have heard you say that your carriage driver is getting too old to see the roads. Let him teach Solomon before he loses his sight, and you will have a mannerly, strong, hard-working driver for many years to come," proposed Tessie.

Shaking his head with a wry grin on his face, Peter chuckled. "You're a hard woman to deal with, Tessie. But for you I will give him a try. My driver must be courteous to my guests at all times.

His duties will require that he bathe every day and wear a fine suit and hat. He will drive my house guests from the coach station and back and into the village for recreation. He will also be sent alone into the village to purchase supplies on my account."

During the months that followed, Solomon learned how to handle the horses, how to bow to the ladies and tip his hat, how to open the coach doors and help a lady or a gentleman inside. He learned how to bargain for supplies with the store clerk, and he learned the roads that were excellent for a warm weather drive. He observed the shop- keepers and the ways of the white men.

Then, one day he drove a lady to the village and never came back.

Peter hated Solomon for the betrayal of his kindness, for the embarrassment, and for the theft of his carriage, and Tessie felt guilty for the first time in her life. She had always been committed to following the rules of her superiors and she had broken the rule of "no deception". Even so, she was not willing to risk being sold to someone else by confessing her deception, so she did not.

She felt compassion for Peter's sense of betrayal, but she prayed that Solomon would never be found. She missed him dreadfully. Regina missed him even more, and she became depressed, although she prayed that he would never come back.

After becoming convinced that neither of them had known of Solomon's plan, Peter began to blame Solomon not only for his betrayal but for the unhappiness of the two women that he loved. He insisted that Tessie move back into the house to care for the Mistress.

The lives of Tessie and Regina passed pleasantly after that. Parties still held the power to delight Regina for a few hours at a time, and the passion between Peter and Tessie was still strong. He slept in Tessie's room every night.

The two women shared their concerns over Solomon and speculated about whether he had successfully established his new identity as a white man. Both lived comfortably in close friendship with one another until Regina was thrown from a horse and suffered a spinal injury. She died within a year.

Tessie missed her immensely. Peter cried a little but, before a week had passed, he asked Tessie to join him in his room and act as his wife for the rest of their lives. The parties ceased; no guests were invited. Peter never left the plantation again as long as Tessie was alive. The Cunningham Plantation was a private place where only one white man and dozens of slaves lived in harmony together. It was whispered in the village that Peter Cunningham had taken one of the slave women as his wife, but no one could ever confirm it.

One day as they sat on the veranda, trying to keep cool with fresh lemonade, Peter began to cry. "I wish Solomon would come home," he said. "I should have let Regina have him. Then you would never have stopped loving me, and Regina would have been happier too. Do you think he was able to pass? Should I hire some men to search for him? I will do whatever you want me to do."

Tessie reached out to take his hand. "I have never stopped loving you, Peter," she said. "Solomon had a plan. He was smart, and he knew how to read. He even knew how to talk exactly like you, and he was going to take the name that Regina gave him, the name of David. His plan was to steal the coach and drive into the next state. There he would hire out to someone who wanted to travel to the north. Once he was in northern territory, he would sell the carriage, keeping only the best horse for himself. He would hire on as a shopkeeper's apprentice and save his money until he had enough to have a shop of his own."

"What kind of shop was he going to have?" asked Peter.

"A shop with books and candles and lamps and oils," said Tessie.

"Perhaps one day soon we will take a trip up north and look for a bookshop that is owned by a handsome man named David," mused Peter.

"How do you know he will still be handsome?" asked Tessie.

"He's my son, isn't he?" said Peter with a brief surge of pride. How could he be anything else?"

They laughed. She was glad that Peter did not reprimand her for having kept Solomon's plan a secret for so long.

Every year they talked about taking a trip up north. They never went. Fifteen years after Solomon ran away, Tessie died of a sudden heart attack, when she was 51.

Chapter 13

MELISSA

England 1875-1921

The child was left in a basket just inside the door of a large Catholic Church when she was only a few days old. Her father had been killed in a factory accident; her mother, without relatives and homeless, had come to the confessional seeking advice.

The priest had insisted that she must place the child in an orphanage, and that he would help her find the right place.

The woman had obviously expected the church to give her money or a home; and she was angered at his advice because of the dreadfully inhumane and impersonal treatment of children in such places. The priest had warned her that this desire to release responsibility for the child was a sin, and now her anger at his advice was jeopardizing her relationship with God and with him. Without a word, she ran out of the Church, leaving the infant behind, and was never heard of again.

The priest found the basket hours later when the child began to cry from hunger. A small convent, adjoining the church, was the closest place for her temporary care that he could think of, so he took her there. His intent was to place her in the orphanage as soon as they would accept her. To his dismay, he was informed that the orphanage did not accept infants under two years old. The nuns agreed to keep the child for two years. One of the nuns was assigned as her primary "nanny" with others available as needed for her care.

It was a breath of fresh air for them to have an infant in their midst. They all agreed that she must be an angel that God had sent to bless them with love. For two years she was given no name, but when it became obvious that the priest had literally forgot that she existed, they all agreed unanimously to keep her. "After all," they reasoned, "it is God's will that she stay with us."

As she grew older, they were even more convinced that the child was an angel.

What else could account for her quiet, serene nature, her eagerness to cooperate with their every request, her piety and enjoyment of the rituals that they practiced, and her pleasant ways? In searching for a deeper reason that God would have blessed them with such a gift, they decided she was sent to them as the embodiment of patience, a quality that they all found most difficult to practice. Some suggested that it was time to give her a name, suggesting that they call her "Patience". Others preferred the name, Melissa, for no reason except that it sounded pretty. "Melissa" was chosen.

After another year passed, the old priest died and another was posted in his place. He knew nothing about the child's existence, and the nuns did not tell. They agreed, again, that it was God's plan that she stay with them. Why else would the knowledge of her existence be so thoroughly forgotten by anyone outside the convent?

This life of prayer and ritual seemed warm and perfect to Melissa. She was given a basic education by the sisters, but had no strong interest in anything. She was content to play quietly or sit reading a book wherever she happened to be. She especially enjoyed strolling the grounds in warm weather, and communing with nature. The legend of her being sent to them as an angel was perpetuated by her total lack of interest in the world outside the convent, her compassionate nature, and the uncanny power she had to attract birds and butterflies at will.

All the nuns spoke in a whisper when they spoke at all, and Melissa preferred the hours of enforced silence more than any other time of the day.

For her this changeless place was a haven of peace. There was nothing to fear, no decisions to make, no conflict; and all her survival needs were automatically met. It was a time of healing from the former life of enslavement, but of that she had no conscious awareness. Her adoration and gratitude toward God, and for the women with whom she lived, satisfied any desire for love that she might have experienced.

She was well aware of the nuns' belief that she was an angel that God had placed with them as a blessing for their piety and to teach them patience. Melissa accepted that role without question. Her self-image was as God's helper, sent by Him to bless the nuns by acting as an example for them. Every morning she practiced a self-reflective examination based on a standard of conduct that she had designed for herself. She found it easy to conduct herself in accordance with that standard, whether alone or in the company of the nuns.

It never occurred to Melissa to wonder about her mother or father. Her whole world was the convent and she was utterly content just to live her quiet life and observe the nuns in their various activities.

The winters were harsh. The rooms in the convent were drafty and cold at times, especially at night. In the winter of her 46th year, Melissa developed a bronchial cough. Before springtime it had deepened into pneumonia. She died peacefully in her sleep ending an uneventful life of rest, freedom from responsibility, peace and frugality. The nuns had tended her with patience and love during her illness, using prayer and herbs from their garden. They buried her secretly in the shade of a tree that had been planted when she was small. Through their tears, they laughed at remembering how delighted she was when the tree became taller than she. One of the sisters, who was good at sketching, made a drawing of Melissa and framed it with willow branches tied together with string. They dared to hang it where everyone who visited could see; when anyone inquired they would say, "It is just a picture of the angel who blesses our convent day and night."

Chapter 14

ROSE

The Now. What Will Cherry Say?

It was a hot summer day. Rose wrote what she thought was a final note in her journal.

Journal Entry 13:

It is obvious from my life as Melissa, that I took yet another lifetime to rest from involvement in the world and to prepare myself for the difficulties of this incarnation. But even in that limited situation, I held a conscious purpose for my life. The purpose was to set an example of peace and acceptance in my environment and to act as an inspiration to those who cared for me. Amazing! I was born in this lifetime with that sense of purpose, and I sustained it as my only goal until I had a vision at age three. The Melissa incarnation also accounts for the silence that I practiced in my preschool days. I get a sense that the situation I left to come to Missouri was an opportunity to complete unfinished business with the dear souls from my incarnation as Tessie; Peter, Solomon, and the beautiful Regina. That would explain a lot. Now I am free and moving forward into my future.

Rose placed the book inside a heavy cardboard box, sealed it with tape, and wrote on the box, "This is ready for your assessment. Please call me when you have finished it. I can hardly wait."

She delivered the box in person to Cherry's front porch, rang the doorbell and left without waiting for a response. Two days later, she received the call with an invitation to share dinner and spend Sunday evening with Cherry. Her excitement was boundless. "I'll bring the appetizer," she said enthusiastically.

Singing a love song to God, Rose prepared a tray of marinated mushrooms, cheeses, gourmet crackers, olives and small spicy meatballs, while a bottle of her best white wine was chilling in the fridge. Dressed in unlined gray silk pants and a sleeveless burgundy tank-top with her favorite chunky jewelry, she balanced the tray on one hand and juggled the wine bottle in the other to push Cherry's doorbell.

The door opened immediately. "Well, well, well," laughed Cherry with a wide, invitational sweep of the door. "It looks like we'll be celebrating tonight."

"And how!" beamed Rose, following Cherry into the kitchen. As she watched Cherry pull the cork and pour generous servings of wine into sparkling amethyst-colored glasses, she picked up some napkins from the kitchen counter and led the way to Cherry's living room.

"I'm all yours," Cherry said.

Rose popped a bit of cheese into her mouth and washed it down with the smooth sweet wine.

"So, what did you learn by witnessing the incarnations?" asked Cherry, sipping her wine.

"I'm not sure that I could give a name to what I learned in those incarnations," laughed Rose, "but, whatever it was, it sure took a heck of a long time. The learning seemed to be gradual with a lot of letting go of former things I thought I had learned. I had to evolve past greed, jealousy, self-pity, timidity, self-righteousness, self-blame and deceit. What interesting paths I took in order to that! It didn't happen overnight and I have a new appreciation for some of the characters that I have spent time with in this incarnation. I see how my unfinished business with them was brought to a peaceful end. It seems to me that that my sense of inner peace, patience, love of creative purpose and dedication to my God were being perfected as I grew in understanding, character and spiritual awareness. Can you put words to that for me?"

Cherry leaned toward the coffee table to spread soft cheese onto a cracker as if she had an eternity to do it. She began to speak with the same indication of timelessness. Rose relaxed and listened.

"You are so right. In that incarnation, everything that you had ever learned, through your episodes of focus on learning and your variety of experiences, all came together for you as Maria," Cherry began. "Until then you were living for the past, often feeling sorry for yourself and quite co-dependent. You felt and acted as if to accumulate and hang onto relationships was your purpose in life, even if the relationships had run their course or were dysfunctional. Some needed to be altered, some needed to be released entirely, but you had to be willing to be honest about your needs."

"Of course," said Rose. "I was not able to self-actualize fully until I was willing to accept myself, accept change, let go of life as I had known it, and rebuild with what lay before me."

"Exactly," said Cherry. "The key that turned that lock, to show you a different perception of yourself, was a major paradigm shift that produced both empathy and awakening. The empathy was developed from all the grief and self-pity and false sense of piety you had stored inside yourself, empowering you to better understand others who were at those gates. The "straw that broke the camel's back" and produced that paradigm shift was one more experience of grief. That mass of self-centered feelings was released, clearing the way for you to really see yourself objectively. It resulted in an immediate sense of deeper empathy toward others and toward yourself."

"Yes, yes, I can see that clearly," Rose agreed.

After they had spent some time discussing various points to prove that theory, Rose felt even greater confidence in Cherry's wisdom.

"It is obvious that accumulated grief, based on a false perception that relationships are possessions" and that life is supposed to be stable, brought me into accepting that these premises are simply not true," observed Rose.

"And, it follows that once we release a false belief, a new one forms to take its place," suggested Cherry. "The reason people classically hold the same co-dependent beliefs that you held for so long is their need for security. Until God is discovered to be the only constant in one's life other than their own existence, a person will look for stability in the environment or in their collection of things, money or even relationships. They will tenaciously hang onto whatever "good" has come their way and lament its loss, instead of being grateful for what it contributed to their life's journey."

"Ah," speculated Rose. "From the perspective of gratitude instead of possessiveness one can appreciate even the unpleasant relationships, disappointments, losses and disillusionments that we face, especially if we accept that they might have been unfinished business from a past incarnation. Is that a fair statement?"

"More than fair," said Cherry with a smile. "I repeat: with the insight that your own being and God are the only two constants in your life, while everything and everyone else is transient, there comes an acceptance that your relationship with God is your only security. That becomes your treasure.

Knowing the truth of the matter makes it so much easier to let go with love and forgiveness, and become centered in the current conditions of your life. Once that is done, you can begin to move decisively into your future with both expectation and courage."

"So, when are we liberated from that unfinished business and those unpleasant relationships of the past? Must we continue trying until there are no control issues on either side?" asked Rose.

"Certainly not!" exclaimed Cherry. "Some people are not even trying to evolve in character, and there is no need for you to continue in relationship with an individual once you have let go of all animosity toward that one. As long as you think they "owe" you something you are not free from the dynamics that produce bondage. If you are finished with the "game" and others are not, they will find someone else to engage in the same struggle with them once you have moved beyond it. Evidence of true forgiveness is not forgetting, lest you forget the lesson and have to learn it again through the same or a different involvement. The evidence of true forgiveness is to release all sense of animosity or thoughts of unfinished business in a situation. This releases attachment. Only then are you liberated from unpleasantries of the past and ready to self-actualize through investment of your time, energy and attention in your next adventure of life, whether it be in this world or the next."

"Okay," said Rose, washing down a meatball with a huge gulp of wine and pouring them each another glass, "I see how my belief was changed through the school of grief, but how was my ability to reason and make proactive choices made so clear all of a sudden? It was as if everything I had learned in those incarnations of focus on learning was fused into one great understanding of relativity in relation to the absolute."

Savoring a mouthful of wine, Cherry closed her eyes and sighed with pleasure, letting it trickle slowly down her throat as if that was all she ever had to do. Then she began the second statement of her assessment.

"So true. In some incarnations you focused on learning, while in others your focus was on just "flowing" with the situation in which you were born, without any effort to learn or make changes. In those alternating cases, one incarnation might have been to struggle against life and the next to choose the opposite way by giving up your right to creative thinking and merely living a responsive existence. Without balance, there is no real understanding demonstrated in either way of living. If we are to mimic God, and I believe that we are, it seems that being creative is an inseparable component of self-actualization, but so is going with the flow. During those lifetimes in which you tried making choices that were based on co-dependency and false beliefs you were just jerked around by your feelings. You believed, and hoped, that once you chose some person or some way of living it was meant to remain a part of your "collected good" for the rest of your life. In those incarnations, when losses came, you never completed your cycles of grief. You remained invested in the past, to the point of depression in many cases, and depression is self-defeating."

"That is so clear to me, now," said Rose. "In those incarnations I did not empower myself to use the knowledge I had to reinvest my life force, but kept lamenting over my losses and sometimes even clinging to hope that a miracle would restore what I had lost. What an energy leach I must have been to the stronger people around me."

"The restoration of what was lost always comes," mused Cherry, "but seldom in the same form as before. It comes as a new opportunity to learn the same lesson again and again until we stop clinging to the past. When we try to build our future by trying to recapture the past, we circle back to the same lesson that we had before. On the other hand, when we invest in current situations, using new components and our latest understanding, we can walk forward one step at a time into Divine Timing for ourselves and feel a new sense of order."

"How can you say that the restoration always comes, when some losses are permanent?" challenged Rose.

"Granted, some losses such as health, relationships and situations are permanent in the current incarnation, but these losses are of situations in the world. Everything of the world is transient. A single incarnation with its window of experience is such a small portion of one's eternal life from creation to infinity," remarked Cherry. "The permanent collections are those of spiritual qualities, spiritual knowledge, spiritual understanding. Altogether they constitute spiritual enlightenment which produces spiritual wisdom for use in this world or even in eternity."

Cherry caressed the stem of her glass gracefully before continuing, "I think that accepting the concept of reincarnation adds to the potential for happiness and progressive, creative living, but it isn't necessary as an incentive for collecting the gifts of spirit. Some people are committed to religions or belief systems that prohibit a belief in reincarnation. In those cases, there is a need for total faith in an afterlife of happiness.

Even that is basically reincarnation of the soul but in a different dimension of reality. I grant you that as life moves on in its continuum, holding one of these two beliefs is most helpful; especially if one is to detach emotionally from the past in a healthy manner. If both beliefs are accepted: reincarnation and an afterlife of happiness, then rapid recovery from grief is assured."

"I hold both beliefs; do you?" asked Rose.

"Oh, yes. And it tickles me inside to know they are true," said Cherry with a smile.

"It seems to me that the atheist view, that religious and spiritual beliefs are merely for hiding from reality, and that only cowards cling to such things, is about as far off center as any belief can be," concluded Rose.

"Indeed," said Cherry. "When tunnel vision blinds one to the ultimate reality of their own and everyone else's eternal life, they become either so intense about worldly life that they can't take time for savoring it; or they go the opposite way and become so confused about their own life that they get too involved in the lives of others."

"To keep the balance between thinking and feeling seems most advisable," said Rose.

"I'll drink to that," laughed Cherry, lifting her glass for a toast. "Here's to the order of life: breathing in and out, action and rest, accepting and releasing, etcetera, etcetera, etcetera."

Rose lifted her glass in a gesture of agreement, "Thinking and feeling, playing and working, giving and receiving, speaking and listening, etcetera, etcetera, etcetera." "Wait," said Cherry, "Don't drink to it yet. What about movement and stillness, night and day, loss and gain?"

"And what about life and death?" added Rose with merriment.

"Whoops! We've come to the end of our Platonic investigation," said Cherry. We have found something that has no opposite. Of life there is no opposite. There is no death, only change which gives the appearance of death. There is no end. Life is an absolute. It is eternal, and so am I."

"And so it is, and so am I," said Rose. Their glasses touched, and a lovely sound of tinkling glass was born. They listened as it diminished, and laughed with the knowledge that it did not die.

That sound had been a potential before their glasses met, and it would remain a potential forever. Just the right combination of actions at the same time could produce it again and again.

"Sound and silence," said Rose.

"Yes, yes," said Cherry, "The Substance and its potential, but before the potential can be produced there is the interplay of actions, the dance of movement and invisible energies combining in a variety of combinations. Both the silence and the sound are life. One is life in action; the other is life in potential. One is knowing; the other is expressing. Which do you prefer?"

Rose answered with playful exaggeration, "Knowing without opportunity to express would result in depression. And expressing without knowledge would result in chaos and loss. I choose both."

"Hear, hear," said Cherry, as she lifted her glass in merriment.

Finishing the last marinated mushroom from their plate of appetizers, Cherry licked her fingers and refilled their wine glasses. "What about the lifetime as Tessie, and of Melissa following her, my dear? Would you say you focused on self-actualization or a Taoist type of attitude toward life in those incarnations? And why?"

Night had fallen, and the two women sat comfortably in silent semi-darkness while Rose pondered the question. At last, she spoke with conviction. "My life as Tessie was self-actualization or self-expression of what I had learned about reality and spirituality up to that point. I had learned acceptance of the changes in life, acceptance of myself, my right to choose yet be cooperative at the same time. In that lifetime I didn't give up the reins of my own life to others. I was proactive within the context of my life as a slave. I applied the appropriate knowledge to my chosen way of life. It seems I always believed in reincarnation, and I knew this was not my last opportunity to choose or re-choose. As for the incarnation as Melissa, I seem to have reached a plateau of sorts, or perhaps I was tired. In any case, I was not in a development phase during that incarnation, but in a phase of consciously resting from development for a time, and just expressing the spiritual qualities that I had already developed."

"I see that," agreed Cherry. "As Melissa you rested from the mainstream of life and claimed a time to practice the best qualities of yourself within the boundaries of a hermit's life. That resulted in holding your energies within, and reenergizing your soul for the enormous spurts of growth that you've experienced in your current incarnation. Would you say that you are self-actualized now?" asked Cherry.

Rose's response was immediate, "I am aware that I remained in my self-created cocoon" of consciousness, hiding away until I was three years old in this lifetime. Through a dramatic spiritual experience that I will write about in a book someday in the future, called *Windows of Life and Death*, I became restless to engage proactively in life again. I set some goals, pursued a chosen path, prepared myself, and made a plan of how to serve that purpose without doing harm to anyone else. As with all things in this world the steps in that direction were a matter of opportunity and timing."

Cherry rose to give Rose a quick hug. Heading toward the kitchen, she said over her shoulder, "Now, I want you to connect the dots by taking the next hour to make one last journal entry while I prepare our dinner. This entry should be about the beginning of your current incarnation."

Rose settled into an altered state of consciousness using the method that she had learned from Cherry. Soon she opened her notebook and began to write.

Chapter 15

ROSE

Mid-20th Century A small town in Louisiana, USA

> *Journal Entry #14*
>
> *I see the early years of my current life objectively, through the Akashic records.*
>
> *They verify the numerous stories that I was told by my parents and other relatives as a child.*

I was born in a swamp shack in southern Louisiana. My 26-year-old father, Ben, was a man of genius IQ but with only a fourth-grade education. Taking care of his family and providing for them was everything in life to him. He worked as an independent logger in the swamps, reporting daily to a foreman at a makeshift log- cabin in the woods to request work and be sent on jobs.

My mother, Magdalene, was a beautiful, energetic half-Indian, half-French gypsy with a nurturing and playful personality. She was a known psychic as well as a young woman with a past when she met Ben. She believed that to keep a husband happy was the God-assigned purpose for a wife and that the gentle rearing of his children under his supervision was secondary only to her duties and services to him.

She was not sure she wanted to give up the single life for just an ordinary man, but after dating Ben for three months and a night in the back seat of his car, she decided he was not an ordinary man. She loved being his wife.

Their first-born, Jeannie--precocious, jealous of her father's affection toward her mother, and demanding attention incessantly--was 18 months old when Magdalene gave birth to yet another rival for his attention: a white-haired infant that they named Rose. That would be me.

It was around 10 p.m. the last day of October.

Stumbling to the bed, Magdalene said calmly, "Get the midwife, Ben. Our baby is coming."

Ben jumped up from his sleep, stepped into his pants as he walked out the door and ran half a mile to the home of the midwife.

Banging on her door, he did not wait for her to answer but kicked it open and grabbed the startled woman by her arm. "Maggie's in labor," he explained as he all but dragged her to the log cabin that was his home. Magdalene lay on the bed in obvious pain while the midwife examined her.

"This one won't be easy," she said with controlled panic. "Better go into town and fetch Doc Arnold. It's a breech."

The railroad had deliberately left a hand-pump car on a piece of dead-end track near Ben's cabin. When it was not in use, the swamp dwellers were free to use it. Giving thanks to God that the railroad ran past their house, Ben jumped on the pump-car, and moving along the track toward town he pumped the handle up and down as fast as his muscular arms could go while he prayed for his wife. Arriving at the edge of town, he jumped off the pump-car, startling a group of three men who were drinking beer outside the doctor's office that also served as his home.

"No sense in going in there, Ben," one of the men said as Ben raced toward the door. "Ol" Doc is in the saloon. Prob'ly floatin'on clouds by now."

The men laughed.

Ben ran to the saloon and saw the doctor right away. He was hanging onto the bar and pawing the waitress, who was laughing and teasing him.

"Get your hat, and let's go, Doc!" demanded Ben.

"Who the hell is talking to me that way?" drawled the drunken doctor.

He spun around to see the panic in Ben's eyes, and his attitude changed. "Oh, my God. Something's happened out in the swamp."

Ben half dragged, half carried the stumbling doctor to the pump-car, pushed him onto it, and started the trip back to his cabin.

As they opened the door to enter the shack, the baby was just arriving. The midwife shouted with alarm, "She's dead! Black as a darkie and cold as stone, with the cord wrapped around her neck."

A huge pot of water was steaming on the pot-bellied wood stove in the one-room cabin.

When the drunken doctor picked the dead child up by her feet and began dunking her up and down into the hot water, Maggie screamed.

"Stop that," yelled Ben. "You'll scald her."

"Well, either she's already dead or she ain't," drawled the doctor. "If she is, I reckon this won't hurt her none. But if she ain't she might start to warm up a little."

After 10 full minutes of rhythmic dunking in the hot water, the baby began to turn pink. She gurgled and opened her eyes. Looking at his watch the doctor pronounced to the midwife: "Time of birth, November 1st at 12:05 a.m.", indicating that this should be recorded on the birth certificate.

He wrapped her in a blanket and placed her in her mother's arms. "She was a bluebaby," he explained. "Might want to bring her to see me in a few months so I can check her over."

Taking a blank birth certificate out of his ever-ready briefcase, he scribbled on it and presented it to the midwife to witness.

"That's not right. She was born 5 minutes before midnight on October 31st," murmured the midwife grumpily.

The doctor glared at her for her insolence, "She didn't breathe until November 1st.

She was born dead and came alive on November 1st. That is her day of birth." The midwife signed reluctantly, after the parents. Doc Arnold stuffed the document into his briefcase, then grabbed his hat, saying, "Now, if you don't mind, I'll take myself back to town."

Mother and baby slept. Ben cried with relief.

After a few minutes he took his first close look at the infant. "I ain't never seen such white hair on a young'un," he said. "I'm gonna call her cotton."

"Her name is Rose," protested Magdalene.

"Don't matter. She can have a nickname if I say so," said Ben and he left the room.

When 18-month-old Jeannie awoke the next morning and was shown to the cradle of her new baby sister, she pushed the cradle hard and almost overturned it. "I hate her," she cried. "I'm the baby; she's not."

Her father took her on his lap and dried her tears. "You are our baby," he said to Jeannie. "This one is a living doll. We got her just to keep you company. You can feed her and rock her cradle and help change her diapers."

"And tell her what to do?" asked Jeannie.

"Yes, when she's older you will be her big sister and she will have to mind you, or you can spank her behind," said Ben. They laughed together.

This set the trend for their family system and, although Maggie silently disagreed with it and was into more equality, she would not think of overriding anything that her husband said.

The four of them stayed in that harsh environment of the Louisiana swampland, living mainly on squirrels, rabbits and poke-salad greens until Rose was two years old. Magdalene carried their water from a pond, boiling the portion that went into the drinking bucket. The woman knew no kind of life other than the country life, but this swamp life was the closest to nature she had ever been.

As the infant grew older, Ben worried about her silence and the fact that she was not thriving. She had never cried until she was three months old, and then just a little whimper. She had walked at eight months, but for the life of him he could not see how those skinny legs could hold her up. She looked like a new born, though she was nine months old. When he took her into town to see the doctor and pick up a copy of the birth certificate, the news was not good.

"She's got a heart murmur, and her lungs are weak. Some kind of bronchitis I'd say. And she's anemic and malnutritioned, too," announced the doctor. "Ain't you feeding her at all?"

Ben looked at his feet with embarrassment. "Maggie ain't got no milk, so we just give her juice from the cookin' of greens."

"Poke salad and water ain't enough for a baby to grow on. She's gotta have milk or she'll die," said the doctor with indifference.

Ben traded his pocket watch for a cow that day and tied it to the railing of the front porch. After that Rose began to "fatten up" and grow at a normal rate.

One day, when she had just turned two, Rose was walking randomly on the bare ground that served as their yard and munching on a biscuit when a wild boar bravely came out of the woods. He stood still, watching her. "Hi", said Rose, approaching the wild beast.

Holding out her hand with the biscuit she asked, "Are you hungry?"

The boar darted forward just as Ben came around the cabin with an armload of cut firewood.

"Git away," he yelled in panic. The boar charged, swallowing Rose's entire hand with the biscuit. Running through the woods to escape the man's threatening voice, it dragged the child by her hand and headed toward the dense forest. Ben was horrified. For the third time in her life this child was near death. His only potential for saving her was to try to stop the boar with a stick of firewood. He had been the champion baseball pitcher among his playmates growing up and a Golden Gloves wrestler in his teens and early 20's. His uncommon strength and accuracy would now save his daughter's life, or it would kill her. Either way he would save her from the horror of being eaten by the boar. He threw a stick of firewood and hit his mark. It missed Rose only by inches, striking the boar on his hip. The animal squealed in pain, released the girl and went racing toward the swamp. Ben carried her into the house where he and his wife bathed her and rocked her to sleep. She did not cry.

When they had placed her under the blanket and tucked her in to rest, Ben said to his wife, "Throw everything you can into sheets and tie it up. We're moving to your Mama's house tomorrow. I'll get a job in a sawmill; then we'll move to a house in town."

Within a month he had a job as saw-mill foreman in the nearest town. He was given lumber and tools free of charge, along with a small parcel of land on which to build a house near the sawmill. Some of the men who worked for him helped build the house; then he went to bring his family home.

They joined a Pentecostal Church, made friends with the neighbors, and began to live a more "normal" lifestyle. Soon people began to comment about how "sweet, quiet, and mannerly" Rose was, but Ben was disturbed.

"She never speaks above a whisper, and mainly she just watches other people unless someone tells her what to do. It ain't natural. She's plumb spooky and too quiet for my liking." He was determined to "get a rise out of her."

There was never any reason to punish her, and that irritated Ben. She was obedient and polite and helpful to the point of being sickening to him. She seemed to have no desires at all and never asked for anything. The only things she seemed to enjoy were going to church, and listening to music on the radio. He knew she had a good mind because she had a quick understanding of anything that was said to her, her vocabulary was much greater than that of her older sister, and she could sing every word of a song after hearing it only once.

Then, to make matters worse, the summer before she was four years old, she had told her mother that Jesus spoke to her and that some kind of Light had come into her head to tell her that she was supposed to become a teacher, and teach people the truth about God. It made him shiver with revulsion to know he had such a strange child in his house, and he said as much to Magdalene, who seemed overly protective toward the girl.

"Cotton acts like some kind of nun or something," he said. "It ain't natural, and I want you to make her get out and play with Jeannie every day. She needs to learn how to run and jump and climb around."

In respect of her husband's wishes, Maggie made a rule. It was that Rose had to stay with Jeannie everywhere she went, and play whatever Jeannie wanted her to play. Rose obeyed without question, but it infuriated Ben even more when he saw that she was just as agile and strong as any child her age.

She had another irritating habit that he was determined to put a stop to. She would sit very still on the floor with her eyes closed, then in slow motion begin to stretch this way and that, twisting her body into strange contortions. When she was all finished, she would stand on her head for 5 minutes or so.

He decided he had had just about enough of her irritating silliness, so he said sternly, "I want you to quit that stretchin' and wrapping yourself up in a knot and standin' on your head, Cotton. You act like a cat, and it gives me the creeps. How come you do such things?"

Innocently Rose said in her quiet even voice, "It's something I used to do, and I like to do it."

"When did you used to do it?" asked Ben with a fierce frown on his face. "When I was old; I used to do it," Rose said.

Ben was so angry he turned red in the face and thought he was going to have a stroke. "Maggie," he called to his wife, "take this young'un out of here and make her quit that stretchin' and twistin'. She's plumb spooky the way she never cries or complains about nothing. It's like she's got no feelings at all. You better teach her to act more like a normal young'un, or I'm gonna teach her how to cry, myself."

Because Ben didn't believe in her psychic skills, Maggie never mentioned her insights to him, but she knew his fears about Rose were unfounded. She felt a sense of spiritual peace around the child, and she permitted Rose to spend time in the house with her when Jeannie did not want her around. They had many lovely conversations while Maggie taught Rose to cook and do kitchen work.

Jeannie was the apple of her father's eye, and Rose was always glad when he was home because it took Jeannie's controlling attention away from her so that she could spend time in silence. Singing was the only thing that she enjoyed doing with Jeannie.

Both girls had lovely clear voices, and every time someone visited, they would ask the girls to sing for them.

The third child came along when Rose was five. Jeannie was in school, and it was a breath of fresh air for Rose. She spent as much time as she was allowed helping to feed and care for her new sister.

When Rose was in the first grade, Ben took a job driving a bus, and the family moved to a larger town nearby. Rose's teacher gave Maggie the phone number of a voice teacher in their neighborhood saying that Rose had an exceptional singing voice and this woman often gave free lessons to children who were talented. Miss Norman accepted both Rose and Jeannie free of charge, which led to five years of public performances on local radio and stage shows for them.

Rose's white hair had turned to a pale silky yellow. She was small with thick blonde curls, sky-blue eyes and clear translucent skin. Jeannie had the dark coloring of her Indian mother and, although she was equally pretty, she envied Rose's storybook blondness.

Jeannie's jealousy of her sister was increased when the voice teacher said that Rose's voice was the best of all her students, and she offered Rose more opportunities to perform. By this time, Rose had gotten the message from her father: If Jeannie was not included equally; Rose was not permitted to accept anything from a party invitation to a stage performance. For this reason, Rose frequently refused opportunities, asking Miss Norman to pass them on to her sister. By deliberately making sure that Jeannie was included, Rose gained permission from Ben to go on the bus trips for performing at Army camps throughout the state. It reminded her of something, but she dared not think about it because Ben forbade her to have such memories.

As they progressed through their early scholastic days, their preteens, and the first dating years, Jeannie's jealousy became a smoldering fire of constant anger toward Rose. She hid it from her father by using subtle cattiness, gossip to her friends, hostility when she and Rose were alone and gushy sweetness to Rose when their parents were close by.

Rose had inherited her father's IQ, and to be in school away from her sister where she could be an individual, apart from the family setting, was heaven to her. She loved learning and immersed herself in the lessons. Jeannie hated school and made very poor grades.

Ben and Maggie frequently moved the family from one neighborhood to another, seeking the lowest rent; and each time they moved a change of schools was required for their girls. Knowing that her school friends would be temporary associations, Rose never became dependent on them for happiness. She received her gratification from study, helping her mother in the house or her father with outdoor work, church, singing, meditative activities, praying, and witnessing the actions of other people with curiosity.

Ben often challenged her when she sat quietly observing her sisters and mother and him. Once he asked, "What are you doing in that sneaky mind of yours?"

"I'm watching people," said 10-year-old Rose.

"What makes you want to watch people so much?" he demanded. "I want to figure out why they do what they do," said Rose. "Why don't you just ask them?" he said.

"Because they don't always tell the truth, and I finally figured out why that is," said Rose.

"Do tell!" said her father. "Anybody knows people lie to keep from getting in trouble. You ain't as smart as your teachers say you are."

Rose ran to get her journal; excited to be sharing what she thought was a real conversation with her father. "Look," she said, handing the spiral writing pad to Ben.

"People pretend to be compatible with other people so they can get approval. Even in the Bible people are always trying to get God's approval, because they believe rewards come with approval and punishment comes with disapproval."

"Well, it does," said Ben.

"With people that is the way life works," said Rose. "But with God, It's not." "What kind of world would it be if everybody went around not caring whether they had anybody else's approval or not?" scoffed Ben, ridiculing her idea. "They'd all be killing and stealing and hurtin' each other every time you turn around."

"Some would, and some wouldn't," said Rose. "But if people are always pretending to be different from what they are inside, how does anybody ever get to live with people who are really compatible with them instead of just pretending to be?"

"Where did you get all them fancy words like compatible?" laughed Ben scornfully.

"It's a new word in my spelling book for this week. I always look up the new words in the school dictionary so I can understand what they mean. When things are compatible, it means that they mix together without doing any harm or damage to each other, and when people are compatible, they are comfortable when they are together," said Rose.

"Well, you see, then," said Ben, "People ain't really compatible", so they have to all have the same rules to make them be compatible."

"We have rules for our family," said Rose, "and I obey all the rules, but you and I are not compatible, and Jeannie and I are not compatible," said Rose. "I don't try to make you or Jeannie be like me, but you and Jeannie are always making fun of me for being different from you."

"I guess you have to do more than mind the rules to get approval then," sneered Ben. "You have to be more like us."

"I don't want your approval enough to quit being like myself," said Rose with the quiet dignity that annoyed her father so much. "I would rather be like God, then I can get my own approval."

Ben roared with laughter until tears rolled down his cheeks. "You'll end up in a loony bin someday with a bunch of crackpots, girl."

Rose stood up and took her journal from her father's lap. "I think people in loony bins are just people who pretended so long they got tired of it and now they are just trying to figure out how to express how they really feel without getting in trouble."

"You'd probably be more compatible with them," said Ben.

"At least I wouldn't tell them they are wrong just because they are different from me," said Rose.

"That's enough," said Ben. "You quit sassing me. And I better not catch you watching me again. You give me the creeps."

"I'm sorry," said Rose.

"See what I mean," Ben said. "You really get on my nerves. Quit saying you're sorry every time I scold you. You ain't gonna get my approval until you start acting like a human being."

"I." Rose caught herself before she finished. Tears rolled down her cheeks.

"Well, lookee here," said Ben. "She does have some feelings after all." He was very pleased to see proof that she could cry.

Rose went into the bedroom that she shared with her two sisters and sat down in a corner to write in her journal.

"I had a talk with my Daddy and it helped me make up my mind about something. When I grow up I will not live with anyone that I am not naturally compatible with. My Mother and I are compatible when she's not pretending for Daddy's approval. I will not be like her in that way. I'll be the same all the time. My sister Jeannie and my Daddy are compatible. They have the same ideas about everything I will marry for compatibility and not for anything else. If a boy is compatible with me, I won't have any trouble loving him."

The child closed her book and began to daydream about the kind of man she would marry someday.

Cherry called cheerfully from the kitchen. "Dinner is ready, my Friend. Come and tell me what you wrote. I do hope you have enjoyed the results of our Divine Appointment."

Rose closed her notebook gently. "I will write the rest of the story someday," she said aloud as if to confirm it for herself. "It will be filled with spiritual fulfillment, spiritual inspiration, romance and adventure."